Hickory Flat Public Library
2740 East Cherokee Drive
Canton, Georgia 30115

# THE
# DREAM
# DRESS

Center Point
Large Print

Also by Janice Thompson and available from
Center Point Large Print:

*It Had to Be You*
*Picture Perfect*
*The Icing on the Cake*

**This Large Print Book carries the
Seal of Approval of N.A.V.H.**

Weddings by Design, #3

# THE DREAM DRESS

## Janice Thompson

CENTER POINT LARGE PRINT
THORNDIKE, MAINE

This Center Point Large Print edition is published
in the year 2014 by arrangement with Revell,
a division of Baker Publishing Group.

The author is represented by MacGregor Literary Agency.

The text of this Large Print edition is unabridged.
In other aspects, this book may vary
from the original edition.
Printed in the United States of America
on permanent paper.
Set in 16-point Times New Roman type.

ISBN: 978-1-62899-048-5

Library of Congress Cataloging-in-Publication Data

Thompson, Janice A.
The dream dress / Janice Thompson. —
    Center Point Large Print edition.
pages ; cm
ISBN 978-1-62899-048-5 (library binding : alk. paper)
1. Wedding costume—Fiction. 2. Weddings—Fiction.
    3. Large type books. I. Title.
PS3620.H6824D74 2014b
813'.6—dc23
                                                        2013041096

To Debbie Maddox, costume designer extraordinaire! For the hundreds of hours you've spent designing, pinning, tucking, altering, and sewing costumes so that I could see my characters come to life on the stage—thank you! The only "stitches" you've given me over the years are the ones in my side from all the laughter! Thanks so much for your encouragement with this book, girl.

And to my mama, the best seamstress I know!

In memory of Fred Astaire and Ginger Rogers. The chapter titles in this fun-loving tale are all Fred and/or Ginger movies or songs.

# 1

## The Sky's the Limit

I'm a material girl— want to see my fabric collection?

AUTHOR UNKNOWN

When a seamstress uses the phrase "coming out of the closet," it takes on a whole new meaning. I still remember the day I spilled the beans to my grandmother, Mimi Carmen, that I wanted to be a designer. She took it pretty well. Mama, not so much. Knowing my mother, she was probably worried about my job security.

I understood her concerns. In fact, that's why I decided not to share my aspirations with my boss at the dress shop where I worked. It was one thing for a girl who specialized in alterations to tell her family that she was a closet wedding dress designer. It was another thing altogether for her to come clean with an emotionally charged man like Demetri Markowitz, one who held her career in the palm of his slick, haute couture–filled hands.

Nope. My eccentric boss wouldn't be hearing about my passion for A-line silhouettes and empire waistlines anytime soon, or the hours I spent sketching out designs in my head during my off-hours. Not if I could help it. My lips would remain as tightly zipped as the size 22 satin crème gown I'd just altered for a bride who insisted she could squeeze into a 16.

*Mental note: Never argue with a bride-to-be who insists on nibbling on a fried pie while trying on her gown.*

Still, sealed lips or not, a girl in my position couldn't take any chances. Not when her mama and grandmother were counting on her to provide a huge chunk of the family's income. And not when she had a boss like Demetri, who would gladly trade her in for a new "material girl"—his words, not mine—at the drop of a beaded bridal hat.

So, in the closet I would stay, pincushion firmly attached to my wrist and measuring tape in hand. Until the wee hours of the night, anyway. That's when you'd find me seated at Mimi Carmen's 1967 Singer sewing machine, eyes glazed over, stitching out what I hoped would be a brand-new life for myself.

Not that I had much time to design my own wedding gowns. As much as I wanted my own line of dresses, my day job consumed most of my energy. It also zapped my creativity, at least from eight to five. If not for the ongoing support of Bella Neeley, the island's most illustrious wedding coordinator, I probably would've given up by now. She knew my passion and fueled it in every shared conversation by offering encouraging tidbits. If only my own confidence level could be as high.

I contemplated my insecurities as I made the drive to Haute Couture Bridal, Galveston's finest wedding dress shop, on the hottest August morning I could remember in years. The heat caused my 2001 Ford Focus to sputter along. If I could afford to get rid of the rust-covered old thing, I would, but who would take it off my hands? No one in his right mind.

The goofy car gave me fits at nearly every stoplight along the way. When I finally reached the dress shop on the far north end of the Strand, I sighed with relief. So did the car. It hiccuped to a stop . . . literally.

After a quick glance in the chipped rearview mirror, I emerged from the car, ready to begin my day. I slammed the door shut and the side mirror fell off. Perfect. I picked it up, opened the door, and tossed it inside.

One of the shop owners happened by and pointed at my car. "Better get that fixed before you get a ticket."

"Yeah, I know."

She told me a story about her brother-in-law's 250-dollar ticket for a broken taillight, and I nodded politely.

The woman headed off to the confectionery just

a few doors down, and I turned to face the now infamous Haute Couture Bridal. I drew in a deep breath, preparing to head inside and face whatever the day happened to bring, good or bad.

*Please, God, let it be good.*

From above, the store's sign caught my eye. Apparently a seagull had left behind some icky remains on it. Demetri would be beside himself, no doubt. He would see it as a blight on his business and call for someone to clean it right away. Hopefully that someone wouldn't be me. Grunt work usually went hand in hand with alterations, at least in his world.

I paused to look at the gowns in the front window, amazed at the professional display. To the right of the front door, two wedding gowns— one pure white silk and one satin crème—flanked a deep purple bridesmaid dress. In the window to the left of the door, Demetri's pride and joy—a multifeathered number—took the place of honor, nestled between two, in my opinion, outdated flower girl dresses. The crystals on the bodice shimmered as a carefully placed light in the floor of the window, angled just so, hit it. Ah, the joy of showcasing. Demetri excelled at it. Not that he actually dressed the windows, of course. Lydia and Corinne, two of our salesclerks, usually took care of that. He'd taken to calling them the Dynamic Duo because of their high energy level.

Before walking inside, I happened to glance

down and noticed that the hem of the satin crème needed to be adjusted. Should I mention it or let it go? To mention it would mean more work on my end. Still, as I stared through the crystal-clean glass at the beautifully presented gowns, I knew that I must. My conscience wouldn't allow me to let it go. No designer in her right mind would allow such a travesty.

I entered the store to find my high-strung boss in one of his moods. In typical flamboyant style, the impeccably dressed, overly groomed Demetri waved his manicured hands in the air to get my attention. "Gabi, you're late, and zis is not a good day to raise my blood pressure!" Angst always seemed to exaggerate his Russian accent, and this morning offered no exception to that rule.

"But I'm not late." I glanced at my watch just to be sure. Yep. Ten till eight. "I'm not supposed to be in until eight o'clock, remember?" I slid my purse off my shoulder and shifted it to the other hand.

"On a normal day." Creases formed between Demetri's carefully sculpted brows, and a muscle flicked at his jaw. "But zis is not a normal day. Zis is a Nicolette Cavanaugh day."

"Ah." Our latest diva bride-to-be had already left her mark on more than one occasion, so I understood his concerns. Mostly. "What time is she arriving?"

"Nine o'clock. And her dress *haz* to be ready."

His accent thickened in perfect timing with the narrowing of his eyes.

"Oh, it is. I—"

"Vhen a designer puts as much time and effort into a piece as I did veeth Nicolette's couture gown, he expects it to be perfect." Demetri paused to check his appearance in a nearby mirror and brushed an invisible piece of fuzz off the lapel of his expensive suit jacket. He straightened his dark red tie and resituated the corresponding handkerchief in his pocket, shaping it to pointed perfection.

"Well, yes, but—"

He turned to face me. "The Fab Five vorked like a vell-oiled machine to follow my pattern to a T, and zay executed it beautifully. Now ve have to make sure zee final touches are equally as fine."

I tried not to groan as he mentioned the Fab Five—the well-paid seamstresses who worked in his design studio behind the shop. Despite my attempts to become the sixth player on this illustrious dream team, Demetri wouldn't hear of it. To him, I would always be just the material girl, a position even lower than that of sales-clerk.

He paused to glance in the mirror once again and touched up the already perfect graying hair at his temples, then brushed the shoulders of his Italian suit jacket. "Under my guidance, zay crafted a magnificent gown—one vorthy of a write-up in *Texas Bride* magazine. And zay did it all in less zan four veeks."

"Yes. They're very good at what they do." Though it pained me to admit it, the five women —handpicked from five countries around the globe—were among the best in the business. I had nothing against them. Well, nothing personal, anyway. Still, I couldn't help but feel like Cinderella, slaving away in my tiny closet—er, alterations room—while the evil stepsisters got all the glory in their spacious, state-of-the art studio.

*Deep breath, Gabi. Deep breath.*

"I'm assuming zee alterations have been made?" Turning his attention away from the mirror, Demetri faced me head-on.

"Yes, of course, Demetri. I—"

"Nicolette vill be in a mood, no doubt. She's always cranky at zis time of day. I'm sure you remember her last visit. It took two days and four Xanax to get over zat one." He rambled on about people and their volatile emotional states, to which I could only offer a nod.

"Don't worry about Nicolette." I flashed what I hoped was a confident smile. "I've done every-thing she asked for."

My boss gave me a dubious look. "You raised zee vaistline?"

"Three-quarters of an inch." Though I had to wonder why the Fab Five made the bodice too long to begin with.

"Let out zee bustline?" Demetri crossed his arms at his chest, as if talking about a woman's chest size made him uncomfortable.

"Two and a half inches." I still couldn't figure out why the bride had decided to get breast implants after being fitted for her wedding gown, but that wasn't really my business, I supposed. I'd used every available bit of excess fabric in the seam to accommodate her perky new DDs, and I'd done it all without destroying the shape of the gown. Houdini himself couldn't have worked such magic.

"Hmm." Demetri followed me into my alterations closet at the back of the shop. He reached for a lint roller and ran it across his shoulders, then gave me a stern look. "Veethout destroying zee pleats?"

Okay, now he had crossed a line. Surely my boss knew me well enough to know the quality of my work. Had I ever destroyed anything?

"Demetri, I've done all that you asked and I did a fine job. Nicolette will be thrilled and so will you. As always." I emphasized the last two words. At this point I didn't trust myself to speak further, so I clammed up, ready to be done with this.

"Still, I—" Thank goodness he didn't have a chance to finish his thoughts. Kitty, our head salesclerk, caught him with a comment about a new shipment that had just arrived. He put the lint roller down and headed off to talk to her. I gave Kitty a grateful smile and settled into my private domain. I would have to tell Demetri about the uneven hem in the front window later, after he had calmed down.

Like that would ever happen.

Around 8:15 Kitty came into my alterations room. I gazed up at the fifty-something beauty, taking in the glistening ruby-red lips with their fine tattooed liner, the nicely executed eye makeup, and the shimmering rosy cheeks on top of pancaked skin. Sheer perfection. Exactly the sort of woman the impeccable Demetri depended on as the "front face" of his store. I'd never seen a hair out of place on Kitty's head. In fact, I secretly wondered if she wore a hairpiece but had never voiced the thought aloud.

In other words, she was the polar opposite of me. No matter how hard I worked to get my long black strands to cooperate, they refused to play nicely. And although I considered myself to have a steady hand in the alterations room, my makeup job often left something to be desired. Not that I didn't give it the old college try. I wouldn't dare show up at work without making an attempt at looking professional. I worked for nearly an hour every morning to add color to my otherwise blank pallet.

Still, looking at Kitty's practically-perfect-in-every-way appearance reminded me of my every flaw. Oh well. What I lacked in the way of physical perfection, I made up for in skill at the sewing machine. What did it matter anyway, when Demetri kept me hidden away from the crowd?

Kitty let out a whistle when she saw Nicolette's gown. She stepped toward the dress form and a smile curved her mouth. "Gabi, this is perfect." She ran her perfectly polished fingertip across the delicate Austrian crystals I'd applied to the bodice. "You did an amazing job. I can't even tell that you let the gown out. Amazing."

I breathed a sigh of relief as Kitty continued to stare at Nicolette's dress in rapt silence. Thank God someone in the store appreciated my work.

"Thank you. I like the way it turned out. Hope Nicolette does too."

"She's crazy if she doesn't."

"It still boggles my mind that she had cosmetic surgery so close to her big day." I did my best not to roll my eyes as I thought about it. Who did that?

"From what I read on her Facebook page, she told everyone she was out of the country on an expensive European vacation." Kitty glanced toward the door and then nudged it shut with her foot, pulled up a chair, and took a seat. Leaning my way, she whispered the rest. "Nicolette even posted pictures of the Italian countryside as proof of her trip. But I followed the link and it led to a stock photo site online." She chuckled.

"Crazy." Who went to such lengths to hide the

truth? Oh, wait. I did. At least when it came to my dress designs.

Kitty's brows arched. "Obviously she didn't want anyone to know about the . . . well, the surgery."

"Like going from a barely B cup to a DD wouldn't be noticeable?"

"I know, I know." Kitty giggled. "Pretty shocking difference, to my way of thinking, but I'm sure her daddy pulled out his credit card and covered the tab."

"Must be nice." Well, not to have breast implants, but to have a father who cared enough to stick around and pay for things for his daughter. What would that feel like?

*Focus, Gabi. Focus.*

Kitty gave the closed door another quick glance as if expecting Demetri to materialize on the other side. "Well, here's the good news," she said, her gaze now shifting back to the dress. "Nicolette is gonna look like a million bucks on her big day. That's really all that matters."

"I hope you're right." I didn't mention that I would have gone with a completely different design for the overly curvaceous thirty-something debutante. To my way of thinking, Nicolette needed something more formal. Less Hollywood party girl–like. I felt sure the ladies at the local Junior League would agree.

"Anyway, I just wanted to pop in to remind you that Nicolette's not the only special guest today. I've already prepped Lydia and Corinne. We've got that reporter coming from *Texas Bride*, so everyone needs to be on their game."

"Reporter?" Demetri had mentioned something about a magazine, hadn't he? But . . . today?

Kitty rose and smoothed her skirt. "Yeah, he's coming this morning at 9:15 for an interview. Not sure if he's bringing a photographer with him, but be prepared just in case."

"Oh, wow. Well, Demetri's got to love the free promotion." I did my best not to let the sarcasm in my voice ring through.

"Actually, the article is specifically about Nicolette's gown, which is why he's so keen on getting it finished before the reporter gets here. It's going to be the star of the show."

She pointed to the exquisite beaded dress, and I looked at it again with new eyes. If I'd known the gown was going to be photographed, I would have . . . Hmm. I wouldn't have changed a thing. Not a thing.

"The reporter's actually interviewing several designers across south Texas, each with a unique point of view, and we're thrilled to be on the list."

"I see." Must be nice, garnering that kind of acclaim for your work. I shoved aside the teensy-tiny bit of jealousy that threatened to erupt. "Well, I'm sure Demetri is pleased. I would be."

"He's nervous, I think." Her thinly plucked brows narrowed, and for the first time I noticed the color did not match her hair. Very suspicious. "But you know how he is. He tends to run on the excitable side. Even on a normal day, I mean."

To say the least. The man was more emotional than a mother of the bride on her daughter's wedding day, and I'd met more than my fair share of those.

"The key here is to leave a lasting impression so that the reporter never forgets Haute Couture Bridal," Kitty said. "We want to be memorable, to stand out."

"Stand out, eh?" I couldn't help the giggle that rose up. "Well, I could do a song and dance number when the guy gets here. I was in musical theater, you know. And I worked at the Grand Opera Society." I didn't mention that I'd only worked behind the scenes, sewing costumes for the cast members. Instead, I gave what I hoped looked like a confident smile.

Kitty laughed. "No song and dance necessary, except the usual from Demetri. He'll be all politeness and smiles when the reporter is here."

In other words, he'd be faking it, as always. I bit back a sharp retort and smiled weakly. "Well, if you change your mind on the song and dance number, you know where to find me."

"Yes, I know where to find you." She glanced around my small janitor closet turned work space and sighed. "I keep telling Demetri you need more room. I'd go crazy cooped up in this little . . ."

"Closet." A hint of a sigh escaped as I finished the sentence for her.

My gaze shifted to a photo of Ginger Rogers I'd fastened to the wall. I read the words beneath for the thousandth time: *The only way to enjoy anything in this life is to earn it first.*

I pondered Ginger's journey—how she'd served as a prop in Fred Astaire's arms as he'd waltzed her across the dance floor in movie after movie. How the spotlight had shone brighter on him, even though she'd done all of the same dance steps. In heels. Backwards. With the edges of her lips curled up in a relaxed smile, seemingly at ease with her role.

In that moment, the weirdest image floated across my brain. I saw myself gliding across the floor with Demetri taking the lead, the tips of his polished Versaces tromping on my aching toes. His smile—forced, of course—was my cue to keep dancing. And so I did, while onlookers lavished him with praise for the exquisite routine and he pulled the red silk handkerchief from his beautifully tailored coat pocket and swiped glistening beads of sweat from his wrinkled brow.

"Gabi? You okay?"

I snapped back to attention and saw the look of concern on Kitty's face. "Oh, yeah. Just thinking."

Kitty said something about having to clean the

bird droppings off the front sign, but I didn't hear most of it. I kept thinking about that image of Demetri waltzing me across the room and then posing for the cameras while I nursed my bruised toes . . . and pride.

Left alone in my little closet, I did my best to shake off my frustrations. If Ginger could hang on while she paid her dues, I could too. I would go on biding my time in this tiny janitor closet until a larger one came along. In the meantime, I would bend over backwards to make sure Nicolette Cavanaugh and her DDs were happy with my services, and I would do it all with a smile on my face . . . no matter how much my toes ached.

# 2

## Perfect Strangers

My mother told me I was dancing before I
was born. She could feel my toes tapping
wildly inside her for months.

GINGER ROGERS

At a quarter of nine I finished steam-pressing
Nicolette's gown and made my way to the break
room at the back of the shop. With the diva
bride coming, I needed to stiffen my backbone
in preparation. Caffeine would do the trick.
Demetri's state-of-the-art coffeemaker beckoned,
and I must answer.

I reached for my TIED UP IN KNOTS coffee
mug, placed it underneath the automatic coffeemaker, chose a packet of French roast, and then
pushed the button to begin the brewing process.
As the machine began to hum, my thoughts sailed
back to the conversation with Kitty. No wonder
Demetri had been so worked up about Nicolette's
dress. With the reporter zeroing in on the gown,
he had a lot at stake—far more than I'd been
aware of.

A little hiss sounded from the machine, and my
cup began to fill with the steaming liquid. I added

a couple of packets of sweetener and then reached into the refrigerator to grab the large bottle of Italian Sweet Crème creamer. Most people used a tablespoon or so. Not me. What good was a cup of coffee if not rich and sweet? I poured in a liberal amount, then put the bottle back into the fridge and leaned against the counter, deep in thought.

As I glanced around the break room, something occurred to me. This beautifully decorated space seemed gargantuan in comparison to my closet turned alterations room. I rarely utilized this area except for the occasional cup of coffee or sandwich at lunch. Kitty and Demetri most often headed down the street to Parma John's Pizzeria with the Fab Five during their lunch hour. Lydia and Corinne usually took their lunch to the patio area outside. Seemed like a waste to let the room sit here like this, empty and useless.

Maybe Demetri would consider switching things up. Sure. We could swap rooms. This could be my office. My thoughts began to wander as I played out the possibilities in my mind. I laid out the entire room in my imagination, even placing the furniture and dress forms in place. This, of course, shifted my thoughts to my own dress designs, which propelled my overactive imagination down a different track entirely.

"Gabriella!" I heard Demetri's voice sound from outside the door, and a little shiver ran down my spine.

I'd just opened my mouth to respond when he stormed into the room, the fine lines on his forehead emphasizing his narrowed gaze. He had that wild-eyed look, the same one a hunter gets as he zeroes in on his prey. Not that I'd ever been hunting. And not that I'd ever seen a hunter in an Yves Saint Laurent suit. Not exactly camouflage, but equally as effective in one-upping his prey.

"Zere you are." He spoke the words as some sort of accusation, as if grabbing a cup of coffee was out of line. He pointed to the cup in my hands, still full of the steaming liquid. "Ve don't have time for breaks today, Gabi. And vhatever you do, don't take your coffee into zee alterations room."

"Right." Did he think I was an idiot? I'd never taken my coffee in there before. Why would I start today?

"The last thing ve need is a catastrophe on zis very important day." He walked away, muttering something about how he needed to take another antianxiety tablet. If I'd had one handy, I might've taken it myself. Instead, I slurped a couple of mouthfuls of coffee, poured the rest down the sink, and headed back to my closet—er, alterations room. With Nicolette's dress complete, I turned my attention to hemming another wedding gown for an exceptionally petite bride. If time permitted, I would tackle the hem of the dress in the window.

Nicolette Cavanaugh arrived at nine, as planned.

I could hear her coming and braced myself. She blasted her way into the alterations room, DDs leading the way. I hated to stare at the woman's chest, but it was considerably larger. Hopefully my imagination was playing tricks on me. My gaze shifted up to her face. The austere expression reflected her haughty manner. Ugh. Such a diva.

Demetri followed hot on Nicolette's heels, bug-eyed as his gaze shifted back and forth between her chest and her wedding gown, which I'd prominently displayed in the corner. Behind him Kitty pressed her way inside, looking calmer than the other two.

Nicolette took one quick glance at the dress, and her somewhat pointed nose wrinkled. "Are you sure you let it out enough?"

*Well, hello to you too. Great to see you again.*

I finally managed an abbreviated response. "Yes, I'm sure."

"And if you didn't?" She folded her arms at her chest—not an easy task, from what I could gather—and glared at me.

Demetri brushed past her in the direction of the gown. "Ve vill make it perfect," he said with a flourish. "No charge, of course."

"I'm guessing the waistline will be too large. I've been dieting, as I'm sure you can tell." She sucked in a deep breath and stood a bit taller.

I saw, all right. Her waist did seem smaller. Or was that just an illusion, with the larger chest? The hourglass figure called for a completely different design, but I would never say so.

"I've been off sugar for six weeks." She released a breath and her posture weakened. "You have no idea how hard it's been. I'm a sugar addict. But a girl's gotta do what a girl's gotta do to look great on her wedding day." Fine lines appeared on her brow.

"Amen to zat," Demetri said.

"Which is why I'm still feeling too unsettled about this dress." Nicolette scrutinized the gown once again and breathed a little sigh. "I've already been wondering if I made the right choice to begin with."

Demetri blanched at this news, and I could almost envision the thoughts whirling around in his head. "Zis gown vas made for you, dah-ling," he said after a moment's pause. "Designed vith your personality and your exquisite physique in mind." A fake smile followed.

"I am grateful, of course." She gazed at the dress more intently than before, fingering the bead-work. "Your work is always so lovely, Demetri. Everyone on the island says so."

"On zee island?" he echoed, then fanned himself with his hand.

"In the state." She faced him head-on and grinned. "Which is exactly why I chose you to design my gown."

"Ah, zat's more like it." With a flourish,

Demetri bowed. "I am your humble servant, here at your beck and call."

Demetri, a servant? Hardly.

"Well then, I will call you with a request to design my veil," she said. "I hadn't planned to wear one, but Peter insists. Some sort of family tradition or something. Honestly, I can't imagine messing up my hair with a veil, but he won't hear of anything else."

"I vill create zee perfect veil to match your gown," Demetri said. "No charge. And think of how beautiful zee dress vill look with just zee right one." He shifted into a conversation about silk tulle versus English net, carrying on about his latest shipment of the latter, but seemed to lose her after a minute or two. I had a feeling the girl couldn't care less. In fact, I suspected she wouldn't even wear a veil on the big day.

"Maybe the dress will fit." Nicolette set her Louis Vuitton bag down on the chair and ran her finger across the Austrian crystals on the gown's skirt. "I will have to see it on to make a determination."

With a wave of his hand Demetri gestured for Kitty to remove the gown from the dress form, then announced that he would be in his studio prepping the Fab Five for the reporter's arrival should we need him. No doubt he planned to swallow the rest of the bottle of antianxiety meds somewhere along the way.

Nicolette turned to the sketchpad on my desk. *Oh, yikes!* She picked it up and flipped through the pages while Kitty lifted the gown from its perch in the corner. Nicolette gazed at my designs without saying a word—*Thank you, God!*—but I noticed she paused on one of my favorites and glanced my way as if to ask, "Did you do this?"

I nodded and breathed a silent prayer that she would put the sketchbook back down on the desk. She did. I scolded myself for bringing it here in the first place.

Never. Again.

Kitty carried Nicolette's white satin gown out of the alterations room, across the front of the shop, beyond rows of high-end dresses, and into the spacious dressing room area with its Victorian fainting couch and matching wingback chairs. Nicolette followed behind her, glancing down at the expensive zebra rug before disappearing from view inside one of the little changing rooms.

I followed behind Kitty, hoping against hope that Nicolette wouldn't say anything about my designs. So far, so good. By the time I reached the Grecian statue lamp—*Really, who chooses a naked lady holding a chandelier for their dressing area?*—I was convinced I'd worried for nothing. I paused to fuss with the fresh roses in the large crystal vase on the marble side table, noticing that one of them had a wilting petal.

Demetri would be humiliated. I plucked it off and stuck it in my pocket.

Kitty glanced at me through the open door leading to Nicolette's changing room, and I could read the concern in her expression. "Gabi, Lydia and Corinne are on break. If any customers come in while I'm busy, will you wait on them?"

"Sure." I could scarcely control my nerves at this point, but I did my best to remain calm, at least on the outside. Thank goodness we didn't have any customers at the moment. Hopefully all of the island's brides-to-be had other plans this morning.

Kitty closed the door and then opened it a couple of inches, speaking through the crack. "Oh, and that reporter . . . he's due here any second. Take care of him, okay?"

"O-okay." How she expected me to take care of him, I couldn't say. Keep him preoccupied, maybe. Sure. I could show him around. Likely he would be the studious sort with a pencil behind his ear and a note tablet in hand. I'd watched enough television dramas to know the type.

"Make sure he makes it to Demetri's office," she added from behind the closed door. "He can wait there until Demetri is ready to see him."

"Will do." I paused to glance at my reflection in the full-length mirror that made up the outside of the door, groaning internally when I saw that my eye shadow looked a bit uneven today. I thanked my lucky stars that Demetri hadn't noticed. Yet.

Naturally, this reminded me of a funny scene in *Top Hat*, one of my favorite Fred and Ginger movies. Before long I was completely lost in the moment, whisked to a dreamlike state by the dancing duo.

I snapped to attention when a customer paused at the front window, gazing at the uneven hem on the mannequin. Oops. I headed to the front of the store, ready to play the role of salesclerk and wishing I had perfect hair like Kitty or vivacious personalities like the Dynamic Duo. If I did, maybe Demetri would put me in a place of prominence.

Positioning myself behind the counter, I reached for a tiny compact mirror in Kitty's top drawer and went to work, dabbing at my eye shadow. Somehow I managed to leave a light silver-green streak across my right cheek. Great. I stuck my index finger in my mouth to wet it and did my best to remove the streak. Unfortunately, all of my rubbing left a red mark the size of my thumb. Oh well.

After I put the mirror back in its place, I released a slow breath and reflected on what had just happened with Nicolette. She'd clearly been intrigued by my designs. I could tell as much from the look of interest in her eyes. On some level, that made me feel really good.

Still, what was I thinking? I scolded myself for

bringing the sketchpad to work and vowed never to do so again. If Demetri saw it, I would be toast. Burnt toast.

My thoughts shifted to the goings-on in the dressing room. I crossed my fingers, hoping for the best with the fit of the gown. Surely Nicolette would be pleased as punch when she saw that I'd fitted the bodice appropriately. And maybe the waistline wouldn't be too large. I hoped. If so, I would deal with it.

At that very moment, a shimmer of light from the front of the store caught me off guard. I couldn't help but squint as I looked toward the front door. Streams of sunlight poured in from the open door, making it tough to see.

At first.

After a moment of squinting, I finally got a good look at the fella who'd stepped into the shop. A teensy-tiny gasp slipped out as I stared at the handsome stranger. If Prince William had a twin, it would be this guy—tall, stately, with blond hair. Mama mia, what a surprise. Was this our reporter? Not at all what I'd pictured. More Hollywood glam boy and less Discovery Channel narrator.

*Hello, Mr. Reporter.*

Poor guy. He seemed a little confused, swallowed up by a sea of white satin and tulle. And though he wore a nice suit—moderately priced, from what I could gather from the cut and fit—he looked strangely out of place among all of the top-of-the-line gowns.

With Kitty in the dressing room and Lydia and Corinne on break, I had to play the role of hostess, did I not? I took a few tentative steps toward him, feeling a little discombobulated as the smell of his yummy cologne captivated me. I stared at his eyes—deep sea-green eyes, perfect for a close-up on the big screen—and did my best not to swoon. Swooning was highly overrated, particularly among alterations specialists. We needed to keep our wits about us at all times lest we do damage with the scissors and needles and such.

"Can I help you?" I managed after a couple of seconds of awkward silence.

"Yes." He glanced down at the notepad in his hand as if searching for something and then looked my way once again. "I'm Jordan Singer from *Texas Bride* magazine." He handed me a business card. Low-end quality. Black on white. My boss would hate it. "I'm looking for . . ." He glanced back down at his notepad. "Demetri?"

I smiled, my performance as solid as a rock. "Demetri Markowitz, our owner and one of the country's most renowned dress designers."

"Looks like I've landed in the right place then." The reporter stuck his notepad under his arm and reached to shake my hand. "Is he here?"

With his hand now swallowing mine, I flashed another confident smile. "Yes, he's in his studio."

*No doubt giving the Fab Five instructions on how to impress you, but that's beside the point.*

"His studio?" The handsome stranger gave me a perplexed look.

"Yes." I withdrew my hand and nodded. "He has a design studio in the building behind this one."

"Right, right. I think I knew that. I guess that's where the magic takes place." A hint of a smile curled up the edges of Prince William's—er, Jordan Singer's—lips.

The only magic taking place at the moment happened to be in my heart. I felt a little like one of those women in movies from days gone by, the ones who couldn't seem to walk or talk straight when a handsome fella walked into the room. Visions of Fred Astaire and Ginger Rogers danced through my mind, but I forced them away.

"Um, yes. Demetri. Magic. Studio."

Jordan gave me an odd look and shrugged. "So . . ."

"I'll take you to Mr. Markowitz's office. He will meet you there shortly." *Just as quickly as I page him, anyway.*

I moved in front of the reporter to lead the way to Demetri's exquisitely decorated office. I'd just taken a couple of steps when the bell above the front door jangled. I looked up to see Scarlet Lindsey, owner of Let Them Eat Cake, my favorite island bakery. She entered the store with a tray of delectable edibles in hand, her smile exuding a sunny cheerfulness, as always.

Yum. I drooled when I saw the platter of baked goods. My gaze shifted to the chocolate-covered éclairs, and I could hardly contain myself.

"I come bearing gifts!" she said with a smile.

"Thank you." I couldn't imagine why she'd brought them into the shop. Demetri would have a fit if he saw someone—other than a potential customer, anyway—bringing food in here. I needed to get that tray out of her hands, and the sooner the better. My mind reeled as I fought to come up with a plan. Yes, I would carry the tray back to the break room. That would work. Demetri rarely went in there.

Scarlet's gaze shifted between Prince William and me, and I could read the intrigue in her eyes.

*Don't make assumptions, girl. He's not mine. Not even close.*

"Scarlet Lindsey, this is Jordan Singer. He's a reporter for *Texas Bride* magazine."

"Nice to meet you," Scarlet said, smiling at Prince William.

"You too," he replied.

I eased the tray out of Scarlet's hands, practically drooling as I hyper-focused on the chocolate éclairs. I'd never been able to resist them—especially when they were covered in rich, dark chocolate.

*Don't do it.*

I must've said the words aloud without

meaning to, because Prince William gave me a contemplative look. "I won't, I promise. But it's tempting, I have to admit."

Embarrassment washed over me. "Oh, sorry. Just talking to myself."

Not that he appeared to be paying any attention. No, his gaze was fixed on the tray of goodies.

"Have one," Scarlet encouraged him. "We're celebrating!"

I almost groaned aloud as Mr. Reporter reached to grab an éclair from the tray. "What are we celebrating?" he asked and then shoved the yummy thing into his mouth.

"Ooo, it's the best news ever." She let out a girlish squeal. "I'm engaged!"

"No way." I nearly lost the tray at this point, but the reporter caught the edge and leveled it out. Our fingers touched as he steadied it, and I felt a little tingling in my fingertips. Might've been from the way I now clutched the tray. Or not. Either way, I needed to get this thing back to the break room before Demetri saw it.

"It's true! I'm engaged!" She clapped her hands together. "Armando proposed a few weeks ago at the bakery. That's why I'm here. When I gave Bella the news, she told me to come and see you, since you're the best designer on the island. Thought maybe the chocolate would serve as a nice bribe."

"O-oh?" I could hardly interrupt Scarlet's story

midsentence, now could I? Especially when she mentioned Bella's name. If the island's most illustrious wedding planner said that Scarlet needed my services, I'd better pay attention. I leaned against the counter and gazed down at the éclairs, my stomach now rumbling.

"Well, of course! I need to talk to you about making my dress." Off Scarlet went on a tangent, telling Mr. Reporter what a great designer I was. How my dresses should be hanging on the mannequins in the front window. How I really understood the heart of the bride, being a woman and all, and how nothing any other designer could create would come close to my designs. How Bella Neeley—with all of her sage wisdom—recommended me above all other designers. I appreciated the flattery, but here? Now? Ack!

"You're a designer too?" Mr. Reporter gave me a "now here's a story I didn't anticipate" look.

Panic overtook me, but I couldn't let it show in my expression. Instead, I managed a weak smile and took a couple of steps toward the break room. "I . . . dabble."

"You dabble?" He took another éclair.

"In dresses," I explained. "But nothing like Demetri. Nothing, nothing, nothing like Demetri."

"Nothing is right." Scarlet put a hand on my arm. "Her designs are just gorgeous."

*Oh. Help.*

Scarlet giggled. "Gabi here is so . . . today. I'm

36

telling you, her gowns should be in magazines."

"In magazines, eh?" The reporter's eyes narrowed to slits, and I felt my face heat up.

"Yep. She's the best."

Scarlet continued to sing my praises, even giving details about a dress I'd made for a recent bride, our mutual friend Hannah. I flashed a warning look, but she didn't take the hint. Instead, she rambled on about my talents and abilities, sharing so much that Mr. Reporter finally reached for his notebook and started jotting down notes. Great. Might as well go ahead and plan my funeral now before Demetri had a chance to kill me.

"Did I hear you say that Bella Neeley knows about your designs?" The handsome reporter gave me an inquisitive look. "If so, it must be nice to have her stamp of approval. Bella owns the most popular wedding facility in the state, and her word is law when it comes to weddings."

"Don't you just love Club Wed?" Scarlet giggled. "I've baked cakes for lots of weddings there." She gestured to his notepad. "You can put that in your article if you like. Did I mention that I bake wedding cakes? I do, you know. My shop—Let Them Eat Cake—is just a few doors down. If you ever want to do an article on wedding cakes, I mean."

Another little giggle followed from Scarlet. Me? I wanted a black hole to swallow me up. Instead, I grimaced as Scarlet added an additional nail to my coffin with her over-the-top statement, "Bella just loves my shop, but you want to know what she loves even more? Gabi's designs."

Great. Put me six feet under and call it done.

At this point I went into a legitimate panic. I felt the heat start in my neck and move its way up my face. I managed to say, "I'll be right back. I just need to put these éclairs . . ."

What happened next will forever remain seared in my memory. Nicolette and Kitty emerged from the changing room. In spite of the semi-sour expression on the bride's face, she looked radiant in the dress, which fit to a T.

Er, fit to a DD.

I could tell Nicolette still wasn't happy, but that didn't matter right now. Relief flooded over me as I realized the perfection of the fit of the gown. Well, relief filled with concern about the tray of sweets, which the bride-to-be zeroed in on.

She took several steps in my direction, the large bell skirt on her gown swishing this way and that, her eyes glazed over as she stared at the éclairs. Her sour expression shifted to one of pure bliss as she stared down at the tray.

*No, no, no, no, no!*

"Oh, Gabi!" Her voice trembled and her eyes fluttered closed for a second, as if trying to resist the temptation. "I-I-I told you that I'm off sugar, remember?"

"Yes. Actually, these aren't for you. They're—"

The sour expression reappeared, along with fine wrinkles on her brow. "Are you saying I can't have one? Just one itsy-bitsy, teeny-tiny bite?"

"No, I'm not saying that. I just—"

I couldn't finish the sentence. Instead, I watched in horror as those long polished nails reached for the largest éclair on the tray. I yanked the tray back. In doing so, the chocolate-covered goodies went sailing in every direction—in slow motion, no less.

Nicolette let out a scream just as Demetri and the Fab Five entered the shop from behind us, followed by the Dynamic Duo. A collective gasp went up as the sugary sweets flew high and then took a swan dive, aimed right at the bodice of the bride-to-be's perfectly altered, beautifully fitting gown.

Pinching my eyes shut, I braced for the inevitable. Only when Prince William lunged to grab the glass tray from my slippery hands did I open them again.

He missed, and the tray flew into a mannequin and then dropped to the floor, shattering into pieces.

I happened to glance up as Nicolette reached out to grab Kitty's arm to keep from falling. Three seconds later, my question about whether or not the beautiful store clerk wore a hairpiece was answered as a shock of hair went shooting through the air and landed on Demetri's shoulder. He must've thought it was a rodent or something, because the man went berserk, flinging his body this way and that, trying to shake it off and hollering in Russian all the while.

Somewhere between the Fab Five's multilingual cries, the Dynamic Duo's giggles, Scarlet's profuse apologies, Kitty's tears, Demetri's jerking, and Nicolette's rants, I heard my boss's announcement that I was fired.

Not that he needed to voice this aloud, of course. I knew my material girl status had come to its untimely demise the minute I saw Nicolette Cavanaugh's DDs covered in gooey chocolate. They, like my career, were a catastrophic mess, one that no amount of alterations could fix.

# 3

## Pick Yourself Up

I'm in therapy, and sewing is cheaper than a psychiatrist.

AUTHOR UNKNOWN

Demetri took one look at Nicolette and went into a rage—all of it aimed at me. Me? Did I force the skinny bride-to-be to take the éclair? Of course not! Did I bake the tray of sweets? No way. Still, I took the blame for it all. In multiple languages at once. The Fab Five ranted alongside Demetri, apparently furious that their hours of hard work in designing the gown had ended in chocolate-covered catastrophe. Lydia and Corinne knelt down on the floor, picking up the mess at a fast pace.

Out of the corner of my eye I caught the look of horror on Scarlet's face. She and Mr. Reporter both looked mortified. Of course, the most mortified person in the room, and also the loudest, was Nicolette, who wailed at the top of her lungs and then flew into a rant about how I'd ruined her wedding.

Please. The girl wasn't getting married for months. How could I ruin a wedding in advance?

"Get your things and go, Gabi!" Demetri's brows furrowed, and I could hear the anger through the tremor in his voice. He reached down to pick Kitty's hairpiece up off the floor and shuffled it from one hand to the other. A muscle clenched along his jaw as he looked at me. With a tip of his head, he motioned for me to leave.

I didn't respond. Couldn't have spoken even if I'd wanted to. And who would want to stay under these conditions? Didn't Cinderella run from the ball when fate handed her an ultimatum? Looked like my appointed hour had come. The proverbial clock had struck midnight and there was no turning back.

I ran to my tiny closet space, suddenly overwhelmed by all of the stuff crammed inside. What could I take with me? Most of these things belonged to my boss, after all. I grabbed a handful of things—my pincushion, measuring tape, and emergency sewing kit—and glanced at the two dress forms standing in the corner. They were too large to lug out of here in front of a watching audience. I'd have to come back for them later. If I ever worked up the courage to come back. Finally, but most important, I snagged my sketch-book, which I tucked under my arm.

*Deep breath, Gabi. You can do this.*

With my head held high, I marched across the store, doing all I could to avoid the glares from Demetri and the wails coming from Nicolette. Off in the distance I heard Scarlet trying to pacify everyone and Mr. Reporter—what was his name again? Prince William?—asking for details about Nicolette's upcoming day. And poor Kitty! She stood behind the counter and, with the help of the Dynamic Duo, tried to force the now wild-looking hairpiece back in place. To say it did not end well might've been an understatement.

I made it to the doorway but froze, one foot in, the other out. Inside—a world of chaos and pain. Outside—a yet undiscovered life devoid of a paycheck.

Taking my first step toward freedom, I drew in a deep breath and then sprinted to my car. I climbed inside, the door clunking to a close beside me. Unfortunately, I'd forgotten about dropping the side mirror onto my seat earlier. I sat on it and came up with a start. Tossing it onto the passenger seat, I fought the feeling of heaviness in my chest.

*Don't cry. Don't cry.*

My car refused to start—the icing on my proverbial cake, so to speak. At this point I stopped fighting it and gave in to the emotion. Flinging my upper body onto the steering wheel, I sobbed like a two-year-old who'd been sent to the naughty corner. How could Demetri humiliate me like that—in front of a reporter, no less? And how could he and the Fab Five blame the chocolate incident on me? Surely he could see that

Nicolette was responsible for her own actions. Right?

Okay, so I happened to be holding the chocolate-covered goodies when she grabbed a piece, but that didn't make me responsible, did it? Of course not.

I sat alone in the car, crying it out for several minutes. Every time I thought about leaving Haute Couture Bridal for good, another wave of angst hit me. I vacillated between wanting to smack someone—Demetri, maybe? Nicolette?—and wanting to beg for my job back. Surely I could reason with my boss. Maybe once things cooled down, he would come to his senses. I prayed so. In the meantime, how did I go about dealing with this inexplicable feeling of emptiness and pain that gripped me when I thought about losing my place in the wedding world?

Minutes later, I heard a tap on my window. I peered through the glass to see Scarlet. I tried to roll down the window—*Really? Is the handle jammed again?*—and sighed, unable to speak past the lump in my throat.

I could read the apology written all over her face. "Gabi, I . . . I don't know what to say."

"You don't need to say anything." I hiccuped. "You're not to blame."

"I am." Scarlet's cheeks blazed red, which only emphasized her freckles. "I took the éclairs in there. I had no idea Nicolette Cavanaugh would be inside the dressing room, or that she would be dieting."

"Looks like she fell off the wagon." I smiled weakly, and Scarlet laughed.

"And she took Kitty's hairpiece with her." Another laugh followed from Scarlet, but I didn't find this funny at all. Still, when I pinched my eyes shut, the image of Kitty's hairpiece landing on Demetri's shoulder revived my sense of humor and I snickered.

Scarlet must've taken this as some sort of hopeful sign on my part. She walked around to the passenger side of my car and opened the door. Well, tried to open the door. The broken handle prevented her from accomplishing her goal, so I reached across and opened it for her. She climbed inside. "At least something good has come out of all of this," she said, giving my beat-up old car a closer look.

"Oh? Demetri is giving me my job back? I won't have to tell Mama and Mimi Carmen that we can't make the rent this month?" I sniffled as visions of my elderly grandmother flooded my mind. Poor Mimi! Would she spend her golden years begging for bread on a street corner because her granddaughter couldn't hold down a job?

Scarlet's cheeks flamed again. "Well, no. Not that. But Nicolette is looking for someone to make her wedding cake. It came up in the conversation as we tried to clean the chocolate off her dress. She thought she'd found the perfect cake shop but didn't like the samples. It all fell through. I told her about Let Them Eat Cake, and I think she's interested."

"W-what?" I had visions of Nicolette pulling every red hair out of Scarlet's head, not hiring her to bake a wedding cake. Still, stranger things had happened. Most of them to me.

"It's true. I think she's really going to order from me. I won her over with the Italian cream cake idea. Turns out she loves cream cheese frosting."

"I have a feeling she loves anything with sugar in it." A minuscule sigh followed as I replayed the éclair incident in my mind once again.

Scarlet gave me a sympathetic look. "Man. Forgive me?" Tiny creases formed around her eyes.

"For what?"

"I'm going on and on about my business growing and you're . . ." She shook her head. "I have to believe that God will redeem this situation you're going through. This will end well, Gabi. I know it will. Just give Demetri a chance to cool down. He'll give you your job back. Wait and see."

"I'm not so sure about that."

"Puh-leeze. The man can't make it without you."

"Of course he can. He's got the Fab Five." Tears trickled down my cheeks.

"They're not half as fab as you." Scarlet gave me a winsome look and smiled. "You're the best. And I'm sorry if I got carried away in front of that

46

handsome reporter. Just couldn't help myself. You don't get enough credit for what you do. If they had any idea how good your designs are, you'd be on the cover of that magazine, not Demetri."

"Actually, I don't think he made the cover. They're doing a write-up about Nicolette's dress." I sighed. "Well, they were, anyway. Now it's covered in chocolate."

"Chocolate washes out, no problem. Nicolette's dress will be as good as new before you know it." Scarlet grinned as if it were really just that easy. "Ooo, speaking of chocolate, I have an idea." She snapped her fingers. "Come to the bakery with me and hang out for a little while. We can wash away your troubles with some sugar. You never got to taste those éclairs. I'm using a brand-new recipe, one I came up with to celebrate my new status as an engaged woman. I'm calling them the Wedding Belles. Did you notice they were bell shaped?"

I shook my head. "No, I didn't. Sorry."

"Well, they are. And I'm going to sell them two to an order. Isn't that sweet?" She chuckled. "Sweet. Get it?"

I got it, but I didn't really feel like acting chipper right now. Not with my world imploding.

Still, how could I ruin her day? The girl had a lot to be excited about right now, what with the diamond ring circling her finger and all.

"I'm really happy about your engagement, Scarlet," I said after a moment's pause, "but I think I'd better just go home and skip the sweets."

Then again, if I went home, I'd have some 'splainin' to do. Mimi Carmen would no doubt go into a panic once she heard I'd lost my job. She'd likely call Mama at the travel agency and tell her that the sky had fallen. This would be followed by a trip to her church, where she would light a candle for me. If she could afford a candle, anyway. I wasn't sure about the going rate for plea-bargain prayers these days.

No point in worrying Mama and Mimi just yet. Besides, cooler heads would prevail. Maybe Scarlet and I could come up with a plan of action. And drowning my sorrows with sugar did sound appealing.

We got out of the car, and I trudged along behind my friend to her bakery, where I spent the next hour and a half nibbling on baked goods—first an éclair, then a banana nut muffin, and finally a macadamia nut cookie loaded with white chocolate chips. Turned out sugar really could wash away your troubles, or at least make you forget about them for a spell.

By the time I reached the diabetic coma stage, I no longer cared that I didn't have a job to go back to. Just one more of those Wedding Belles and I might be willing to forget the whole bride-covered-in-chocolate thing too.

Around 11:30 Scarlet passed the reins to her mother, who worked as her assistant in the kitchen. The most amazing spicy aroma filled the air, and I rose in one fluid motion to figure out where it had come from. Parma John's Pizzeria next door. Of course.

"It's the South of the Border special today," Scarlet explained and grinned. "I love the South of the Border. Hot. Yummy. Taco meat. Cheese. Gooey." Her eyes glazed over, and I felt myself swooning all over again. She peeked through the new opening between the bakery and the restaurant. "Bella's there. Let's go."

Scarlet grabbed my hand and practically pulled me into Parma John's. Not that it took much doing. The delicious aroma drew me like the Pied Piper wooing the children into his lair. Until I saw Bella. At that point I erupted in tears. Couldn't help myself. Bella was a wedding pro. I was a failed wedding dress designer. The contrast stared me in the face.

"Gabi?" She drew near and put her hand on my arm. "What's happened? Did someone . . . I mean, has someone . . ." Her eyes misted over. "Died?"

"No." I shook my head. *Only my career.*

"What's happened then?" She gestured for us to take a seat at a nearby table, and I leaned my head down on it. "You're never off work this early."

"I'm off . . . period."

"What do you mean?" She paused from our conversation long enough to holler our order back to her brother in the kitchen, then she turned my way again. "Now, what were you saying?" She leaned in to whisper, "You're taking the day off because of your period?"

"No." I fought the temptation to slap myself on the forehead. "I'm trying to tell you that I'm off because I don't have a job anymore. I've been axed."

"No way. Tell me everything."

And so I did. Bella sat straight as an arrow, clinging to my every word until the pizza arrived. At that point she didn't even give me a chance to grab a slice before taking one herself. She seemed lost in her thoughts. Or lost in the cheese, one or the other.

"There's got to be a solution for this," she said after downing half a slice of the gooey pizza. "God will turn it around, watch and see."

"That's what I said." Scarlet nibbled on the corner of a slice of pizza and gave me a pensive look.

I didn't really need or want any of their religious talk today. If God cared about my career, why had he allowed this to happen in the first place? For that matter, if he really gave a rip about me, why did he let my dad walk out when I was just twelve years old?

Ugh.

I reached for a slice of pizza and shoveled it in, taking bite after humongous bite. It filled the gap in my soul, at least temporarily.

After a few moments of silence, Bella finally spoke. "Well, let's look at this as a blessing in disguise."

"A blessing in disguise? Losing my paycheck?" Had the girl lost her mind?

"Well, not that part, but the obvious. I mean, think creatively, Gabi. This is probably just the opportunity you've been looking for to start your own line. Open your own design studio. You know? If anyone deserves the chance to be showcased, it's you."

"R-really?" I sniffled.

"Yes, really. Now, we'll need a plan, of course, but I feel sure, if we put our pretty little heads together, we can come up with something. We're smart, educated women."

I wasn't sure a year and a half at the local junior college qualified me as educated, but I didn't say so. Instead, I mumbled the only thing that made sense in the moment. "I need an income. I pay the rent on our house."

Not that someone like Bella Neeley could understand the financial woes of a girl like myself. She had a hardworking husband. Lived in a beautiful Victorian home in the historic district. Managed Club Wed, the island's most successful wedding facility. In other words, she had the world on a string. Me? I couldn't even afford a quality spool of thread.

Empathy flooded Bella's eyes as she leaned my

way. "I get it, Gabi," she said, her voice now lowered. "I know what it's like to start your own business. It's scary, for sure. But we'll pray and go from there." She sat up straight, now all business. "In the meantime, you'll need a quick way to bring in money."

"Exactly."

After a moment, she snapped her fingers. "I know. The opera house. Mama was just telling me that they're holding auditions for the Christmas production. She can help you get your old job back."

"Really?"

"Sure." Bella grinned. "I'll talk to her later this afternoon. I don't know where they stand on costumes, but I'm sure she would put in a good word for you. Before long you'll be up to your eyeballs in costumes."

"You think?" I thought about it for a nanosecond before grief washed over me again. To go back to costume design would be fun, but it just wouldn't be the same. My heart, my thoughts, and my imagination were all tied up in the wedding biz, not the theater.

I'd just started to open my mouth to share this when the door of Parma John's opened and Demetri entered with the Fab Five in tow. A shiver slithered down my spine and I hid behind a menu, hoping to avoid the inevitable.

"Wow." Bella glanced over at my boss and

must've noticed his sober countenance. "Someone's knickers are really in a knot today. And the ladies don't look much happier."

I peeked around the menu and gave the Fab Five a closer look. Strained expressions on most of their faces clued me in to the fact that they, like Demetri, hated my guts. Not that they could see me hiding behind the South of the Border special and all.

I lowered the menu and caught a glimpse of Antonia, the baby of the group. Still in her early twenties, this recent import from Spain would surely empathize with my dilemma. She seemed nice enough. Not Beatrix, though. I shivered as I caught a glimpse of the oldest of the designers, the one who used every available opportunity to make me feel like a failure. She'd shoved her reading glasses onto the top of her head. They might as well have been horns. She, along with the other ladies, hovered around Demetri like a colony of ants giving reverence to their queen.

Bella's brother Armando seated the group on the far side of the restaurant, thank goodness. I breathed a sigh of relief and placed the menu back on the table.

"I have a thousand questions about those women." Scarlet's nose wrinkled as she gave them a second look. "But I hate to be nosy."

"There's not much to know," I said. "Just call them A, B, C, D, and E."

"Huh?" Scarlet took another bite of the pizza. "What do you mean?"

"They're all letters of the alphabet—Antonia from Spain, Beatrix from the UK, Chantal from Paris, Doria from Greece, and Emiko from Japan. A, B, C, D, E."

Scarlet leaned my way and whispered her thoughts on the matter. "Well then, I predict that one day you will not only get your job back, but you will also join them. You'll be the sixth in their little circle of champions."

"No way." I released a slow breath as I thought it through. "My name doesn't start with an *F*." A weak smile followed. "But if it makes any difference, Demetri has probably given me a big fat F for my performance today."

"That would be *my* performance." Scarlet groaned and took another nibble. "And just as soon as I finish off this pizza"—here she paused to ask Bella the calorie count of her slice—"I'm going to go over there to your boss and explain what really happened. Tell him that he needs to give you your job back. This is all my doing, not yours."

"No. Please don't." I felt a sudden urge to run. Still, I couldn't be rude to Bella and Scarlet, so I finished my piece of pizza, then slipped out of the restaurant when Demetri's back was turned. With my heart in my throat I raced toward the car, ready to put this awful morning behind me.

# 4

# They Can't Take That Away from Me

I cannot count my day complete
'Til needle, thread, and fabric meet.
AUTHOR UNKNOWN

I jumped into my car and prayed it would start this time. It did. Thank goodness. Something needed to go right for me today. I made the familiar drive to our little house on autopilot, unable to focus on anything but the events of the day. When I arrived home, I tiptoed inside, hoping not to wake Mimi Carmen, who usually napped at this time of day.

After easing my way into the kitchen, I tossed my bag onto the counter. Its contents spilled out, makeup clattering to the floor below. Great. Just one more mess I needed to clean up. On the top of the pile, I caught a glimpse of the reporter's business card with his name emblazoned across the top.

Ugh. He could keep his article on Demetri. I tossed the card on the countertop, my thoughts shifting to the chocolate-covered gown once again. I shivered as the incident replayed itself in my mind, not once, but twice. Was it my imagination, or was this story growing with each new replay?

"Home so soon, Gabriella?" Mimi Carmen's voice sounded from the hallway.

I looked up as she hobbled into the kitchen, her arthritic joints giving her fits, as always. Not that they stood much of a chance these days. Mimi was nearly as round as she was tall. Years of homemade tamales and enchiladas had taken their toll. Not that she was ready to give them up, of course.

"Yes. I—" Tears sprang to my eyes and I could not continue.

The soft wrinkles on Mimi's face drew me in, the comfort of the familiar grabbing hold of my heart. I would feel better after confiding in her, no doubt about it. But still, I hated to burden her. I'd already interrupted her nap, and she looked exhausted. No, I'd say as little as possible and hope she wouldn't press me on the matter. Not until later, when Mama arrived home. That way I could share the news with both of them in attendance. Between now and then I would figure out how to soften the blow.

Mimi ran her fingers across her upswept graying hair and tried to fix the loose bun in the back. This wouldn't be the first time she'd fallen asleep with her hair up, nor would it be the last. It also wouldn't be the last time she'd doze off wearing the housecoat Mama had purchased for her in 1987 as a Christmas gift.

"Did I wake you up?"

"Oh, just dozing a little during the commercials." She took a couple of slow steps my way and shrugged. "I was watching my story."

Her story was *Doña Bárbara*, her favorite telenovela. Classic Spanish soap opera. Loaded with drama, angst, and soured relationships—a lot like my life of late. Only, the people in that story received a decent paycheck for their drama.

"It's been a hard day," I managed. "I'll tell you later, okay?" My emotions were still too raw to share.

"You think your day has been hard!" she responded in Spanish. "You should see what's happening with Cecilia on my story!" Mimi went into a lengthy explanation of the dilemma her favorite character faced, but she lost me about halfway into it. Who had time to talk about a fictional world when the real one presented so many problems?

After a few minutes of rambling, she brought her story to its rightful conclusion. Her gaze shifted to the mess I'd made when my bag spilled onto the counter. "Don't worry about this. You go soak in the tub."

As always, she knew exactly what I needed even before I voiced it. I gave her a hug and then headed for the bathroom. A long, hot bubble bath would wash away the pain of the day.

The bubbly warmth did little to ease my worries, but it did help release the knots in my shoulders. If only my mind could relax as easily. As I rested against the tub, eyes closed, I replayed this morning's nightmare scene over and over again. Éclairs. Chocolate. DDs. Demetri's passionate "You're fired!"

*Stop it, Gabi. Let it go.*

I couldn't change the past, as Mimi Carmen would say. No point in trying. I just had to figure out a plan for the present. And the future. Without my income, we wouldn't be able to make our rent. Mama's paycheck—if one could call it that—hardly covered the utilities. No, her job at the travel agency didn't even make a dent in the light bill, water bill, and groceries. I would have to come up with a plan—and quick. Looked like Bella's suggestion that I apply for my old job at the Grand Opera Society was the only viable one. For now, anyway.

I'd never been a pray-er. Still, I gave it my best shot. I wasn't sure which way to go about it, though—Mimi Carmen's "light a candle and tell it to the priest" way or Bella's "just have it out with God and let him know how you're feeling" approach.

I opted for the latter and offered up an "oh,

help!" prayer, followed by several frustrated rants.

Having it out with God, it turned out, was a little frightening, especially when one was in such a raw and vulnerable state. Hopefully he could handle my tirade and not strike me with lightning. Not that I'd planned to confront him in full voice, actually, but I must have, because Mimi Carmen tapped on the door.

"Gabriella? Who are you hollering at?"

I groaned. "No one, Mimi."

"But I heard you. Something about life being unfair."

*Well, it is.*

"Sorry," I hollered out and then slithered under the water. If my grandmother responded, I couldn't hear her.

By the time I emerged from the once-warm, once-bubbly water, I felt renewed. Duking it out with the Almighty seemed to help, at least on some strange level. I climbed out of the tub, toweled off, and dressed in my workout clothes. Maybe I would go for a run later.

Or not.

As I passed by the spare bedroom, I caught a glimpse of the sewing machine in the corner. It seemed to call my name. I walked into the room, my thoughts immediately captivated by a dress design I'd sketched last night in the wee hours. At once I found myself transported to a happy place. I reached for my art pencils, then settled in to tweak the design, realizing it would be perfect for Scarlet. Yes, indeed. She would love this dress, no doubt about it.

Around 4:30 or so, the doorbell rang. My heart shot to my throat. Had Demetri come to add fuel to the fire, perhaps? Would he confront me in front of my grandmother? The thought terrified me, for all our sakes. This story might just end up on the evening news, with my grandmother in handcuffs.

NEWS FLASH: LOCAL SHOP OWNER TAKEN OUT BY ENRAGED GRANDMOTHER. STORY AT TEN.

I pushed my sketchbook aside and stood. A peek out the window didn't reveal much. I couldn't exactly see the front door from here.

"Gabi, can you get that?" Mimi Carmen's voice sounded from the kitchen. "I'm up to my eyeballs in enchilada sauce and can't stop."

"Okay." In spite of my less-than-perfect appearance, I opened the door. My heart shifted to my throat when I saw—*What's your name again, handsome?*—the reporter from *Texas Bride* standing there. I'd just started to work up the courage to stammer a hello when his gaze narrowed. I could read the confusion in his eyes.

"It's . . . it's you." He crossed his arms and leaned against the entryway.

Strange. I'd almost used the same opening line.

But why did he seem surprised to see me when he'd come to my house? "Yeah, it's me," I managed. "Why are you here?"

Now he really looked perplexed. "I was wondering the same thing. I came because I was summoned. Not sure why, though."

Again with the narrowing of the eyes. What was up with this guy? Was he on some sort of secret spy mission? Had Demetri sent him to scope me out? Confusion wrapped its tendrils around me, and fear quickly set in.

"I-I'm sorry?" I said.

"Oh!" His face flooded with relief. "Is *that* why you brought me here? To apologize?" A beautiful smile lit his face. "Well, I guess that makes sense, but the way you went about it seems a little odd. I would've just made apologies over the phone. Not that you owe me—or anyone else—an apology, by the way. What happened back at the dress shop was not your fault. I still can't believe you took the blame for that, so no apologies necessary, trust me."

He'd started to lose me a few sentences back. "Brought you here?" I sputtered. "What do you mean?"

He tilted his head. "You called me pretending to be an old woman. Accused me of doing a lousy job. On what, I'm not sure. Told me to come over here right away to take care of something I had broken."

"Something you'd broken?" Now he'd lost me entirely.

"Yeah." He gave a little shrug. "That's the part I don't understand. Were you blaming me for the broken glass tray? The one the éclairs were on?"

"No." This whole conversation threw me for a loop, and I couldn't help but think this guy had ulterior motives. No doubt he was on a secret mission, sent by Demetri to further humiliate me. Likely in print. In *Texas Bride* magazine. Well, I wouldn't give him that option. Not this time.

Just then Mimi Carmen appeared at my side, still wearing the homemade housedress I'd seen her in earlier in the day. Lovely. She wiped the enchilada sauce from her hands and glared at Mr. Reporter. "There you are, young man." She pushed past me and placed her balled-up fists on her ample hips. "It's about time you got here. Get in this house right now and take care of this broken sewing machine."

"Sewing machine?" Prince William and I spoke in unison.

"Of course." Mimi Carmen shook her head as if disgusted with him. "What else?"

"But I-I-I . . ." He glanced my way, now wide-eyed.

"Aye, aye, aye is right!" Mimi swung the door wide. "What happened the last time you were here was unforgivable, but this is a new day, and I'm a firm believer in offering second chances."

*Since when?*

"So get in this house, young man." She gestured with a tip of her head. "And do the right thing once and for all."

At that, Prince William stepped inside, and my grandmother slammed the door behind him, ready to take him down a notch or two. For what, I could not be sure.

"Ma'am, I'm really not sure why you called me," the reporter said, looking more than a little confused. "There's obviously been some sort of misunderstanding. Or mistake."

She pointed an arthritic finger in his face. "The only mistake is the one you made last time we were together." The tremor in her voice let me know she meant business. Apparently she frightened him too, from the look on his face.

"L-last time? At the bridal shop?"

"No, not the bridal shop." She rolled her eyes as if his words annoyed her. "Here. The last time you came to fix my sewing machine. You botched it up."

"Botched it up?" Prince William and I spoke in unison once more.

"Yes. You call what you did a repair job?" She crossed her arms and stared him down, then began a lengthy tirade in Spanish about how he'd fouled up a perfectly good 1967 Singer sewing machine—a classic, no less—by over-manipulating the bobbin. "I paid you good money!" she sputtered, now in English. "And you took advantage of my generosity."

"I-I what?" That freckled nose of his—cute as a button already—wrinkled, which only made him cuter. Not that I had time to focus on him. For more than a second. Out of the corner of my eye.

I put my hand on my grandmother's arm and did my best to calm her down. "Mimi, you've got the wrong man." I fought to keep my words steady so as not to further upset her.

"Wrong man, indeed." She snorted in a very unladylike fashion. "I should've called someone trustworthy the first time, and then we wouldn't be in this pickle, now would we?" She turned to face me. "You with those beautiful dress designs, Gabi, and no sewing machine to get the job done." Off she went in Spanish about how important the Singer sewing machine was to my design career, and I ushered up a prayer that this reporter—*Ack! What is your name again, you handsome devil, you?*—didn't speak Spanish.

"Wait. None of this makes a bit of sense to me." This, he managed in fluent Spanish. Great. Go figure.

"It doesn't make a bit of sense to me either." Mimi Carmen shook her head. "How someone could accept money for a job they didn't complete is beyond me. I should report you to the Better Business Bureau."

"But ma'am, I—"

"And another thing—the next time you service a customer's machine, leave a card. I had a doozy of a time finding your number." She gave me a little nudge with her elbow. "Thank God you had his card, right, Gabi? It certainly came in handy."

"Had his card?" This was growing stranger and stranger.

"Yep." She pulled out the business card I'd tossed onto the counter when I arrived home. I glanced at it, more perplexed than ever. Until my gaze landed on his name.

*Jordan Singer.*

In that moment, it all made sense.

Jordan *Singer*.

*Singer* sewing machine.

I got it. Only, how could I tell him without humiliating my grandmother or further irritating her?

Mimi folded her arms at her chest and gave me a knowing look. "Gabriella, this might be a good time for you to admit that Mimi Carmen was right."

"Right? About what?"

"I told you last week that the sewing machine repairman's name started with a *J*." She chuckled, then grabbed Jordan by the arm and pulled him across the tiny foyer. Her attention shifted to his face. "You've lost weight since the last time you were here."

"I-I have?" He shot a bug-eyed look my way,

and I sighed, knowing anything I said would only confuse him—or Mimi Carmen—more.

"Yes, but it looks good on you." She gave him a closer look. "Just so you know, though, I think I liked your hair better the other way."

He stammered, "Th-thank you?"

A grunt followed on Mimi's end. "Might as well get started on this sewing machine. You need to fix what you fouled up, and the sooner the better."

He tagged along on Mimi Carmen's heels into the back room. Arms waving, she rambled on and on in Spanish about his shoddy workmanship. Then, about the time I thought she might just punch his lights out, she patted him on the back and crooned, "There. I've said enough. You work. I'll get you and my sweet Gabriella a lemonade."

She left the room, and I found myself alone with the reporter who looked about as baffled as I'd been. He stared at me with that deer-in-the-headlights look.

Time to offer an explanation. "It's your name," I said as I took hold of his arm. "Your last name is Singer."

"Right," he responded in a hoarse whisper, sounding more confused than before.

"She thinks you're the Singer man." *Wow, is this guy muscular or what?*

"I *am* the Singer man. Jordan Singer."

I groaned. "No, she thinks you're the Singer sewing machine repair guy. The last one who came out to fix her sewing machine—and that was three or four years ago, FYI—was James something-or-other. At least, I think it was James. She remembered that his first name started with a *J.* So I'm guessing she saw your business card and got confused." At this point I realized I still had my hand on his arm, so I pulled it away.

"Ah." He raked his fingers through his beautiful blond hair and shrugged. "So, now what?"

"Now you repair her sewing machine. Or, rather, my sewing machine, though it's technically not mine until she dies. She's willed it to me."

"I see." He paused and glanced down at the antiquated machine with the Singer logo emblazoned across the front in faded letters. "But I don't know anything about sewing. Or sewing machines."

"Well, can you act like you do?" I said through clenched teeth as my grandmother appeared in the doorway. I turned her way and flashed a smile. "I'm sure everything will be fine, Mimi."

"I certainly hope so." She placed two glasses of lemonade on the stand next to the machine. "You, young man, should be ashamed of the shoddy work you did last time. I've never known a repair-man who didn't know a bobbin from a spool pin. I hope you've learned a little some-thing between then and now."

"*Little* being the key word." Jordan eased his way down into the chair in front of the sewing machine and stared at it as Mimi Carmen stormed out of the room. He glanced my way as if to ask, "Now what?"

What, indeed? I had absolutely no idea. But as I gazed into Jordan's handsome face, I couldn't help but think there were worse fates to befall a girl. Like losing her job, for instance. Oh, and ruining a wedding dress for an important client. All of this in front of a reporter for the most illustrious bridal magazine in the state.

A reporter with the handsomest face I'd seen in a long, long time.

And great biceps.

And the kindest smile, which he now gave—a smile that convinced me he would do whatever it took to put my grandmother's mind at ease.

For the first time since his arrival, I found myself relaxing. Yes, indeed. A girl could get completely lost in those gorgeous sea-green eyes. And as they locked onto mine, I felt my breathing return to normal for the first time all day.

# 5

# Follow the Fleet

Keep calm and get the seam ripper.

AUTHOR UNKNOWN

"So, now what?" Jordan asked after a few moments of silence passed between us.

I snapped back to attention, realizing I'd been staring at him for quite some time.

*Awkward.*

"Well, you're in luck," I said.

"I am? Could've fooled me."

"I'm just saying, I happen to know a little something about sewing machines." I nudged him out of the chair and sat down. "And despite what she thinks, the machine's not even broken. The bobbin's just giving me fits. But I can fix that myself. I've done it before. Surely I can do it again."

"Good." He leaned down to have a closer look as I raised the presser foot and opened the bobbin cover. "Glad someone knows what they're doing around here."

I continued to dismantle the metal casing, my mind in a whirl. "We'll just let her think you did it, okay?"

"Fine by me. I have a feeling she might sue me or something if I botch this up."

I glanced over at him as he grinned, his pearly whites catching my gaze. Perfect eyes. Perfect hair. Perfect teeth? Some people had all the luck.

We settled in at the sewing machine, and before long Jordan started offering advice. Helpful advice.

"Are you sure you're not a closet seamstress?" I laughed.

"No, trust me. I'm a reporter through and through. But I like to tinker with mechanical things. I used to work on cars. Before computers took over the world, I mean. Now the technology behind these new smart cars eludes me. So I'll stick with reporting. It pays the bills."

I paused from my work to look his way. "I've actually never met a reporter before. What's that like?"

"It's okay." He shrugged, and I could read embarrassment in his expression. "I know it's kind of odd for a guy to be working for a bridal magazine." He gave me an apologetic look. "Trust me, it wasn't my first choice. I wanted to report the news. The real news, I mean."

"What?" I chuckled. "Debutante brides aren't your idea of real news?"

"I guess some people would think so, but I don't happen to be one of them." He fidgeted with his shirt collar.

"So what happened?" I asked as I turned back to the loose bobbin. I pulled it out and took a screwdriver to the machine to tighten things up, hoping to relieve the poor guy of his embarrassment by keeping my attention on the machine.

"The magazine publisher shifted gears midstream," he said. "*Texas Bride* magazine became part of the *Texas Highways* family, and the next thing you know . . ."

"You're covering caterers, dress designers, and florists?" I tried.

"Yeah. Not exactly my dream job, but I'm doing my best to make it work until I get to do what I *really* want to do."

"Then we have more in common than you know." I gave the screwdriver another turn, laid it down next to the sewing machine, and looked at Jordan with greater admiration than before.

"Oh?" A hint of a smile turned up the edges of his lips. "Is this your way of saying you're not happy with your job at the dress shop either?"

"My *former* job at the dress shop." I did my best not to let a sigh escape as my thoughts shifted back to this morning's events. "But yeah, I guess you could say I haven't been happy for a while now. Maybe this is all some sort of a sign that I should change careers or something."

His dark eyebrows arched mischievously. "Open your own design studio?" He paused, and the playful expression on his face shifted to one of genuine caring. "From what your friend said, you've got the skill. Maybe you should just go for it."

"I dunno." Another uncomfortable silence followed as I thought about his question. Three times today someone had suggested I open my own design studio—first Scarlet, then Bella, and now this guy?

I bit my lip to keep from responding, then picked up the bobbin and settled it back into its cradle. With determination mounting, I gave the handwheel a turn but could tell the tension still wasn't where it needed to be. In fact, I'd actually made things worse. Just one more mess to fix.

From the other room Mimi Carmen's voice rang out in a sweet song, a lovely hymn in Spanish. I listened to the familiar words of "It Is Well with My Soul" and was transfixed.

*De paz inundada mi senda ya esté,*
*O cúbrala un mar de aflicción,*
*Mi suerte cualquiera que sea, diré:*
*Alcancé, alcancé salvación.*

*Alcancé salvación.*
*Alcancé, alcancé salvación.*

Jordan took several steps toward the door, completely silent, as we both listened to my grandmother's shaky but lovely refrain. When she finished, he looked my way. For a moment, I thought I saw his eyes glisten.

"I know that song," he said.

"You do?"

"Yes. My mom's parents are from Puerto Rico. I grew up hearing my grandmother sing her favorite hymns in Spanish." His eyes took on a faraway look, and I could tell I'd lost him to his memories. After a while he seemed to shake it off. "Sorry. Didn't realize how much I've missed them until now. My grandmother had the temper of a boiling teapot much of the time, but just as quickly she would burst into song. Like that."

He nodded toward the door as my grandmother's voice rang out again, this time singing "All My Exes Live in Texas." In Spanglish.

"The only time I ever saw my grandmother's temper flare was when my dad cheated on my mom." I shivered as the memory overtook me. "Trust me, you don't want to get her mad."

"I think I saw a little taste of that temper just a few minutes ago," he said. "She's really mad that I fouled up her *Singer* sewing machine."

I grinned as he stressed the word *Singer*.

"But hey, a fella can't help his name. Right?" He shrugged and then stared at the machine once again.

"Right."

"At least my first name has a good meaning, one I'm proud of."

"It does?"

"Sure. Jordan. As in 'cross the . . .' "

"Cross the Jordan?" It took a moment, but I finally got the reference to the Israelites crossing over the Jordan River into the Promised Land. "I see."

Staring into his twinkling eyes, I had the strangest feeling I really could cross over into the Promised Land. I shook off my swooning and focused on the sewing machine.

Jordan began to whistle "All My Exes Live in Texas" along with Mimi Carmen, who continued to belt it out from the kitchen. I couldn't help but notice the guy had perfect pitch too. After a moment, he stopped whistling and focused on a poster filling the wall space above the sewing machine.

"Ginger Rogers?" he asked.

"Yep. She's my personal favorite."

He gave me an inquisitive look. "You a dancer or something?"

"No. I have two left feet, actually."

He glanced down at my bare feet and laughed. "Now *that* I'd pay money to see." His gaze traveled up to the poster once again, and I could read the curiosity in his expression.

"It's not just Ginger I'm fascinated with, it's Fred too. I've loved them both for as long as I can remember. I suppose I have Mimi Carmen to thank for that. She introduced me to their movies when I was a little girl. I think I'm just mesmerized with their clothing. They had such . . . style."

"Yes. Fred was quite the suave fellow, wasn't he." Jordan phrased the words more as a statement than a question.

"He sure was. And Ginger's dresses were breathtaking." I pointed at the poster. "See what I mean? The waistline is perfect for her figure. And notice the cut of the skirt. See how it flares out at the bottom as she spins? I read that she put weights in the hemline to make it do that." A teensy-tiny sigh followed. "You just don't see dresses like that anymore."

"I guess you're right."

Passion now fueled my words as I turned to face him. "But don't you think you *should* see dresses like this? With a little tweaking, this would make a great bridal gown. At least to my way of thinking."

"Never thought about it."

"I think about it all the time." To prove my point, I rose and walked over to my worktable to grab my sketchpad. After flipping through the various pages, I finally landed on just the right one. "See?"

He took a couple of steps in my direction, then leaned in close, and I noticed the scent of his yummy cologne. As he glanced down at my somewhat messy drawing, I felt his breath on my neck, and a little tingle wriggled down my spine.

"Oh, wow. You're really good." His gaze traveled between my sketch and the poster on the wall. "I see what you mean now."

"Thanks. But I'm really just fascinated with trying some of these older styles in a new way. Not in the same way that Demetri does. My designs are nothing like his."

"Well, your friend was right about that. And now I see why she went to such efforts to sing your praises. You definitely deserve it. Does Demetri know that you—"

"No!" I cut him off with an evil-stepmother glare. "And he won't. Ever. He would . . ." I couldn't finish the sentence.

"He would hire you to do some of his best work?" Jordan tried.

"Hardly. He would probably sue me, claiming that I was trying to steal his clients. Or worse, his designs."

"What makes you say that?" Jordan took my sketchbook and turned the pages, giving each an admiring look. "Maybe he would come to his senses. Carry your line in his store. You never know."

"Oh, I know all right." Should I tell him the story? Share the details about Brenda Wainswright, a former employee who had lost her job after Demetri discovered her "unfaithfulness," as he called it? No, that would be a tale for another day.

"Well, you're too good a designer to be shut up in the back room hemming skirts, that's all I have to say."

"Th-thank you." His words both embarrassed and inspired me. How could he, a perfect stranger, offer such insight and encouragement? Then again, he wasn't a complete stranger, now was he? We'd already shared a tiny bit of getting-to-know-you time at the store.

I shook off my errant thoughts and glanced at the sketchpad. "You just have to trust me when I say that it's better if Demetri doesn't find out. Not that he ever really notices me anyway."

Now Jordan's eyes locked onto mine. "How could anyone not notice you?" His voice carried a hint of teasing, but I saw a definite look of interest in his eyes, and it totally stunned me.

For a moment, I couldn't seem to find my tongue. I finally managed an answer. "I don't think he can see past the Fab Five and the Dynamic Duo, to be honest."

"Fab Five? Dynamic Duo?"

I spent the next several minutes filling Jordan in on the ABCs of the Fab Five and then shifted gears to Lydia and Corinne. I finally stopped, remembering his reporter status. "I . . . I think I've said too much, sorry. Promise me you won't put any of this in your article?"

"I promise, Gabi."

Something about the way he spoke my name

with such tenderness made me believe him. For a minute, anyway. Just as quickly, doubt and fear grabbed hold of my heart. I'd given this guy way too much information. Sure, he was playing nice right now, but would he use this against me later? In print? I could live to regret my vulnerability.

"Don't worry. We're off the record here. I won't be writing about any of this, I promise." His words eased my mind, and the conversation turned back to the sewing machine, which still gave me fits.

Jordan grabbed the screwdriver and gestured for me to give him the chair. "Let me give it a try, okay?"

"Sure."

We worked together until the tension in the bobbin finally evened out. At that point I took his place in the chair, then ran a beautiful row of white stitches down a colorful piece of fabric. Primo!

Holding it up for his approval, I couldn't help but smile. "What do you think of that?"

"Not bad for a guy who knows nothing about sewing," he said as he took the piece of fabric in hand. "Sometimes I amaze myself."

"Apparently you have a real gift."

"Don't tell my dad, all right?" He paused. "He always wanted me to become a surgeon. Might pain him to know the only needles I've worked with are the kind on a sewing machine."

He passed the fabric back to me, and I folded it and placed it on the desk next to the machine. "Well, I promise not to tell."

"You would have a hard time tracking him down, anyway. My parents live in New York. They moved there a couple of years ago."

"Well, that's different." I couldn't imagine leaving Galveston, let alone traveling to a place as busy as New York.

"Maybe I should give up reporting and open a bridal studio in the Big Apple," Jordan said. "Hire you as the designer. What do you think? Would you move up there if it would make you famous?"

"I don't know, I . . ." Before I could think of a proper response, the aroma of Mimi Carmen's enchiladas wafted in from the kitchen and captivated me.

Jordan glanced toward the door and sniffed the air. "What is that?"

My grandmother appeared in the doorway at that very moment. I noticed she had changed out of her housedress into a skirt and blouse. She'd also fixed her hair. Odd.

"It's Mimi Carmen's homemade enchiladas," she said in a singsong voice. "It's a family recipe. You stay for supper." She spoke the words as a command, not a question.

Not that Jordan appeared to mind. Neither did I, for that matter. I'd never had a prince—a real, live prince—stay for dinner before.

"Before we eat, come and look at the machine, Mimi." I gestured to the Singer.

She stepped into the room, sat at the chair in front of the machine, and then stitched a beautiful line onto a scrap of fabric. Her face lit into the loveliest smile. "Perfection! You have regained my trust!" She stood and gave Jordan a kiss on the cheek, then repeated her offer of food.

We followed her into the kitchen, where the aroma of spicy sauce greeted us. When Jordan saw the platter of enchiladas, his expression shifted to one of pure delight. He leaned down over it and drew in a deep breath.

"Smells great. I haven't had real, authentic Mexican food since my grandmother passed."

"God rest her soul." Mimi Carmen and Jordan spoke the words in unison.

"Reminds me of the old days." He gazed with longing at the yummy food.

"Mimi Carmen makes the best enchiladas on the island." My mother's voice sounded from the hallway, my first clue she'd arrived home from work. She entered the kitchen, took one look at Jordan, and the beginning of a smile tipped up the corners of her mouth. "Well now, who have we here?"

"Jordan Singer, ma'am." He gave her a nod.

"The Singer sewing machine man," Mimi threw in. "Come to fix what he broke the last time."

My mother set her purse on the counter and

looked at him with amused wonder. "I see."

I could tell from the expression on Mama's face that she didn't see, but I decided not to chime in. We had enough confusion already. Thank goodness she took her seat at the table, bowed her head while Mimi Carmen offered up a lengthy prayer in Spanish—much of it related to my single status—and then dove in, no questions asked.

I glanced Jordan's way to see if perhaps he had snuck out during the prayer, but he had not. Instead, he sat, eyes ever widening, as my grandmother scooped a large helping of enchiladas onto his plate. As he took his first bite, a look of contentment settled over him and I relaxed. There would be time to sort this out later. Right now, some steaming enchiladas called my name, and I must answer.

# 6

# Top Hat

I love sewing and have plenty of material witnesses.

AUTHOR UNKNOWN

I had a hard time falling asleep the night Prince William came to dinner. Not that I could blame my sleeplessness on him, of course. With a day like I'd been through, sleeping was highly overrated.

When I did doze, the craziest dreams taunted me. In one of them, Bella Neeley and Demetri duked it out in the middle of Parma John's while Jordan—in reporter mode—captured the shenanigans in photographs. I did my best to steal the photos from him, but he escaped me at every turn.

In another dream, my grandmother sang hymns in Spanish with Jordan, who knew every word and harmonized perfectly. Figured.

Strangest of all, perhaps, was the final dream—the one that woke me up. In that one, Nicolette Cavanaugh marched down the aisle wearing not the dress that Demetri had crafted for her but one I had made, which was far better suited to her than the one I'd covered in chocolate.

Like that would ever happen.

Still, when I jolted awake, my conscience felt seared, as if I'd really stolen a customer from my boss. Er, former boss.

Or, make that current boss.

Demetri called at 7:43 a.m. to let me know that I would be expected in my alterations room at 8:00 sharp. No mention of yesterday's fiasco. No apologies for humiliating me in front of the reporter. Nothing. Just "See you at eight sharp, Gabi. Don't disappoint me. Again."

Um, okay. He probably needed a quick fix on a gown and couldn't get one of the Fab Five to lower themselves to material girl status long enough to deal with it. Still, who did he think he was? And who did he think *I* was? Did he really think I'd lower myself to come crawling back after the ugly way he'd treated me in front of people?

Likely.

Still half asleep during our phone call, I found myself saying, "I'll be in as quick as I can."

Really? Who said that the day after being fired? Only someone who had no respect for herself. Someone desperate to pay the light bill. Someone willing to suck it up, tuck her tail between her legs, and crawl back to the dungeon.

Still, on some level, I had to think this was an answer to the frantic prayers I'd hollered up to the ceiling while bathing yesterday. Maybe there really was a God up there who put the rest of the world's problems on hold long enough to deal with one neurotic seamstress. Had he opened a door for me to return to the land of hyper-ventilating brides and over-the-top designers? If so, then he had a fascinating sense of humor.

When I got to the shop, Kitty greeted me just as she did on any normal day. If not for the chocolate stain on the carpet, I might've thought I'd imagined the whole incident. I'd just started to wonder if she was going to mention the situation at all when she chuckled.

"After you left yesterday, Demetri disappeared into his office and we never saw him again," she said. "Not sure when he came to his senses and decided to hire you back, but you'd better offer up a few Hail Marys as a thank-you for that one."

"I'm not Catholic," I said.

"Yeah, I know. But don't you find it weird that he seems to be moving ahead as if nothing ever happened? Very strange indeed. For Demetri, I mean."

"Right, but we haven't come face-to-face yet, so I'm not counting out a confrontation. No telling what he might do to me when he sees me in person."

"I'd bet the farm he won't do anything. He needs you too much."

"True. I'm the only material—er, alterations girl he's got."

"Speaking of which, you might want to go by the studio before you settle in," she said, looking prim and proper with every hair in place. "Beatrix needs to give you some instructions about Nicolette's dress. Sounded pretty important."

"Okay, I'll do that." The words came out a little shaky. And I couldn't stop thinking about Kitty's hairpiece flying through the air. How surreal it all seemed now.

After offering her a hope-you're-not-mad-at-me smile, I walked through the dress shop, beyond the hundreds of lovely dresses, past the Dynamic Duo as they reeled in a new customer, to the door at the back. I crossed the little alley and entered the door leading to the back entrance of Demetri's prized studio. Though I hated to face the Fab Five, especially after yesterday's fiasco, it had to be done, and the sooner the better.

Seconds later, after swallowing hard and offering up another frantic prayer for mercy, I entered their hallowed territory.

To my right, Antonia—from Spain—cut out a pattern for a new design. She was the dreamer of the group, the youngest and the most inclined to lose herself in over-the-top creativity. Still, I always admired her work.

To her right, Beatrix pinned fabric pieces on a dress form. Ack. I hated to bother her, especially since the wrinkles on her forehead ran so deep.

Across the room, Chantal, the one I most

envied, spoke to a client on the phone in fluent French. No surprise there, since the svelte blonde, who could've had a career in modeling, had arrived from Paris just six months ago. What would it be like, I wondered, to live in Paris? To study fashion among the greats? I'd love to pick her brain . . . if only she liked me.

At least one of the Fab Five did.

I smiled as I clapped eyes on Doria, the motherly one in the bunch. The plump older woman fussed with the bodice of a new design, talking to herself all the while. Her lovely Greek accent held me spellbound, and the sweetness in her voice was palpable. As she looked my way, I saw compassion in her soft blue eyes.

And then there was Emiko, fresh off the plane from Tokyo. The petite workaholic labored away on a panel of intricate beadwork exquisitely done. I'd never seen anything but sheer perfection from her. She might look like a teenager, but in reality, she probably had more skill than all the rest of us put together. Talk about weirdly smart. And reclusive. The woman had never spoken a word to me that I could recall. She leaned down over her work, the lights overhead casting a lovely sheen on her long, black hair.

Not that anyone seemed to notice. They were all too preoccupied with their work. Well, all but one. I felt relief flood my soul as Doria swept me into her arms.

"My little Gabi! You're back! What a blessing. God is smiling on us!"

From the smirk on Beatrix's face, she didn't feel the same. Her snide comment, "So it's true —the black sheep has returned to the fold," left little to the imagination. No doubt she saw my rehiring—if one could call it that after only missing a half day's work—as a mistake on Demetri's part. Or maybe she just felt I didn't belong in their hallowed territory.

But wait—wasn't she the one who had summoned me to come to the studio?

"Yes, I'm back," I managed after finding the courage to speak. With my head held high and my backbone stiff, I added, "Kitty said you wanted me?"

"Well, I'm not sure I would've phrased it *that* way exactly." Beatrix shoved her reading glasses on top of her head as she turned to face me. "I need to speak with you about Nicolette's gown. We've sent it to be cleaned, and it is expected back this afternoon at three. When it arrives, you must completely rework the hem."

"Rework the hem? But it's the perfect length."

"It was, before the . . ." Beatrix rolled her eyes. "Accident. You are obviously unaware of the fact that Nicolette caught the hem in her shoe when the unfortunate incident occurred. The entire front section pulled loose. The stitching is a mess."

"Oh no!" I could hardly believe it. On top of

everything else, now I had to tackle Nicolette's gown again?

"Demetri, as you might imagine, is beside himself over this." Beatrix began to carry on about our boss's fragile nerves, but she lost me about halfway into it. I just couldn't get the image of the ripped hem out of my mind.

Squaring my shoulders, I thanked her for the information, then headed back to the safety of my little closet.

Minutes later, Demetri stopped by my room long enough to give me choppy instructions regarding an incoming bride who needed an emergency fitting. No mention of yesterday's incident whatsoever, no lecture about repairing Nicolette's hemline. So weird. He left the room muttering about his nerves, and life as I knew it shifted back to normal. Well, the Haute Couture version of normal, anyway.

Until midafternoon, when an unexpected visitor arrived at my door. As the words "Singer man at your service! Need any sewing machines repaired in here?" sounded, I glanced up from my project. Jordan stood in the open doorway, a boyish grin on his face.

I couldn't help but return smile for smile, and all the more when I noticed the playful look in his eyes. "Well, hello. Long time, no see." My words came out a little hopeful sounding, but he didn't seem to notice. I gestured for him to enter the tiny room and pushed my alterations aside. "Sorry, but your services will not be required today. My sewing machines are all in working order."

"Well, that's a shame. I happen to be an expert in bobbin . . . bobbin . . . what do you call it again?"

"Tension?"

"Yes. I'm an expert in tension." He took a couple of tentative steps inside, likely boggled by the tight space. "So, you're back at work, I see."

"Looks that way."

"Told you he couldn't function without you." Jordan's right brow elevated mischievously.

I put my finger to my lips to encourage him to lower his voice, but he just laughed.

"You're too good for this, you know," he said as he gestured to the closet space filled with dress forms and half-finished projects. "But I've got to believe you're supposed to be here until God opens a door for you to do your own thing."

*Seriously? More God talk?*

If I didn't know better, I'd think that Bella, Scarlet, and now Jordan were conspiring against me. Maybe they'd teamed up with the Almighty to . . .

To what? Encourage me?

I relaxed, and a feeling of contentment washed over me as I realized they were all on my team.

I'd never really had a team before, and it felt good.

"So, Demetri and I had a long chat this morning." Jordan reached over to touch a long strand of crystals I'd loosely pinned to a satin bridal hat. "We went to breakfast and I interviewed him for my article. But I also did something else."

"You did?"

"Yeah. I told him that he was wrong about what happened yesterday with the éclairs. Made him see the error of his ways."

"Really?"

"Yep. Didn't seem fair that you would take the blame for something you didn't do."

Aha. So Jordan had arranged all of this.

"Well, thank you for that." I gave him a sheepish look. "I mean, this might not be my dream job, but it's a way to pay the bills and gives me an opportunity to sew, so that's good. Keeps me in the wedding business, which is the idea. I can't imagine stepping away from that. It would kill me."

"Happy to be of service." He sat in the chair across from me and gave me a thoughtful look. "Anyway, I've already got the info I need from Demetri for my article, and I plan to visit with the Fab Five and the Dynamic Duo"—he smiled—"a little later. But I thought it might be a good idea to interview you as well."

"Wait . . . interview me? Why?" What could I possibly offer? I hadn't designed Nicolette's dress. I'd only altered it and then coated it in chocolate. Surely he knew that.

Jordan pulled out an iPad and turned it on. "I want to get your take on the industry. Maybe I could follow you through a day's work to get your perspective on the alterations angle."

"Are you serious?" I fought the unladylike snort that threatened to escape. "I'm just the material girl. My work is pretty dull, trust me. I can't think of anyone who would be interested in reading about my life."

"Even a material girl has her story." He waggled his brows in playful fashion. "I want to know the untold tales. The dark secrets."

"Dark secrets?" My hands trembled and I pressed them to my sides. Hopefully Demetri wouldn't happen by and hear about my passion for design.

"Besides, life isn't all work and no play. Surely you get out. Do things."

"Well, yeah." I lowered my voice. "When I'm designing my own stuff—or sometimes when Demetri's on a roll and needs something—I go to the fabric store. Woo-hoo."

"The fabric store. Well now, that sounds intriguing."

"Puh-leeze. It's anything but." I gestured to the messy room and sighed. "But I'm always happy to get out of here when I can. You can see how it is. This is my . . . domain, and I'm stuck here much of the time. Kind of like Cinderella locked in the dungeon on the night of the ball."

"Cinderella in the dungeon. I'll have to use that in the article."

"Do so at your own peril!" I laughed. "You can call it anything but that. Please."

"Okay, okay. I might use the Cinderella angle, though." His eyes—those dancing, joy-filled eyes—met mine. "But if I do, I'll probably throw in a dashing prince. The ladies always like that sort of thing."

"Very funny."

He chuckled and fidgeted with his iPad. "Hey, I feel bad for you working in here, but I'm sure this space must feel like home after a while. It's small but cozy." He glanced around and shrugged. "Okay, more small than cozy. But things could be worse."

"I suppose."

"Sure they could. I did a story last month about a group of women in China who work for pennies on the dollar, sewing wedding items to be sold in America. You should see the photos of their work space. I feel horrible for them."

Suddenly, shame washed over me. I wanted to find those women and help them in some way.

Jordan messed with the icons on his iPad. After a couple of seconds, he glanced my way. "Okay,

I'm ready to start. Is it all right to ask a few questions?"

I looked over at the open door, wondering when Nicolette's dress would be delivered. Until it arrived, I might as well take a few minutes to answer some questions, right?

Decision made, I set my work aside and focused on the handsome young man seated across from me. In that moment, the oddest thought occurred to me. Maybe, just maybe, his joke about adding a prince to my Cinderella story was more than just a far-fetched idea. Maybe this guy had arrived with glass slipper in tow.

Slipper in tow. Ha!

Then again, what would a girl with two left feet do with a glass slipper?

I allowed the idea to percolate as I settled in to answer his questions.

# 7

# A Damsel in Distress

Stitch your stress away.
AUTHOR UNKNOWN

Staring into Jordan's gorgeous eyes was the easy part. Staying focused proved to be more difficult.

He balanced the iPad on his knees, fingers perched and ready on the keys as if expecting me to give him some sort of breaking news story. "Okay, first question: how did you get the job working for Demetri?"

Ugh. He would have to start there. To answer this question would bring a certain degree of humiliation. "I, um, well, I applied to be one of his design seamstresses."

"Ah. One of the Fab Five." Jordan typed the information and then looked at me. "You told me about them."

"Yes. But there were only three of them at the time. I wanted to be the fourth. Didn't happen. But to answer your question, I had originally applied to be one of those seamstresses, not an alterations specialist."

"I see."

"Even though I came in with a really strong

portfolio and good samples of my work, Demetri still felt I should start here and work my way up." Memories flooded over me as I spoke. Turned out Demetri's idea of working my way up involved several years of paying my dues with a pincushion attached to my wrist and a measuring tape in hand. "Please don't put that last part in your article, though. Okay?"

"Gotcha." Jordan's eyes lit up. "But I have to believe it's just a matter of time until he comes to his senses."

"Comes to his senses?" *Have you met Demetri Markowitz?*

"Yeah. I've really been thinking about this, ever since I looked at your sketches. They're really good, Gabi. It won't be long before you end up in his studio, creating dresses like the other ladies."

I shook my head and attempted to offer an explanation. "It's been three years." Three long, difficult years buried in hems and waistlines. Three years of proving myself, of wasting my efforts trying to please an unpleaseable boss. "Trust me, I'm not moving up the corporate ladder here. If anything, I've been nudged farther down the rungs." *Relegated to the dark recesses of the janitor closet.*

I gave myself a proverbial slap in the face to stay focused. *Snap out of it, Gabi. Chin up.*

No point in getting down, not with Jordan looking on, anyway. He glanced across the room at the female dress form adorned with an ivory tulle gown and rose to have a closer look. "This is fascinating. You use these a lot?"

"What? The dress forms?" I nodded. "Yeah. They're adjustable, so I set them to the bride's measurements and then tweak the gown to fit it. Those forms are mine, by the way. I brought them with me. They belonged to Mimi Carmen." I'd never made the connection until I spoke the words aloud. She had given them to me when I was twelve. The same year my father left. Interesting.

"I see." He shoved his iPad under his arm.

"They're like old friends." I couldn't help the smile that followed. It warmed my heart to know that Mimi Carmen had used the dress forms even before I was born, and her mother before her. They were a part of our family, and their presence brought a certain degree of comfort.

"So, if they're old friends, do they have names?" He sat once more and perched his fingers on the digital keyboard, poised to type.

"Of course." I laughed. "Some people name their cars. I name my dress forms." I pointed to the one with the ivory dress. "I call this one Ginger. But you might've guessed that after our last conversation."

"Oh, right, right. I almost forgot you've got a thing for Fred and Ginger." He jotted it down on the iPad and chuckled. "Because you're secretly a dancer."

"With two left feet."

"Still dying to see that." He glanced down at my feet, and I felt my cheeks warm in embarrassment. His gaze lingered for a moment on my ankles, then eventually moved up to my face. He pointed at the male dress form, which I'd shoved in the corner. "So, I'm going to take a wild guess here and assume this must be Fred?"

"No, actually."

"Interesting. I would've gone with the whole Fred Astaire/Ginger Rogers angle. He must have a name too, right?"

Jordan returned his attention to the digital keys, ready to type my response, and I flinched. I couldn't share this answer with him. Instead, I opted for, "Yeah, he's got a name, but it's not important."

"Not important?" His narrowed gaze clued me in to the fact that he didn't believe me.

"Well, you know what I mean. What's so important about a name, anyway? It's just silly. It's kind of like naming your car. Doesn't really have a lot of significance."

"I named my car after my first dog, Lucky, who got run over when I was seven. But you're avoiding the question." Jordan leaned in so close the smell of his cologne made my head spin. "The reporter in me smells a story here."

*The single girl in me smells someone's yummy cologne here.*

He leaned a bit closer, his voice now lowered to a sexy drawl. "You gonna tell me his name, or am I going to have to weasel the story out of you?"

"Not a chance." I flashed what I hoped was a please-end-this-conversation-right-here smile. If the guy knew I'd named the male dress form Demetri, he'd want to know why. "Because I get to stick pins in him" would be a dead giveaway about how I felt about my boss. That was a whole different article, one for a mental health magazine, not *Texas Bride*.

"Just trust me when I say that I've given him a fitting name," I said at last. "For a guy, anyway."

"For a guy? Dying to know what *that* means."

"Sorry." I groaned. "I'm not a man hater or anything. But if I tell you his name, you'll think I am."

"So, you're not a man hater, but you have issues with men? Maybe that's the real story here. Now that would be a fascinating slant for a bridal magazine. Most of our readers are happy to have a guy in their life."

Could this situation slide downhill any faster?

"I'm really not a man hater. It's just that . . . some things don't seem fair. You know?" A deep sigh followed as I gestured to my office space. "The size of my workroom should clue you in.

I have to work twice as hard to get half the recognition."

"Gotcha."

"But at least I take comfort in the fact that I'm not alone. Lots of other women throughout time could relate to what I'm going through. Take Ginger there." I pointed to the female dress form. "Poor thing. She did everything Fred did, but backwards."

"And in high heels. I've heard that one before."

"Well, it's true. She was a hard worker." *Like me.*

"Right. Got it. So, back to this battle of the sexes thing . . ."

"Wait, I didn't call it that."

"Didn't have to." He typed something and then looked back at me. "Tell me where it started. In your situation, I mean."

"No way." Embarrassment rushed over me. "You're not putting anything personal about me in that article of yours."

"No, of course not." He laid down the iPad. "I'm just being nosy now, that's all. We're off the record. Just dying to know why you have such a thing against guys."

"I don't."

"Sounds like you do." He gave me an accusing look, but I could still read the teasing in his eyes.

Frustration settled over me like a dark cloud.

"I won't say I'm biased against men. It's just that . . . surely you see how things are at my house. Mama. Mimi Carmen. Me. It's just us. Not that that's a bad thing. We're the Delgado women, after all. We're tough."

"Sounds like the name of a television show: *The Delgado Women.*"

"We've had enough drama for a TV show, that's for sure."

"Really? So you ladies have your own *Jersey Shore* thing going on?"

"Um, no. The furthest thing from it. We're just three generations of women who all live together and try to make the best of things with no men in the picture, so I probably have a skewed perspective. Our experience with men, as a whole, has not been favorable."

"I see. So, the Delgado women. You, your mom, and your grandmother?"

"Yeah."

"Interesting." He paused and his tone grew more inquisitive. "By the way, your mother looks nothing like her mom. I mean, I know they're twenty years apart in age."

"Thirty," I said quickly.

"Thirty. But I never would've guessed them to be mother and daughter."

I couldn't help the laugh that came rippling out. "Oh, they're not related." I quickly collected my thoughts. "I mean, they're related, of course, but not like you think. Mimi Carmen is my father's mother."

"Oh. Your father is . . ." I could practically hear the wheels clicking in his head.

"No, no. He's alive." My heart twisted as I spoke the words. For no more often than I heard from him, I assumed he was alive. Shaking off my reverie, I continued with my explanation. "He and my mom got divorced years ago when I was just twelve."

Impressionable, tender twelve. The worst possible time for a girl to lose her father. And to watch him slip so easily into a new, ready-made family—one complete with two sons and a daughter my same age—was horrible. Many times I'd cried myself to sleep at night, wondering what the new daughter had that I didn't.

"Man."

"My memories of my dad are vague, but I've heard Mimi Carmen use the words 'he thinks he's God's gift to women' enough times to get the picture. He's quite the ladies' man. Only, not the sort to do right by the ladies, if that makes sense."

"I'm sorry, Gabi." Jordan's expression showed me that he really cared.

"We don't see him much," I explained. "Trust me, there were at least a dozen reasons he had to go."

Jordan's brow wrinkled. "So, your father left but forgot to take his mother with him?"

I had to laugh at that. "No. Just the opposite. My mom booted him out and Mimi Carmen helped her do it. They packed up his bags and put them on the front porch."

"Wow. Must've been a tough night for all involved."

"Yeah." I sighed as the memory of that awful night flitted over me. "And yes, my grandmother stayed. I think it would have devastated me to lose her too. It was bad enough . . ." I shook off my frustration. "Anyway, she stayed and has been a lifesaver for Mama and me. She's quirky, as I'm sure you noticed, but we love her."

"That's good. I get the feeling she'd be easy to love."

"My mother still struggles with being single, I think. Even though it's been years." My mind reeled back to the day she got her job at the travel agency. She'd always dreamed of traveling the world with my dad. These days she sent other people off on trips that she would never get to go on.

Sadness swept over me. It must've shown on my face, because Jordan gave me a sympathetic look. I figured I'd better get back to talking or else I might just spring a leak and spout a few tears. That would make this awkward conversation even more nerve-racking. I'd already given him far too much information, anyway.

I gave him a curt nod. "Anyway, like I said, we

are the Delgado women. One for all and all for one. It's what binds us together."

I didn't bother mentioning that I flinched every time I heard the Delgado name. Of all things— to carry the name of a man who'd walked away from my life. Should I tell Jordan about how detached my dad had always been? How he couldn't hold down a real job? How he never offered a penny of child support?

"I like that you're so close to your grand-mother." He sighed. "I miss mine. She was the hardest-working woman I've ever met in my life." Jordan glanced around my alterations room. "Until now, I mean. I'd have to say you're a pretty close second, based on all of the dresses in here."

"I do enjoy my work." For whatever reason, I yawned. "But I enjoy my nighttime more, because that's when I get to design my own gowns." This prompted a lengthy, joyous conver-sation about the hours I spent with my sketch-pad and at Mimi's Singer sewing machine in the wee hours of the night. At some point along the way I realized how animated my voice had become and decided to lower the volume a bit. What if Demetri happened to be standing outside the door, listening in? Ugh.

"Enjoying your work isn't a problem, espe-cially when you get to focus on what you love," Jordan said. "But it sounds like you work around the clock."

"I pretty much do." Another unexpected yawn followed.

Really? I had to embarrass myself in front of him?

"Just promise me you'll get the rest you need," Jordan said, his eyes reflecting concern. "Keep things in balance."

"Me? Balanced?" I chuckled. "Hardly."

"Well, remember, even God took one day off. Ya know?" He grinned. "That's a challenge, by the way. When you're able to step away for a while, take a day off. Get out. Think about something other than work. Live a little."

"But I have my own work to do when I leave here. That's what I was trying to explain just now."

"I know." He put a finger up. "I'm not saying you should give that up. Just take one day. Or, if you can't spare a day, take one hour. Go to . . ." His brow creased. "The beach. Or the park. Someplace where you can get alone with God and just . . . be. It will free up your creativity, I promise."

Getting alone with God would free up my creativity? How did one go about getting alone with the Almighty, anyway? Climb a ladder to heaven? Ask Saint Peter for a private audience in the inner sanctum? I'd learned enough from Mimi Carmen to know that people couldn't even get in to see the pope without special dispensation.

"Spend time with him, Gabi. You might be surprised at what happens."

Strange how Jordan talked about God with such ease, as if the two of them were BFFs or some-thing. For that matter, Scarlet and Bella had the same free-spirited way of talking about the Lord, like he was sitting in the chair across the table sipping sweet tea and chatting about the weather.

I thought back to my rushed prayer time in the bathtub and how good it had felt to cry out to someone. Something. Talking to myself was highly overrated, to be sure. And I did have the sense that my ceiling-bound pleas had led to my rehiring. Still, the idea of this buddy-buddy God thing felt weird.

As Jordan continued to share his heart, I couldn't help but find myself captivated. He was my polar opposite in every respect—blond, tall, eyes as sea-green as the Caribbean. His polished speech told me that we traveled in different circles—he in the wide-open places where planes, trains, and automobiles would take him, and I in the coziness of my own little corner. In my own little chair.

Yes, we definitely came from different worlds, but as I gazed into his sparkling eyes—eyes that ushered me into the comfort of his presence— I realized how inviting his world felt to me.

*Face it, you don't get out enough, Gabi.*

Oh, but I wanted to get out now. As he smiled—that beautiful, boyish smile—I found myself wanting to summon up a fairy godmother to turn my sewing machine into a carriage that would carry me to the ball. Or at least throw in some mice to hem Nicolette's dress.

*Nicolette!*

From outside my workroom I heard Demetri ranting to the Dynamic Duo about our incoming bride-to-be. Apparently her dress had arrived from the cleaner's, ready to be hemmed.

He hollered through my open doorway, clearly oblivious to Jordan's presence. I knew this because he called Nicolette a couple of choice names, complete with expletives, and ranted about how she wouldn't be happy with the gown even if we cleaned and hemmed it to perfection. Lydia and Corinne responded with a few not-so-nice things to say about Nicolette, one of them—Corinne, maybe?—commenting on her new DDs. After that Demetri lit into a frantic talk about how he planned to wrap Nicolette around his little finger before day's end in spite of her hesitations about his design.

All of this from just outside my door.

Jordan shifted in his chair and cleared his throat.

This must've captured Demetri's attention. He stuck his head in the door and blanched when he saw the reporter sitting there. At once my boss's tight jaw flinched, and he nearly dropped the gown. He shifted from ranting mode to polished pro.

"Hello, Meez-ter. . . Meez-ter . . ."

"Singer."

"Right. Meez-ter Singer. I didn't realize you'd come back. Good to see you again."

What a faker.

"Yes." Jordan pivoted around to face him. "Hope you don't mind, but I'm trying to get a thorough look at your place of business so that I can write a . . . well-rounded article."

Was it my imagination, or was the guy fishing for words?

"Vell, surely you don't need to spend time here, in zee alterations room." Demetri rolled his eyes. He hung the gown from the top of my open door. "Come, and ve vill talk business. Then, if you like, I vill take you back to my studio, where zee real seamstresses work. Gabi here is just zee material girl. Nips and tucks. That sort of thing."

My self-confidence flew out the window—not that I had a window in this dungeon. How dare he denigrate me in front of the reporter? Didn't he see that Jordan found my work fascinating?

To his credit, Jordan didn't appear interested in jumping to attention at Demetri's command. "Tomorrow, maybe," he said with a wave of his hand. "Right now I'm fine. Here. With Gabi." He gave Demetri a pensive look. "Besides, it sounds like you've got some wrinkles to iron out with Nicolette Cavanaugh." Reaching for his iPad, he added, "And a wrinkled bride is never a good thing, especially not one with a feature article in *Texas Bride*."

Demetri squirmed and then muttered something under his breath about the Fab Five needing his help with something. Seconds later, he disappeared from view.

Jordan looked back my way and smiled. "Now, where were we again?"

After his "gotcha!" comments to Demetri, I figured we were halfway to heaven. At least from my perspective. But I couldn't tell him that, now could I? Instead, I flashed him a thank-you smile and leaned back in my chair, suddenly feeling better than I had in ages.

# 8

## Vivacious Lady

I adored Fred. We were good friends. Our only problem is that we never aspired to be any kind of a team. We didn't want to be Abbott and Costello. We thought of ourselves as individuals. We didn't intend to be another Frick and Frack. But it happened anyway, didn't it? And I'll be forever grateful it did.

GINGER ROGERS

The following morning I awoke in a panic. The hands on the clock showed a very clear 9:30. I'd obviously slept through my alarm. Ugh!

No. As reality hit, I released a slow breath and willed my racing heart to calm down.

*This is Saturday. No work today.*

No Haute Couture work, anyway.

While flinging the sheet back, I accidentally knocked the clock off the bedside table. It clattered to the floor. I reached down to scoop it up and caught a glimpse of the sun peeking through the window. After a long night of work, my bleary eyes could hardly stand the glow. I squinted and turned the other way.

"Good morning, sleepyhead." Mimi Carmen's voice sounded from outside the door. "I hear you stirring in there. Everything okay?"

"Yeah, I'm fine. Just knocked over my clock, but it didn't break."

She opened the door a crack and peeked inside. "You were up late again last night, weren't you?"

"How did you know?" I did my best to stifle the yawn that threatened to work its way out.

She gave me a knowing look. "I saw the light from under the door of the guest room and heard the sewing machine. Glad it's running again. That Singer man really knows his stuff."

"Yes, he's good at what he does." What else could I say, really?

Her eyes twinkled. "And he's mighty cute too, if you don't mind an old woman noticing such things." A girlish giggle followed and her cheeks flushed.

"I don't mind a bit. And yes, I'm glad the machine is running well again." No point in telling her the truth about Jordan's real job. It would probably just complicate the matter. "And I didn't mean to stay up so late. It's just that I'm meeting with Scarlet today to talk about her wedding dress, and I'm loaded with ideas."

Too many ideas, actually. By three in the morning I'd sketched out four completely different ones.

Mimi fussed with the covers on my bed, pulling them up as she talked. "I'm sure she'll love whatever you come up with. You're the best."

"Thanks, Mimi." I helped her finish making the bed, smiling as she fluffed my pillows, then followed behind her to the kitchen, where Mama worked at the stove, flipping eggs in a skillet.

"Morning, sunshine."

"G' morning, Mama."

"Hope you're hungry. Mimi made chorizo and I've got eggs cooking. I'll warm up the tortillas and we can dive in."

"Okay. Smells great." Then again, if I continued to eat like Mama and Mimi, chances were pretty good I'd end up a size 3X too. Not that the size of either really bothered me, but it did occur to me that I'd better be careful, starting now.

As we ate, my mother quizzed me about my meeting with the bride-to-be.

"You're meeting at Club Wed?" When I answered with a yes, her eyes took on a dreamy look. "One of these days I want to go there. See the inside of the chapel and the reception hall for myself."

"Oh, I'm sure Bella would love to show you around. Or maybe her aunt Rosa. She's so sweet." Well, sweet and feisty.

"Rosa? The one with the cooking show on the Food Network?" Mimi Carmen spoke around a mouthful of chorizo and eggs.

"Yeah."

My grandmother's eyes lit up. "I would love to meet her."

"You two have a lot in common, from what I can gather. Maybe I can arrange it."

Mimi looked as if I'd just offered her the moon. "Really? Then I must take her some enchiladas. I think she would like them, don't you?"

"Oh, I'm sure. She'd be crazy not to."

"Oh, but she's a professional. I would embarrass myself. I'm just a home cook."

"But that's how she started too, Mimi," I said. "In fact, that's what makes her so appealing to the television audience. They can relate because she's all about home and family."

Mimi rambled on and on about the possibility of ending up with a show of her own on the Food Network someday. I couldn't picture it, to be honest. Not because of her cooking skills but because of her tendency to slip into Spanish. Was there such a thing as a Spanglish cooking channel? I'd have to look into that. Right now, however, I had other things to think about.

I turned my attention back to the matter of Scarlet's wedding dress. "I'm just loaded with ideas for Scarlet's gown. I'm sure she's got a design in mind, but I'm hoping to win her over with what I've been working on. I've come up with a few that would be perfect for her."

"How can she help but be won over by your

designs, Gabriella?" Mimi Carmen said. "They're prettier than any of the dresses I see in magazines."

"And certainly more normal-looking than anything I've ever seen in that so-called high-end store you work for," my mother added, then rolled her eyes. No doubt she felt I didn't belong in the couture world.

"You're brilliant, Gabriella." Mimi smiled and filled another tortilla with eggs and chorizo.

"Thanks, Mimi, but you're supposed to say things like that. You're my grandmother."

"I only say them because they are true. Even the Singer man sees your talent. He said as much at dinner the other night."

My heart quickened as she mentioned Jordan's name. Well, his last name, anyway.

"True." Mama gave me an inquisitive look. "That very handsome young man did seem interested." She cleared her throat and took a sip of her juice. "In your designs, I mean."

*Gee, thanks, Mama.*

"Let's invite him over for dinner again soon," she added. "He seems to like Mimi's cooking."

"Good idea. I'll make my tamales." Mimi Carmen rose and walked to the refrigerator, where she grabbed a jar of homemade salsa. "I'm guessing the Singer man loves tamales. His mother is Puerto Rican, you know."

"Do they eat tamales in Puerto Rico?" I asked.

Mama shrugged and took another bite of her breakfast taco.

"What time is your meeting with the bride-to-be?" Mimi asked as she dumped a large mound of salsa on top of her food.

"Three o'clock."

"Ah." She took a bite and talked around the mouthful of food. "I need to make a run to the store."

I knew which store she meant, of course. Walmart. And when Mimi Carmen said she had to "make a run" to the store, she certainly didn't mean she needed to get there in a hurry. Neither did she mean that she would shop in a hurry. Or check out in a hurry. Or unload the car in a hurry. No, she moved at a snail's pace, enjoying every second of the adventure.

Not that I'd ever considered a trip to Walmart an adventure, but she certainly did. I'd never seen a woman so enamored with the various food products as my grandmother. She read every label top to bottom before buying a thing. This slowed down the process considerably and basically made me want to smack my head into a wall, but I usually coped by going to the candy aisle.

Visions of myself wearing a size 3X floated through my brain again. Maybe I should find a new way to pacify myself.

"Would you drive me?" Mimi asked. "You know how much I hate to go by myself."

"Sure." I bit back the sigh that wanted to escape. Looked like I'd be spending my morning at the local Walmart instead of touching up my sketches. "Give me a few minutes to get up and running, okay?"

Half an hour later, Mimi and I joined approximately a thousand other rushed and frazzled shoppers as we perused the store. It took over an hour, but we finally made it to the register, and I congratulated myself for avoiding the candy aisle.

Once there, my grandmother used her coupons to get reduced prices on nearly half of the products. One of these days we wouldn't have to live like this. I hoped. I dreamed of a day when the woman could purchase a bottle of laundry detergent without having to fret over the price.

*Is that too much to ask, Lord?*

There I went praying again. I'd been doing a lot of that lately.

When we returned to the house, I dove back into my work, finalizing my designs for Scarlet. Hopefully she would like my ideas.

By 3:00 I could hardly wait to meet up with her at Club Wed. I always looked forward to spending time at the island's most beautiful wedding hot spot.

Turned out I wasn't alone. I pulled up to Club Wed just as a bride and groom emerged from the front door.

In that moment, the weirdest thoughts ran

through my mind. Would I get married at Club Wed one day? If so, would my rickety old Ford Focus end up covered in multicolored streamers, with the words "Just Married!" etched in shoe polish on the back window? How did one go about covering rust spots with shoe polish, anyway? And would it matter that I still hadn't fixed my side mirror? Would my groom and I get arrested on our way to the honeymoon?

Hmm. Maybe my new life—the one with the handsome prince in it—would include a car that actually ran. One could hope.

Thinking about the car must've jinxed it somehow. It sputtered to a stop about three feet short of where I'd planned to park. Oh well. With the wedding coming to an end, no one needed the space anyway. At least I hoped not.

I paused to give the wedding facility a closer look. I'd been here before, of course—on Hannah and Drew Kincaid's big day a couple of months ago. In fact, I'd gotten to know Scarlet better on that special day. Her bridesmaid dress had required a last-minute alteration, thanks to her weight loss.

Seeing the facility now, fully loaded with guests I didn't know, made me realize the significance of Bella Neeley's impact on our little community. She and her ever-growing family were responsible for hundreds, possibly thousands, of blissful wedding days.

Who wouldn't want to get married at Club Wed? The gorgeous old Victorian stood tall, a fresh coat of white paint causing it to shimmer under the afternoon sun. The gingerbread trim, intricate in its design, had won accolades from the historical society a few years back. Even now it captured my imagination. For a moment, anyway.

My eyes gravitated to the beautiful veranda and the stately columns flanking the wide front steps. Talk about inviting. How many brides had scurried up and down these steps on their wedding day?

Off to the side, a lovely rotunda area, framed by half a dozen oleander bushes, beckoned guests to spend time visiting and relaxing. The scent of flowers floated on the breeze, a lovely perfume. Just one more reason why I loved it here.

The Rossi home, though elegant, offered an invitation to sit and rest awhile. To step away into a peaceful place, one complete with oversized doors and lovely wooden shutters, open and welcoming. I had to give it to the Rossi family. They knew how to draw the eye . . . and the heart.

Thinking about the Rossis made me smile. Though I didn't know them very well, I already loved Bella's family. Loud, wacky, over-the-top in every way, they radiated pure joy and devotion. Watching them at work gave me hope that a girl's business really could succeed. I would learn from their example and grow my business with equal zeal.

Surely if one family could handle all of those brides, I could handle one diva designer. Demetri Markowitz would not get the best of me, no matter how hard he tried.

After watching the crowd for a moment longer, I got out of the car and wove my way through the mass of people on the veranda. As I entered the spacious foyer, my attention shifted to a group of ladies oohing and aahing over the rich mahogany staircase with its carpeted steps. I didn't blame them. This place deserved every bit of the praise, and so did the family responsible.

Still, I must find Bella. We had much to discuss.

I located her in the opening between the foyer and the reception hall, giving instructions to the photographer, Hannah Kincaid.

Hannah glanced my way and grinned. "Well, hello there. If it isn't the island's best dress designer!"

"Good to see you again. I—"

Before I could complete my thought, she took off chasing after the bride and groom, hollering something about catching the picture-perfect shot.

"That's how she is," Bella said. "Never misses an opportunity. But you'd better watch out or she'll run you over."

"She's very fast," I observed as I watched her

disappear across the veranda through the throng of people.

"You have to be, around here."

Bella took a couple of steps through the opening off the foyer, and I followed her, now finding myself in the gorgeous reception hall. My gaze traveled up to the chandeliers above and then back down again to the heavy wooden floor, polished to perfection. Lovely.

A couple of lingering guests visited at one of the tables, and the mother of the bride cried as she helped Bella's mother dismantle the intricate centerpieces. I couldn't help but notice Bella's aunt Rosa and uncle Laz working in the kitchen off to the side of the room. I recognized them from television, though they appeared slightly less rotund in real life. My conversation with Mimi resurfaced and I smiled, hoping she could one day meet these two in person.

At this point Rosa approached. "You! Eat. Cake." She waved what appeared to be a knife in my face.

"Um, okay."

Turned out the knife was really one of those triangular cake-serving thingamabobs. Still, an armed woman wanted me to eat cake. I would eat cake.

And that's exactly where I ran into Scarlet . . . at the cake table. She passed me a yummy-looking slice of white cake with raspberry filling and spouted her instructions. "Eat up, Gabi. Those folks left over half the wedding cake behind. It's a travesty, I tell you. A travesty."

I couldn't help but think the butchered cake looked rather sad in its current state but didn't say so. It certainly tasted great. So much for skipping the candy aisle at Walmart.

*Size 3X, here I come!*

I spoke around a mouthful of the sweet stuff. "Now I see why you and Bella suggested meeting here. You were both here anyway for a wedding." I took another bite. Then another. I could feel my hips growing with each tasty morsel.

"Yeah, I'm getting more and more gigs at Club Wed now that I'm marrying into the family." Scarlet giggled as Armando, her intended, walked up.

It still made me smile to see Scarlet and Armando together. Did two more different people exist on the planet? Armando, Bella's older brother and former Italian bad boy, marrying Scarlet, the laugh-a-minute Lucille Ball look-alike? Crazy. Still, they seemed blissfully happy, as was evidenced by the lip-locking going on right now in front of me.

*Awkward!*

"You meeting with us, Armando?" Scarlet asked as she nuzzled into his embrace.

"No, I'm just here to help Uncle Laz clear out the leftovers in the kitchen and then clean up.

120

He's having a hard time getting around these days."

She gave him a little kiss on the nose. "Well, you're a good man to help out like that."

"This is family." He smiled and joy flooded his face. "And you know I'd do anything for family."

And that pretty much summed up why I loved Bella's clan. They all shared a common love for family. My dad could certainly learn a thing or two from these people.

"Let's meet in my office, okay?" Bella's voice came from behind me. "Guido is in there, so we'll have to talk around him. Hope you don't mind."

I didn't know who Guido was, but I didn't really mind regardless. I tagged along on Bella's heels with Scarlet at my side, chattering all the way. Oh, not about her own wedding. No, her thoughts seemed firmly planted on today's ceremony and reception.

Until we settled into the plush wingback chairs in Bella's office. At that point Scarlet's focus shifted and she dove headfirst into a lengthy explanation of how and why her wedding would be vastly different from the one she'd just attended today. About every other sentence, Guido—who turned out to be the Rossis' colorful parrot—interrupted with a bizarre song, followed by a Scripture verse about forgiving others. He seemed to be following her conversation better than I was.

"Wait." I shook my head, confused. "Are you getting married here? At Club Wed?"

"Club Wed!" the bird echoed from his perch in the corner of the room. "Club Wed!"

"No." Scarlet shook her head. "My dad's a pastor, you know, and our church has the prettiest sanctuary on the island, just the right size for my guests. I wouldn't dream of getting married anywhere else." This sent her off on a tearful tangent, talking about how much she loved the beautiful old building.

"Right, right." I shifted in my chair, wondering how anyone could be that enamored with a church building. "That's what I thought. I guess I'm just confused. You're talking about the wedding like it's taking place here."

"Ah, not the ceremony. The reception. Our fellowship hall at the church is too small to add a dance floor, so we're going to use Club Wed's grand ballroom."

"The perfect compromise, since the groom's family owns Club Wed," Bella threw in. "That way it's a win-win situation for all involved."

"Yes." Scarlet sighed. "It's going to be beautiful, and I want a dress that somehow fits in at both places—our homey little church and the big, fancy reception hall." She gave me a pleading look. "Can you pull that off?"

"I think so. I've been working on some ideas, actually. I was hoping maybe you could look at—"

I wanted to finish my sentence, but Guido interrupted by bursting into a rendition of "Ninety-Nine Bottles of Beer on the Wall," which totally threw me off track.

"Speaking of looking at things, I think it would be helpful if you saw our little church first-hand. Then you'll see why it's important to have a dress that matches the comfortable feel of the church." She snapped her fingers. "I know. You should come to service tomorrow morning. Then you can kill two birds with one stone." She glanced up at the parrot and said, "Sorry, Guido. Don't take it personally."

Killing birds in church didn't sound like much fun. Still, she'd piqued my interest.

"You can hear my dad preach—he's pretty amazing, you know—and you can take a little tour of the church."

"Hmm. Maybe." But we'd come to talk about dresses, not churches, right? Looked like I needed to get this train back on track.

# 9

## Chance at Heaven

Intelligence, adaptability, and talent. And by talent I mean the capacity for hard work. Lots of girls come here with little but good looks. Beauty is a valuable asset, but it is not the whole cheese.

GINGER ROGERS

Corralling Bella and Scarlet turned out to be tougher than it looked. Somehow they shifted from talking about weddings to sharing their thoughts on dieting to reminiscing about Brock Benson's recent win on *Dancing with the Stars*. I didn't mind talking about the hunky Hollywood star, but really? Didn't we arrange this meeting to talk about Scarlet's big day? Between their tangents, the lengthy dissertation about the church, and the bird's singing, I'd pretty much decided the whole day was a wash.

After a few minutes, I cleared my throat, which served to bring them to attention. "Let's talk dresses," I suggested, hoping they would take the hint that I was ready to move on. Opening my sketchpad, I glanced down at the first of my sketches and smiled. Hopefully Scarlet would like this one. I certainly did.

"Yes, let's!" Scarlet scooted her chair closer to mine, all smiles. She oohed and aahed over the first sketch. And the second. And the third. Still, she never used those words I always longed to hear: "Ooo, that one's perfect!"

After glancing at all of my sketches, she still hadn't used the key phrase I'd been waiting for, so I decided to go another route.

"If you don't mind my asking, what's your theme?"

"Theme?" Her nose wrinkled. "I guess I haven't really thought about the wedding in themes before."

"I find it helps keep you focused." I closed my sketchbook so as not to be distracted.

"Good idea." She paused and appeared to be thinking. "Well, you know me. I'm the queen of sweets, so it has to be something light and fun. Fairy-tale-like."

My thoughts began to churn, and I pulled the sketchpad close to my body, realizing that what I'd already drawn certainly didn't fit that theme. Maybe I needed to come up with a new design angle.

For whatever reason, my gaze shifted to the parrot. He appeared to have fallen asleep sitting up. I knew that feeling well.

"And I hope you won't think I'm vain for what

I'm about to say . . ." Scarlet's eyes twinkled. "I've lost quite a bit of weight over the past few months, but I'd like to lose another twenty or so before the big day, so I hope we can come up with a design that will, you know . . . make me look like a normal girl instead of like a giant marshmallow."

"A giant marshmallow?" These words came from Bella, who looked stunned.

"Yeah." Scarlet sighed. "I've never looked great in white. It's not the most slimming color, you know. But this is my wedding and I'm wearing white, even if I look like the Goodyear Blimp floating down the aisle."

At this, Hannah appeared in the doorway, camera in hand. "Don't you ever let me hear you say anything like that again. You're gorgeous, Scarlet." Hannah leaned against the open door and slung her camera over her shoulder. "And you are a normal girl. All girls are normal, whether they're tall, short, chubby, thin . . . whatever."

"That's right. But you really do need a dress with a great fitted waistline to show off your new physique," Bella added. "A real Cinderella-like gown." She looked at me and smiled. "On a budget, of course."

If anyone understood budgets, I did. Still, with my workload growing at the bridal shop, I'd have to burn the midnight oil a bit longer to accomplish a fairy-tale dress that didn't look like a giant marshmallow. Something in a lovely shade of non-slimming white. I would need to create an elongated silhouette with a higher than usual waistline to showcase her figure. The skirt? Flowing, not fitted. That was a given, considering her body type.

Or maybe I needed to go with a fitted bodice. Hmm. My imagination kicked into overdrive, and before long I started sketching out a design in my head.

"You can do this, Gabi," Hannah said, snapping me back to the present. "You're the best designer I know. Better than Demetri by miles."

"You think?" Her words boosted my confidence, but I still doubted my abilities, especially in a situation like this, with a dieting bride. Hadn't I just walked this road with Nicolette? Her changing figure had almost proved to be my undoing.

"I don't think, I *know*." Hannah crossed her arms and stared me down.

A teensy-tiny sigh escaped before I spoke. "I think I've just been overlooked so many times that I can't envision it." My gaze shifted to my hands and then back up again.

Hannah looked stunned. "Who could possibly overlook you? Your dresses are better than most I've seen in magazines. People have to sit up and take notice when they see your work."

"You might be surprised." How many times had Demetri walked right by me without complimenting my efforts? And how many times had brides-to-be given me seemingly impossible tasks that I had completed to a T? Nine times out of ten they just took their wedding gowns and headed on their way without so much as a word of thanks or praise.

My stomach began to churn, and I decided it might be time to change the subject.

*Think of something clever to say, Gabi. Anything.*

Bella gestured for Hannah to close the door and then looked my way, eyes narrowed. "I know what's wrong with you, you know."

"You do?"

"Yes, and I got all the proof I needed when I used the words *Cinderella gown*. You flinched."

"I-I did?"

"Yep, and I know why. You've got a Cinderella complex." Bella nodded as if that settled the issue.

"Cinderella complex?"

"Yes. Demetri has kept you in that awful little room, hemming skirts and letting out waistlines, when your real talents and abilities lie elsewhere."

I did my best not to sigh. Bella's comment—completely true in every respect—didn't deserve an argument from me, so I simply shifted gears, hoping to distract her. "Is there a prince in this story somewhere?" My thoughts reeled back to my earlier conversation with Jordan. He'd mentioned a prince, hadn't he?

"Maybe." Bella chuckled then grew serious. "But that wasn't my point. I think the whole prince and cinder-girl theme is really about God's love for us, not man's."

Well, that totally threw me. I'd never considered the Cinderella story to be a Bible tale in disguise. It figured that Bella would try to turn it into one.

"Anyway, I was just trying to say that Cinderella was made for more than grunt work, and so are you." She leaned back in her chair and gave me a nod.

A nervous laugh wriggled its way out. "I'm going to embroider that on a sampler and hang it on my wall."

"Good. It's true, you know. Cinderella was made for bigger things, and I think she sensed it all along. That's the only reason she struggled so much, because she realized her future was destined to be greater than her present." Bella's eyes now sparkled with merriment.

"Greater?"

"Yeah. Like living in a castle," Hannah chimed in.

"With a handsome prince?" I asked again, unable to hide the smile that rose up.

"Someday your prince *will* come." Bella paused. "A prince of a guy who will see you as valuable, not some tyrant who works you to death to further his own career while sabotaging yours."

"Well, yes, but—"

"In the meantime, just realize that the real Prince Charming is already here."

I looked around, half expecting to see a fella dressed in regal attire standing behind me. Ha! Wouldn't that be something?

Bella's phone rang, but she didn't answer it right away. Instead, her eyes—now misty—zeroed in on mine. "He's loved you even before you were born and will go on loving you every day of your life, even on those days when you feel most unlovable."

I never got the chance to respond. She answered her phone with a quick "Hey, babe, can I call you right back? I'm right in the middle of a—" Then her face lit into a smile. "Oh, Tres! How's Mommy's sweet little boy? . . . You did what with Daddy and baby sister today? . . . You went to the zoo? . . . You saw a zebra? What was his name? . . . Oh, you saw a tiger too? You weren't scared, were you? . . . What about Rosa-Earline? Did she cry?"

We lost Bella for about five minutes after that as she chatted with her son about his trip to the zoo. While they talked, I had time to think through what she'd just said about Demetri. In that moment it occurred to me that perhaps Bella thought Demetri and I were . . . a couple? Really? I needed to remedy this, and the sooner the better.

As soon as she hung up, I did my best to explain.

"Bella, Demetri and I were never . . . I mean, you know he's . . ."

I didn't say the word. Turned out I didn't have to. She quirked a brow and then chuckled. "I know, I know." With a wave of her hand she dismissed any further explanation. "I'm just saying that he hasn't treated you like royalty, and that's why you've got a Cinderella complex."

"Well, I didn't exactly *agree* that I have a Cinderella complex," I muttered.

"You didn't have to." Scarlet gave me a knowing look.

"Just saying, you deserve better, whether it's in your working relationship, your personal life . . . whatever." Bella released a sigh, a gentle smile evolving. "You need a fella like my D.J. One who loves me unconditionally and who loves our kids so much that he would give his life for them. A man who uses his day off to take his kiddos to see zebras and lions so that Mommy can coordinate a wedding and then have a meeting afterward."

"Tigers," I said.

"Tigers." She shrugged. "And when those tigers scare the babies, he's there to sweep them in his arms and kiss their tears away. The babies, not the tigers." Bella's smile lit the room.

Still, it did little to squelch the pain I now felt as I pondered my father's absence in my life. I couldn't remember him ever kissing a tear away, and I'd shed plenty over the years.

*Shake it off, Gabi. Shake it off.*

"You need a guy like Armando." Scarlet's hands went to her heart, and I could read the bliss in her expression. "One who stops everything he's doing just to come and help his family out when they need him. I can't tell you what a big help he's been to me at the bakery, and what a blessing he's been to people at the church." She began to share a story about a young man named Devon that Armando had helped, then dove into a story about a recent missions trip they had taken. She paused to wipe her eyes. "He's pretty great."

"So is my Drew." Hannah's eyes pooled and she reached for a tissue. "He merged his business with mine so that we would have the best possible chance at succeeding. And we have, thanks to him."

"I don't suppose I really need a guy. Period." I put my hand up, ready to bring this conversation to an end. Had they brought me here to talk about this? Of course not. I was supposed to be here designing a dress.

"It's true that you don't need a man in your life to be successful." Bella leaned forward and put her elbows on the desk. "Having Demetri in your life hasn't helped in that regard. For that matter, you don't really even *need* to have a father figure to be successful. Millions of kids have made it without having a dad in the picture, and they've gone on to do just fine. The real Prince Charming tops all of that, anyway. So spend time with him, and he will give you the desires of your heart."

"The desires of my heart?" I sighed as I reached for my sketchbook. "I suppose. Hey, aren't we supposed to be talking about Scarlet's—"

"Yes, but here's my point." Bella's eyes sparkled again. "Sometimes life gives you the opportunity to add a fella to the picture. And sometimes, just sometimes, those relationships do work out. They do lead to something memorable. Something that stands the test of time. Do you get what I'm saying?"

"You're saying I'm Ginger and there might be a Fred out there for me?"

"Exactly!" She clasped her hands together and grinned. "I'm saying you're Ginger and there's going to be some great fella who's going to come along and sweep you off your feet. You don't have to have him to be successful, but God can use the two of you to create something even better than what you could do on your own."

"So . . . I don't need a Fred to be successful, but I *do* need a Fred to be memorable?" When she groaned, I laughed. "Kidding, kidding. I get it, Bella. And I know it's probably a good thing to have a strong relationship with a guy. I'm not saying I'm opposed to the idea."

"That's great news, Gabi." Scarlet reached for my sketchpad and began to thumb through it. "Because your turn is coming, trust me."

"It happens faster than you might think," Hannah said as she leaned over the back of Scarlet's chair to look at my sketches.

"Maybe," I said. "But finding guys as great as yours doesn't come as easily to some of us. And to be honest, I've never actually known a man with sticking power."

Bella rose from her spot behind the desk, the expression on her face growing more serious.

*Uh-oh.*

She walked up next to me and put her hand on my shoulder. "Gabi, trust me, there are men out there with sticking power. You have to find one who's solid in his faith. If he's in a good place with God, he'll be in a good place with you."

Again with the God talk. Seemed like Bella inserted it into just about every conversation. Made me feel like she half expected the Almighty to chime in with his thoughts on the matter. I glanced at her chair just out of curiosity. Nope. Empty.

"I have one more thing to add to my Cinderella theory. After that we'll walk away from this conversation and talk about our bride-to-be here." She gestured to Scarlet, who offered a little "don't worry about me" look.

Me, on the other hand? I definitely wanted to stop talking about this foolishness and focus on the bride, the real reason for my visit today.

"I think you're like Cinderella in all of the

ways that matter." Bella leaned against the desk.

This certainly got my attention. "What do you mean?"

"Well, she was always kind and thoughtful to people, even when they were rude to her. You're one of the kindest people I know." Bella crossed her arms.

"You think so?"

"Of course."

"Ooo, and she's industrious," Hannah added. "A hard worker. I've never met anyone as hard-working as you."

"Please." I gestured to Bella. "We're sitting in the office of the hardest-working woman I've ever known." I now spoke directly to Bella. "Between the wedding facility and the kids, you're going around the clock."

"Well, maybe I've got a Cinderella complex too." She gave a little shrug. "Mostly, though, I think you're like Cinderella because you're so patient. You're willing to wait on God's perfect timing."

Ugh. She had to go there.

"Trust me, I'm not patient." I didn't mean for the words to come out through clenched teeth, but they did.

"Of course you are. When you're designing a dress, when you're meticulously seaming and reseaming a gown for a bride, when you're analyzing the length of a hem."

"When you drive to a wedding facility at the last

minute to fix a bridesmaid's dress that's too big," Scarlet chimed in. "Like you did for me at Hannah's wedding."

"Well, yes, but—"

"All of this requires extreme patience." Bella gave me a knowing look. "And think about when you're sewing a dress together. You cut out the pieces and work them together one at a time. Patiently. You don't actually see the whole dress until it's done, right?"

"Right."

"That's patience. In your mind's eye you see it, but in the real world it's just a hope. A dream."

Scarlet, the dramatic one, lit into the song from *Cinderella* after that, the one about a dream being a wish your heart makes. With a smile, she took to dancing across the floor with a pretend partner. Pretend for a moment, at least. Hannah eventually joined her, and before long Bella and I were laughing. Until Scarlet stopped cold and glanced down at my wrist.

"Um, you do know you're wearing a pincushion on your wrist, right?" She laughed.

"O-oh." I glanced down at my left wrist and sighed. "It's a part of me. Kind of like a growth. I can't seem to shake it."

"I like it on you," Bella said. "Nice accessory."

Should I tell her that I'd almost bathed with the goofy thing on a few times? Nah.

"I'm probably the only girl I know who has

fallen asleep with a pincushion on her wrist," I explained.

"No way." Bella's lips parted in surprise at this announcement. "Are you serious?"

"Yeah." I chuckled as a memory overtook me. "Happened just the other night, actually. I woke up in the morning with pins all over the bed."

"Well, just pull it off before Prince Charming comes along," Scarlet said as she started dancing once again. "You don't want to accidentally stab him before the wedding night, you know."

"Or *on* the wedding night," Hannah added. She brought her hand up to stifle her giggles. "That would be *really* awkward!"

We all got the giggles after that.

I thought about Bella's little speech on patience long after we parted ways that afternoon. Come to think of it, I did spend much of my time waiting. It didn't really bother me to move slowly with a project—to get every little detail right. Maybe waiting wasn't such a big deal for me after all. And if I didn't mind waiting to piece together a gown, maybe waiting to see my dreams come to pass wouldn't be so tough either.

Ginger Rogers had waited, hadn't she? Sure. Maybe that was why her journey resonated with me so much. It wasn't just the whole dancing backwards thing, it was the "I'll hang on for the ride and eventually see my dreams come true" part as well.

But what about waiting for love? What was the point in that?

Then again, Bella had waited, and she'd found D.J.

Hannah had waited, and she'd found Drew.

Scarlet had waited, and she'd found Armando.

Okay, maybe waiting for Mr. Right to come along worked for some girls. And maybe God— aka Prince Charming—would help with the loneliness in the meantime. Again, for *some* girls. But what about girls like me? Seemed like all of my waiting just got me one thing: more time alone in the closet.

# 10

## Carefree

I like making a piece of string into
something I can wear.

AUTHOR UNKNOWN

I awoke early on Sunday morning in a completely different frame of mind. Instead of rushing
to jump out of bed, I rested comfortably and
reflected on yesterday's conversation with the
ladies at Club Wed. When I closed my eyes, I
could almost see an image of Prince Charming.
The God version.

Very odd . . . for me, anyway. Maybe others
sensed the Almighty's presence, but I rarely
claimed to feel it like I did today. With my eyes
closed, I could see him, hand extended, ushering
me into the ballroom. Asking me to dance.

What a lovely Fred and Ginger–like image.

It stayed with me as I grabbed a bagel, penciled
a quick note to Mama and Mimi Carmen, and
slipped out the back door. It lingered as I drove
from our little house to West Beach several miles
away. Something—or someone—was calling me
away today. Calling me to be alone. To just . . . be.

Minutes later, I sat at the water's edge, staring

out over the vast expanse of the Gulf of Mexico. I watched, transfixed, as the waves lapped the shore. As I observed their repetitive pattern, how they left lovely etchings in the sand, I reached for my sketchpad. Something about the ripples put me in mind of a dress design.

Before long I'd sketched the most beautiful fairy-tale-like gown complete with a fitted waist, one my bride-to-be was sure to adore. One that didn't look like a giant marshmallow but would easily sweep her away to a sweet fairy-tale kingdom.

After shoving my sketchbook back into my bag, I closed my eyes and listened to the sound of the waves. They inspired me once again, and I found new ideas flowing. I pulled the sketchbook back out and added the finishing touches to the dress, the rhythm of my pencil against the paper as soothing as the sound of the water gracing the shoreline.

Afterward I sat alone with my thoughts, thinking about my life. In spite of my whining about the lack of a father, I had to admit God had given me a pretty great family. Where would I be without Mimi Carmen? Sure, she was a challenge at times. Half Spanish diva, half buttercream frosting. But I loved her with an undying love.

And Mama? I'd never known a harder worker. Other than myself, anyway. Okay, and Bella. But Mama proved her love by getting out of bed every day and trudging off to a job that blessed others. And she did it all for little pay.

Between the two of us, we got it done, didn't we? Sure.

God had blessed me with some amazing friends of late too. No complaints in that department, especially when it came to the ones in the wedding biz. Bella. Scarlet. Hannah. They all gave me the encouragement I needed and somehow kept me grounded. Kitty too, for that matter. It felt good to know I'd grown enough in my skills to hang out with people like Bella. The more I got to know her, the more I realized how crazy I was about her—not in a "she can further my career" sort of way, but in more of a "wow, she's successful and still normal" way.

*Just . . . be.*

Jordan's words flooded back over me, and I found myself gazing out over the water again. Maybe he had something there.

I took in the beauty of the scene before me, but my heart seemed to capture more than what could be seen with the eyes or heard with the ears. Utter stillness, interrupted by a seagull overhead. The soft rhythm of my heartbeat, dancing in tune to the gentle motion of the water.

I closed my eyes and felt that same sensation I'd noticed earlier in my bedroom. Some would call it a presence, I supposed. To me, it just felt like . . . like a lovely cloud sweeping down over me and cocooning me in a gentle embrace.

That cozy feeling remained as I sat and listened to the waves lap against the shore. It sang in a chorus with the seagulls and whispered in my ear through a conch shell. It danced along the water's edge in graceful lines and blew soft against my cheek in the morning wind.

A delicious shiver worked its way over me as the sensation continued. After a few moments, I could deny it no longer. This moment—this holy moment—was a special gift, one I needed with every fiber of my being. How had I lived on Galveston Island so long without experiencing this kind of moment at the shore?

After lingering in the stillness for a few more moments, I thought about Scarlet's invitation to visit her church. Something quickened inside of me, and I felt myself wondering about the possibilities. A quick glance at my cell phone revealed the time—9:55. The service started in twenty minutes.

An internal argument began at once. Why would I bother going to church? Hadn't Jordan encouraged me to get outdoors? Spend time with God in nature?

Still, the idea wouldn't leave me alone. Besides, I really needed to show Scarlet the new sketch and talk about fabrics. Sounded like as good an excuse as any to go to church.

After a couple of moments of wrestling it

through, I rose and brushed the sand from my backside. I hadn't exactly dressed for church, but maybe they wouldn't mind my jeans and T-shirt. These days people paid little attention to such things, right?

I climbed back into my old car and glanced down at the passenger seat, realizing the side mirror still sat there. Oh well. I would have to deal with that later. Right now I needed to double-check my appearance, so I gave my reflection a quick glance in the rearview mirror.

Ugh. I reached into my bag for my brush and pulled it through my hair, working out the tangles the wind had caused. After a few strokes, I pulled up the sides of my hair, fastening them in place with a clip I found in the bottom of my purse. Two minutes later I'd added mascara and lipstick to my otherwise blank slate of a face and was on my way.

To church. For the first time in . . . what? Ten years? Surely things hadn't changed that much in ten years' time, right?

A few minutes later, I pulled into the parking lot and observed the people around me—young, old, and in between. Thank goodness many of them wore casual clothes, so I relaxed about my attire.

My car sputtered to a stop, drawing the attention of a slightly rotund older fellow with a jolly smile and thinning hair. He approached with a con-cerned look on his face.

"If you need a mechanic, I've got a pretty good eye for engines. Sounds like this one's needing a little TLC, but I'll be glad to take a look if you need me to. Just name your time."

"Oh no. I appreciate the offer, but it's not really necessary. Sometimes it just does that."

He gave me a funny look. "If you change your mind, look me up. I offer discounted rates for church members, but if that doesn't work for you, I might just be willing to give it a look, no charge."

"Why would you do that?"

"Why not?" He shrugged. "I'm blessed to be a blessing."

Okay then. Maybe things *had* changed over the past ten years.

I made my way through the crowd of people into the church, where—after being officially greeted by at least ten or twelve overwelcoming people—I managed to snag a seat on the back pew. I didn't remember much about church life, but I did remember that the back pew was the place to be in case you needed a clean getaway.

Oh! Getaway! I sent Mama a quick "I'm in church" text and shoved my phone in my purse. Just as the music kicked in—*Wait . . . they have drums and guitars in churches now? What happened to pipe organs?*—Scarlet took notice of me.

"You're here!" She plopped down into the spot next to me.

"I'm here."

"Well, there's no way you're sitting all the way back here by yourself. C'mon." She extended a hand and led me to the front row—*Really? The very front row?*—where her fiancé Armando greeted me with a smile.

I took my seat and tried to appear invisible. It worked pretty well until Scarlet's father, now in full preacher mode, asked all visitors to stand.

Was he kidding?

Scarlet nudged me, and I somehow rose to my feet and gave a funky little wave. It didn't help that I was the only visitor. And the sermon that followed really made me sweat. Forgiveness? Seriously? He had to speak on forgiveness?

The service carried on, but I could hardly get my heart to slow its beat.

By the time the band played the last worship song, I had to conclude Scarlet's church was pretty cool. Well, all but that "Visitors, please stand!" part. And the shaky feeling I got whenever her dad mentioned forgiving those who'd hurt you.

After church I called Mama to let her know that I would be joining Scarlet's family for lunch at Casey's Seafood on the seawall. Scarlet's father, it turned out, was quite the character. He kept us laughing every step of the way.

About halfway into the meal, Scarlet leaned my way and whispered, "You have to forgive him, you know."

"Forgive him?" I felt a nervous flutter in my stomach. "You mean, your dad? For making me stand up in church in front of everyone like a goober?"

"No, you goof. I'm talking about Demetri. You have to forgive him for not seeing your gifts. And for thinking of himself above you."

"Well, I—"

"I'm right. Admit it." She took a nibble of her fish. "If you don't let go of this frustration, it's going to eat you alive. Ask me how I know." She lit into a story about the animosity she'd once felt against her aunt Wilhelmina, going on and on about how it nearly destroyed her psyche.

"Anyway, it's not good to put up walls," she said. "And forgiving him—even when it doesn't make sense—is the best gift you can give yourself."

Now she'd lost me entirely. How could forgiving someone else be considered a gift to myself? That made no sense at all.

At this point she reached for her phone to look up the calories in her grilled fish, and before long we were talking about dieting. Thank goodness.

When the meal ended, Scarlet walked me to my car, and I pulled out my sketchpad. She took one look at this morning's sketch and her eyes filled with tears. "Oh, Gabi, it's perfect. Absolutely perfect. You really listened to me. I can tell."

"I thought you might like it."

"I can't wait to see it done up. What sort of fabric will you use?"

"What do you like?"

She shrugged. "Ask me anything about cakes—flavors, decoration, fondant, frosting—and I'd have an answer. But I don't know fabrics like you do."

"We should meet up—maybe Tuesday after work—at the fabric store. Sound good?"

"Perfect."

We made arrangements to do that, and I filled her in on the store's whereabouts. As I climbed into my car, Scarlet remained at my door, so I knew she must have something else on her mind. I rolled down the window—well, I tried to. Turned out the handle didn't work again, so I had to open the door.

"Everything okay?" I asked.

"Yeah." She shrugged. "I'm just still thinking about my dad's sermon on forgiveness."

Ugh. I thought we were done with that.

"I've decided that holding someone in unforgiveness hurts you worse than it hurts them," Scarlet said. "Keeps you bound up on the inside."

"I-I guess." My hands began to tremble, so I steadied them on the steering wheel.

"I heard a story once about a woman who was abused as a child," she said. "It was horrible. Her parents had physically abused her to the point where she almost lost her life. She now speaks to women across the country. About forgiveness, I mean."

"You're saying she forgave the people who beat her?"

"She did. But here's the real kicker—she said that forgiveness is like a key that opens a prison cell."

In that moment, I had a little vision of my dad locked in a prison cell. I stood outside, holding the key in my hand. He stared at me through the bars.

"Not to say that you control the other person's actions," Scarlet went on. "But you get the idea. You can unlock the door with that key you're holding, and the person who really gets freed up is you. You don't have to dwell on the pain anymore. You release it to God."

"Um, okay." So, I was the one in the cell, not my dad? Interesting. Still, I couldn't quite figure out how to go about releasing something to the Almighty, though it sounded lovely in theory.

"He's the keeper of all keys." She grinned, then turned and gave me a little wave. "Think on that."

I thought on it, all right—all the way from the restaurant to my house. When I arrived at home, Mama quizzed me on my church experience. Mimi Carmen turned up her nose at the drums-in-church part, commenting that the pope probably wouldn't approve of such a thing, but I told her I rather liked it.

Afterward Mama followed me into my workroom and took a seat on the chair in front of the sewing machine. She seemed to have something on her mind. After a couple of moments of awkward silence, she spoke up. "I've given some thought to going back to church myself. What do you think?"

"I think . . . it's good."

"I've spent a lot of years working myself to death. And the only friends I have are my co-workers. Might do me good to get out and meet people."

"No doubt. And they're really friendly there. They greet you to death." I chuckled. "And beware, they make the visitors stand."

With a wave of her hand she appeared to dismiss any concerns about making a public spectacle of herself. "Might be worth it as long as I'm standing among the living again. It's been a long time. You know?"

Wow. She rarely opened up to me like this, so I drank in every word.

"I don't know if going to church will change some of the things I struggle with, but I'm willing to give it a try." At this proclamation she rose, gave me a kiss on the forehead, and walked out of the room.

I'd barely had time to ponder her words when my phone rang. I answered it, surprised to hear Jordan's voice on the other end.

"Hem-ry!"

"I-I beg your pardon?"

"Hem-ry. That mannequin thing in your office. His name is Hem-ry. Get it? *Hem*-ry? Because you hem dresses." He laughed and then came back with, "See, I'm good!"

"No." I laughed. "It's not Hem-ry, but that's a good try. I guess."

"I'm going to get this, you know," he said. His voice carried a hint of flirtatious playfulness, which really intrigued me. "I won't give up."

I had a feeling he was talking about more than dress forms and names now. As he lit into a fun story about his latest interview with a bride in Houston, I found myself caught up in his easy, cheerful chatter.

A girl could get used to this.

Very used to this.

# 11

# Tight Spot

May your bobbin always be full!
AUTHOR UNKNOWN

Monday morning dawned like any other day, but my perspective seemed to have improved. Was it just my imagination, or was the sun shining brighter than usual? As I drove to work, my car sputtered all the way, but it didn't really bug me. It did, however, remind me of the fellow at Scarlet's church, the one who had offered his services. Nice guy. I would have to ask Scarlet for his contact information later and then give him a buzz. I might even ask him to replace the side mirror before I got a ticket.

Yes, everything on this Monday morning felt just plain . . . peachy.

Until I arrived at work.

Kitty greeted me at the door, her brow knitted and lips tight. "Gabi, I'm so glad you're here. I just couldn't think of what to do."

"What to do?" I stepped inside and put my purse on the counter. "What do you mean? Has something happened?"

"It's Demetri. He's . . . he's . . ."

My heart quickened as I envisioned the worst. "W-what?"

Kitty took hold of my arm and lowered her voice as she pulled me past the mannequins with their fancy gowns, past the Dynamic Duo as they worked their magic on a customer, toward the break room at the back of the store. "He's in the hospital."

"Hospital?" No way. "I didn't even know he was sick." Shame washed over me as I took in this news. Had I known all along that Demetri was ill, would it have changed my perspective?

"He's not really sick," Kitty said. "He's had a . . ." Her gaze swept the length of the little break room. "A nervous breakdown. I mean, he didn't come out and call it that, but based on what he said . . ."

"Wait, a nervous breakdown?" Huh? Sure, he was a little high-strung, but when it came to business, Demetri Markowitz was the most together man I'd ever met. He scheduled everything. Surely we would've known if he'd planned a nervous breakdown. I would've seen it on the calendar. He simply didn't have time for a nervous breakdown right now, not with the Nicolette Cavanaugh situation and all.

"He's scared to death that reporter is going to find out where he is." Kitty's words sounded strained. "In fact, he's so worried about it that he's registered at the hospital under an assumed name."

"Wow." I paused as I thought it through. "I'm sure Jor—the reporter would never do that."

"You don't know that for sure, Gabi," she said. "I mean, getting the story is a reporter's business. I have no doubt in my mind he's out to get the most sensational tale possible, and this one's pretty sensational." She raised her hands in the air as if displaying her next words. " 'Dress designer melts down after bride-to-be leaves him at the altar.' "

"Wait . . . Nicolette canceled her wedding?"

Kitty's face blanched. "No, that's not what I meant. I'm trying to tell you that she's not wearing the dress he designed for her after all. That's the reason for his breakdown. Well, partly. I'm sure he has other issues going on too. But she's dropped him like a hot potato."

"Oh no." Guilt swept over me as I thought back to the incident involving the tray of éclairs. "Because of the chocolate stain?"

"Nothing to do with that. We got the chocolate stain out. Every bit of it. And you did a fine job on the hem, so it had nothing to do with anything related to that day. Nothing that concerns you, anyway."

"What then?"

"None of this solved the ultimate problem. Turns out she was never keen on the design in the first place. In her heart she wanted something different from the very beginning, but she went

153

along with Demetri because of his popularity. She felt sure that wearing a Demetri Markowitz gown would solidify her role as a debutante." Kitty shook her head. "Not that she phrased it like that, but you get the idea."

"Right."

"She didn't want to hurt his feelings, and she thought the design would grow on her once she went through with the . . . well, you know."

"The surgery?"

"Yeah. But having the surgery just solidified in her mind that she wasn't a fan of the dress. She now considers the chocolate incident a sign that it was never meant to be. She called this morning and talked to me at length about all of this. We had a very frank discussion, actually."

"Ack." No doubt Demetri considered the chocolate fiasco a sign too. One that I should look for work elsewhere. Why oh why did this have to happen now, after I'd lost and then regained my job?

"So, now what?" I dropped down into a chair.

"Now we have the task of diverting the reporter. He can't find out." She shrugged. "He's already done his interview with Demetri, and as far as he knows the bride is happy, so if we don't say anything, no one will be any the wiser."

"Wait. Are you saying Demetri is going to let the article run as is? He's going to let *Texas Bride*—and all of its readers—think that

Nicolette actually walked the aisle in his dress?"

Kitty released a loud sigh, one that mirrored my concerns. "I guess. I just know he's not in any shape to let the reporter know the truth yet."

"They're going to find out." I knew from past experience that situations like these always had a way of coming to light. "Better to be a little humiliated now, in front of Jordan, than to be publicly humiliated in front of thousands of readers when the truth emerges."

"True, but—" She gave me an inquisitive look. "Wait, did you just call him Jordan?"

My heart quickened. "Y-yeah. That's his name."

"Well, yes, but you say it as if you guys are good friends or something." Now she gave me a funny look. "*Are* you good friends or something?"

"I wouldn't say we're good friends, really." I cleared my throat and tried to look nonchalant. "More like acquaintances. He interviewed me to get extra tidbits to add to the article, so I've spent time with him."

*Alone. In my office. And at home. And on the phone.*

"What did you tell him?"

For whatever reason, her question felt more like an accusation. I'd never known Kitty to be anything but kind, so I did my best to write this off as anxiety on her part.

"I certainly didn't say anything about Demetri's nerves or his visit to the hospital. Not that I knew anything about Demetri being hospitalized, anyway. All of this is news to me."

"Right, right." She paced the room, then looked my way. "I guess you should know that the Fab Five . . ."

"What about them?"

"They're not taking this news very well. Turns out they don't function well without their fear-less—er, fear-filled—leader."

"Are you saying the *vell*-oiled machine isn't so *vell*-oiled?" I couldn't help but smile as I tried to mimic Demetri's accent.

"They're frozen with rust at the moment. That might be a better description." She paused. "Look, I know this is asking a lot, but would you mind going over there? I've tried to talk to them, but they're pretty much stuck right now. They need some sort of motivation."

"And you think I can provide it?"

"I don't know, but at this point I'm willing to try just about anything."

Alrighty then.

Sucking in a deep breath, I turned to face the studio, ready to make the trek. Before taking one step, though, I offered up another one of those frantic prayers. Seemed like the Lord was hearing from me a lot lately.

Turned out I didn't have to go to the studio. The Fab Five came to me. We met in the break room. Well, just outside the break room, actually.

I watched as Beatrix stumbled across the room, knocking down one of the mannequins and nearly taking a tumble herself. Emiko tried to grab the mannequin but failed. Only when I stuck out an arm to catch it was the catastrophe averted.

A normal person would've thanked me for saving her neck. Not Beatrix. She glared at me as if I'd somehow caused the whole thing. Emiko, however, gave a kindly nod and said, "Thanks."

Wow. Her first word to me. Ever. A crack in the veneer. I took this as a hopeful sign. But just as quickly, the young woman's gaze shifted to the floor.

Doria gave me a hug, but her eyes glistened with tears. The other two ladies looked . . . lost. Vacant.

I wanted to say something motivational to the group but never got the chance. They huddled around the cappuccino maker, all whispers and sighs, and left me to the outer fringes. Again.

I made my way to my office, where I plopped down on the floor at Ginger's feet to hem the gown she happened to be wearing. The owner of said gown would arrive in a couple of days to pick it up, so I'd better get busy.

I gazed up at her and sighed as I asked the question, "Ever wish you had a different sort of life?"

Ginger did not respond.

"Sometimes I think about having a different

life," a familiar voice said from the doorway. "But I don't really know what I'd do. Open a bridal shop and show off your creations? Or maybe take up sword fighting? Become a professional wrestler?"

Glancing in the direction of the voice, I saw Jordan standing in the open doorway, looking more adorable than ever in a blue button-up shirt and dark jeans.

"But sword fighting doesn't pay much," he added with a shrug.

"That's what I hear."

"So maybe I'll stick with reporting." Jordan took a step into the room. "We've already established that I'm pretty good at that, especially when it comes to all things bridal."

"That's true," I said. "You know your brides."

"And their gowns." He pointed at Ginger.

As his smile lit the room, I was transfixed. Still, I wondered why he had returned to the scene of the crime. Had he heard about Demetri's hospitalization, perhaps? Was he here to glean more info for his article? Get the inside scoop? The very idea made me a nervous wreck.

The twinkle in his eye spoke otherwise. "I think my real calling is eater of great Italian food."

Now he'd lost me completely.

"I'm asking Ginger to lunch." He extended his hand. "If she has the time."

"Ah." I looked back and forth between Ginger

—half hemmed—and Prince William. Er, Jordan.

"Ginger is drowning in work at the moment." I sighed as I gestured to the dress in front of me. "She's not sure she can spare any time away."

"Oh, well, that's a shame, but I've got the perfect solution. Mice!"

"Mice?" I leaped up, brushing loose thread from my backside as my gaze traveled the floor from one side of the room to the other. "You saw a mouse?"

"No." He chuckled. "I'm asking if you have mice like the ones that helped with Cinderella's dress the night she went to the ball."

"Ah." I felt the tension go out of my shoulders. "I sure hope not."

"Well, they came in handy, if memory serves me correctly. Didn't they help sew her dress?"

"True, true. But I somehow doubt the real deal would prove to be as helpful." In fact, the very idea of mice in the workroom made me shiver.

I did my best to steady my breathing as Jordan carried on about the scene in the animated *Cinderella* where the mice worked as a team to put together Cinderella's ball gown. Suddenly I pictured Demetri running through the shop, chased by a passel of baby mice that knocked down dress mannequins all the way. I had to chuckle at the image that presented.

"Ooo, you like my idea. And you have to agree, it's the perfect solution." Jordan nodded.

"Cinderella had a Fab Five too. Only, they were much smaller. And kind of sneaky."

"Not much different from the ones I know." I instantly bit my tongue. Really, I had to quit blaming Beatrix and the other designers for my plight. They weren't the wicked stepsisters and I wasn't Cinderella. They were just five women who'd caught a break—a great break—from an important designer.

"So, about that lunch date . . ." He offered his hand again. "If I promise to have you back before the clock strikes midnight, will you come with me?"

I reached to take his hand and gave a little nod. "I guess so."

"Not the most enthusiastic response, but I'll take it." He held my hand a bit longer than the situation would have called for. Not that I felt like complaining. Oh no. I made no effort to withdraw it. I looked into his ruggedly handsome face, and those compelling eyes drew me in. Made me a little weak in the knees, frankly. A girl couldn't help but be captivated by his strong but gentle face, the confident set of his shoulders, and those kissable lips—always curled as if on the edge of laughter.

Kissable lips? Where had that come from? Oy! I'd seen one too many of Mimi Carmen's tele-novelas, apparently.

I found myself saying, "I'd love to go to lunch,"

which only served to broaden his smile and draw my attention once again to those lips.

*Focus, Gabi. Focus.*

Not that anyone could focus just now, with all the noise coming from outside my workroom.

Jordan turned and released his hold on my hand. "What is that?"

" 'Who is that?' might be a better question." I knew, of course, but didn't want to raise his suspicions.

Outside the door, the Fab Five argued among themselves about a design project. Their voices rose higher and higher in pitch. Then Kitty got involved. I could hear her trying to shush them, but it didn't appear to be working. No, they only grew louder, and within seconds, one of them— Emiko?—started crying. Man. Now what?

"Are they okay?" Jordan asked, his words lowered to a hoarse whisper.

"I think they just don't know what to do without Demetri guiding the ship. You know?"

"Demetri's not here?" Jordan asked.

Yikes! I'd totally forgotten *not* to tell him.

"He, um, well, he stepped out this morning, and they seem a little lost without him." I smiled faintly. "You know how it is, a ship without its rudder and all that."

"You're saying this ship has lost its rudder?" Jordan's eyes widened. "That's not good."

"Well, no. Not really." My heart thump-

thumped. "I mean, no, it's not true that they've lost their rudder. I just think they're waiting for someone to give them instruction. And Demetri will be back. Soon. Very soon. I feel sure of it."

"That's good, because I was hoping to connect with him today to ask a couple of questions about Nicolette's dress. Once I get these notes plugged in, the article will be good to go."

*Oh. Help.*

Outside my room, Kitty finally managed to get the ladies calmed down. Before long I could tell that they'd left the building, likely headed to lunch at Parma John's, their usual spot.

"You ready to go to lunch? I think it's safe to pass now." Jordan grinned. "I'm dying for some pizza, and it's Monday. You know what that means."

"The Mambo Italiano Special," we said in unison.

Only, now I didn't feel like eating. Ever again. I wanted to climb in a hole and pretend I hadn't just told him that Demetri—our rudder—was gone. At least I hadn't mentioned where he'd gone.

Had I? Right now I couldn't remember.

"I can't believe I get to go to lunch with the prettiest girl on the island. I'm one lucky guy." Jordan offered me his arm—à la Fred Astaire—and I took it, mesmerized by his flattering words. We walked out of the workroom together, but I could hardly think straight.

When we got to the front of the store, Kitty

looked our way, her eyes growing large as she saw my arm looped through Jordan's. Her words, "*Are you good friends or something?*" ran through my mind. I'd denied it, hadn't I? And yet here I stood, looking like more than just friends. Much more.

She shook her head as if to offer some sort of subliminal warning, and panic swept over me. I pulled my arm free and stopped walking.

"You okay?" Jordan looked my way, clearly confused.

"Actually, I . . ." *Think of something, Gabi.* "I have a lot of work on my plate, and I don't know if I have the time to grab lunch today."

"Oh." His expression shifted, and those lips— those gorgeous, kissable lips—turned down. Strange, I'd never seen him look sad before. Kind of broke my heart, especially his quiet "I understand."

He didn't, but that was probably a good thing.

"I'm sorry, Jordan. I really am. But I really need to stay here." My gaze shifted to Kitty, who seemed to relax at this statement. "And work."

We said our goodbyes, and I did my best to answer Kitty's barrage of questions. My explanation seemed to pacify her, at least on some level, and she left me to my own devices once again. With my heart in my throat, I sprinted back to my workroom, my nerves more frazzled than the loose threads hanging from the hem of Ginger's dress.

# 12

## The Way You Look Tonight

*Asking a seamstress to mend is like asking Michelangelo to paint your garage.*
AUTHOR UNKNOWN

I stopped by Let Them Eat Cake early Tuesday morning to grab a quick breakfast. Scarlet's mother waited on a host of customers at the front counter but finally got to me. She smiled and commented on how much she loved my ideas for her daughter's wedding gown, which totally made my morning.

After ordering a kolache, I walked back to the kitchen to say a quick hello to Scarlet before heading off to work. I found her gabbing with Hannah, who filled her ears with newlywed chatter.

I nibbled on my kolache as the ladies giggled and talked about Hannah's honeymoon a couple of months back. She blushed as she referred to the wedding night.

After a while Scarlet looked my way. "Sorry, Gabi. Just quizzing Hannah to see what my future holds." She released a wacky laugh and almost went face-first into the bowl of batter in front of her. The whole thing reminded me of an *I Love Lucy* episode.

Before long I found myself chuckling too, and all the more when Hannah informed us that the wedding night was definitely worth the wait.

"Ah, love." Scarlet sighed and poured the cake batter into a pan. "It's so divine. So . . . perfect."

"What about you, Gabi?" Hannah gave me a pensive look. "Any love interests we don't know about?"

At once heat rose to my face. I shifted my gaze downward so that my inability to maintain a good poker face wouldn't give me away.

"Aha." Scarlet waved her batter-covered spoon my way. "You have a secret crush. I can tell from the look on your face."

"C'mon now," Hannah said. "Fess up. Who is he?"

"Ooo, I'll bet I can guess." Scarlet let go of the spoon, and it clattered down into the now empty bowl. "It's that reporter. Am I right?"

I shook my head. "Please. I hardly know him. We've only seen each other a couple of times."

"That's all it took with Armando and me," Scarlet said. "Sometimes God moves really fast."

I let the God comment slip right by.

"If not the reporter, then who?" Hannah's nose wrinkled. "Oh, I know! It's that guy who works at the fabric store. The one who makes the deliveries to the shop."

"Yep. That's it." I smiled and nodded. "You guessed him. Okay, next question." I somehow managed to steer them in a different direction, and before long we were talking about tonight's visit to the fabric shop.

A couple of minutes later, Scarlet gave me a "you're not fooling me" look, and I knew she would be asking me for more details later.

Not that I had details. I really didn't have much to share. Except for that one really great conversation with Jordan at my house, we hardly knew one another. Besides, I didn't have feelings for Jordan Singer, not really.

Okay, maybe I did, but they weren't the kind I needed to be sharing with anyone. I wasn't the sort of girl who got what she wanted anyway, so why bother?

"You okay over there?" Scarlet asked.

I startled to attention. "Hmm? What?"

"I don't know, all of a sudden you looked kind of . . . distracted."

"Nope. Not distracted. Completely focused and ready to get rolling on this dress of yours. So, I'll see you tonight? We'll meet at the fabric store?"

"Yes."

"Awesome." I offered the brightest smile I could muster. The moment I'd said the word *dress,* the world seemed right again. Who cared if I didn't have a sweetheart? Or a designing career?

I had my real secret crush—designing—and it suited me just fine.

Suited me just fine. Ha!

Scarlet and Hannah dove back into a conversation about wedding nights—my cue to leave—and I said my goodbyes. I waved to Scarlet's mother, who was up to her eyeballs with customers, and then headed outside to go to work. Then an idea came to me, one I couldn't shake.

I walked down the Strand to the local confectionery and purchased a box of sweets—fudge, chocolate-covered caramels, truffles, local taffies, and more. Then I pointed my car in the direction of the hospital, not the bridal shop. Demetri would fuss at me, but I didn't care.

Sure enough, he fussed. Still, as he laid eyes on the truffles, his personal favorite, he seemed to forgive me for invading his personal space. I didn't want to make him more uncomfortable, so I remained standing. No point in him thinking I might overstay my welcome.

"I got a call on my cell from zat reporter." He gestured to his phone. "I didn't take it. But Kitty told me he stopped by zee store yesterday unannounced."

"Yes, he's wanting to ask you more questions, I think."

He groaned. "You didn't tell him, did you?"

"Of course not. But you don't need to run from

him, Demetri," I said. "I suggest you do the opposite, in fact."

"Zee opposite?"

"Yes, give him a real story. A heartfelt story. Jordan is a great guy. He won't use your situation to hurt you in any way."

Demetri grunted. "Puh-*leeze*. Ve are in zee wedding business, you know. Ve live to stab one another in zee back."

"Not everyone lives to do that," I said. "Some of us just want to help others. Jordan falls into that category."

"Jordan." Another groan followed. "Now zee two of you are on a first-name baze-ese? Kitty told me you looked like a couple. Is it true?"

"A couple? No way."

"Good." His dark brows slanted into a frown, but this did not weaken my resolve.

"I think you should call him, Demetri. I really do. He'll do right by you. I know he will. And you'll have the advantage, because you called him, not the other way around." I picked up his cell phone and handed it to him, impressed at my boldness. What could he do from the hospital bed, anyway? Throw a bedpan at me?

Demetri stared at the phone for a moment and then put it back down. "Give me zee mirror." He pointed to a crystal-encrusted hand mirror on the bedside table. I reached for it, mesmerized. "If zat reporter is coming, I must look presentable." He glanced in the mirror and groaned. "Vell, as presentable as possible." He licked his fingertips and then used them to shape his already perfect brows.

I couldn't help but notice the intricate crystal design on the mirror. "This is beautiful, Demetri," I said as he passed it back my way with a grunt.

His eyes seemed to fill with sadness. "It vas my mother's." Total silence followed. I'd never heard the man comment on his mother before. Strange.

"Well, it's lovely. I've never seen anything like it."

"It is from my homeland." His eyes took on a faraway look, and I thought maybe I'd lost him to his memories. Just as quickly he snapped back and reached for his phone. Seconds later, he and Jordan were engaged in a jovial conversation, one that seemed to end on an upbeat.

I headed out of the hospital minutes later, after promising Demetri approximately a thousand times to keep spirits up among his employees. Strange how concerned he seemed about all of us. I'd never seen him as a father figure, but perhaps he felt that way after all.

When I arrived back at Haute Couture, I found Kitty distracted with a phone call. "It's Nicolette," she mouthed, then covered the phone with her hand. "And she wants to talk to you."

"M-me?"

"Yeah."

"Why?"

"I don't have any idea." Kitty pressed the phone behind her back and whispered, "Whatever you do, don't tell her about Demetri. He'd be humiliated if she found out."

"What if she asks to speak to him?"

"Tell her . . ." Kitty's eyes narrowed. "He's on a European vacation."

I pulled the phone out of Kitty's hand and groaned as I whispered, "That one's already been done, remember?" I turned my attention to the phone with a polished "Hello?"

"Gabi, this is Nicolette."

"Yes, Kitty told me you—"

"I need to talk to you. Soon. I'll be in the area this afternoon and would like to drop by."

"Oh?"

"Yes. I hope you're able to give me a few minutes of your time. I know everyone's in a tizzy about my decision not to wear Demetri's gown, but I think maybe there's an answer that all of us can live with."

"Really?" I breathed a sigh of relief in preparation for whatever she might say.

"Yes. So can you make some time for me later this afternoon? I'll come by just before you close. Maybe quarter of five?"

"I'll be here," I assured her.

Her brusque "See you then" brought the call to an end.

I turned to Kitty, suddenly feeling much better about the situation. "She's coming to see me at 4:45."

"Why?" Kitty paced the space behind the counter.

"I'm not sure, but she said there's an answer to the problem, so I'm thinking she wants me to alter the dress again, maybe make it more to her liking. Do you think Demetri will mind?"

"I don't know." Kitty bit her lip. "But it would help him save face if she decides to wear the dress after all." Her face lit up. "Yes, I think this is just the news Demetri needs to brighten his day. I'm going to call him and let him know that she's coming in. You just . . . just . . . do what you can to make her happy, promise?"

"I always do."

"I'm sure Demetri's pride won't be too wounded. Just keep her smiling, and then we won't have to worry about the reporter finding out anything. He won't notice if the dress goes through a bit of a transformation. Somehow I doubt he pays much attention to dress design, anyway. You know? Men rarely do."

*You might be surprised.*

I didn't say the words aloud but certainly thought them. Jordan had not only paid attention to Nicolette's gown, he'd paid specific attention to my sketches as well. Talk about someone who noticed the details. He would know if her dress was changed, no doubt about it. Should I do as Kitty said and not tell him? Just let it ride?

I went about my business, but thoughts of Nicolette's impending arrival were never far from my mind. She entered the shop at exactly 4:44, one minute before expected.

She brushed past me in the break room and mumbled, "Gabi, I need you," as she breezed toward my little closet. I followed on her heels. When we arrived inside, she turned to face me, her gaze falling on the sketchpad on my desk. "Oh, good. It's here."

"W-what?"

She reached for the sketchpad and held it close. "This. You see, I've been fretting over this for days."

"Over my sketchbook?"

"Yes." She groaned. "Well, no. Not the sketchbook, exactly. I've been fretting over how to go about getting what I really want without hurting Demetri's feelings. But I think it'll be okay. I mean, you already work for him, right, so how mad can he be?"

"R-right." What that had to do with anything, I couldn't be sure.

"Perfect. We can still tell the reporter that the dress came out of Demetri's studio. He won't have to know that it's not technically Demetri's design."

Okay, now she'd lost me completely.

I twisted a strand of my hair between my fingers as my nerves took over. "Nicolette, I'm not sure I get your meaning."

"Then let me make it clear."

I felt my breath catch in my throat as she opened my sketchbook and thumbed through the designs inside. "What are you doing?" My hoarse whisper felt more like a yell. I reached to close the door, terrified that Kitty might peek inside.

"It's awful, I know, but I saw your sketchbook that day I came to your workroom for a fitting." She glanced up, giving me a sheepish look. "There was a sketch . . . it was sheer perfection—a one-shouldered number with a ruffled skirt. Absolutely breathtaking and exactly the sort of look I was going for from the beginning."

I knew the gown she referred to, of course. I'd sketched it, after all.

She went into a lengthy dissertation about the dress, about how perfect it would be for her new figure, how the fabric would be ideal for her skin tone, how the featherweight ruffles at the bottom captured her zeal for life, her fun-loving side. I realized she'd not only seen my sketch, she had spent serious time analyzing the complexities of the gown.

She continued to thumb through my sketchbook until she landed on the design in question. "That's it!" She let out a squeal and pointed. "That's the dress I want."

"B-but . . ." I glanced at the design, my thoughts now tumbling madly. "It's not an actual dress. Not yet, anyway. It's just in my imagination."

"I figured." Her nose wrinkled. "And that's a problem, I guess, since my wedding is just a couple of months away. So how fast can you take it from your imagination to the altar?"

"Nicolette, I don't know. It's not just the timing. Demetri will kill me." Murder me in my sleep was more like it.

With a wave of her hand she appeared to dismiss that idea. "Don't be silly. You work for Demetri. The dress will be produced in his design studio. Why would he kill you? Having your own line will just bring more attention to him. Surely he can see that."

"That's what Bella said." Why I spoke those words aloud, I could not say. I hadn't meant to bring Bella into this.

"If anyone knows her wedding dresses, it's Bella Neeley." Nicolette's smile exuded confidence. "Now I *have* to have it. I'll pay whatever price you like."

*Cha-ching!* Maybe I could stop worrying about the rent for a change. Let Mama cut back on her hours. A world of possibilities opened up as I thought it through.

"Demetri can keep the money I've already given him, so everyone will be happy. See?" Nicolette giggled, and for the first time I saw her as a giddy bride, not a debutante with something to prove to her friends. "Well, everyone but Daddy. He'll have a fit, but we'll cross that bridge when we come to it."

"I really don't know what to say."

"Say yes, Gabi." Nicolette placed her free hand on my arm. "We'll make things right with Demetri, I promise."

"How?" There weren't enough prescription meds in the state of Texas to cover this one.

"I don't know, but we will. I'll handle it." She gazed at the sketch again, and her expression shifted from concern to pure bliss. "You just get busy and make me the dress of my dreams, okay?"

I swallowed hard, unsure of how to answer.

"Yoo-hoo! Ginger!" From outside the door Jordan's voice sounded. "I went to visit Demetri at the hospital, and he said I should swing by and check on things at the shop." Jordan's volume increased, and I could tell he was getting closer. "I told him I'd be glad to."

"Demetri's in the hospital?" Nicolette clamped a hand over her mouth, then pulled it away, lowering her voice to a whisper. "Why didn't you tell me?"

"I-I-I . . ." *Aye, aye, aye.*

Jordan entered the room, all smiles until he saw Nicolette standing there. Then he managed a wide-eyed "Oh no."

Yep. My thoughts exactly.

# 13

## The Pleasure of His Company

If Fred Astaire made a great dancer out of Ginger Rogers, it is equally true that Ginger made a successful romantic lead out of Astaire.

LINCOLN BARNETT

For a moment, none of us spoke a word. Jordan glanced at the sketchbook in Nicolette's hands and then up at me with a look of terror in his eyes.

She slipped the sketchbook onto my desk, her gaze shifting to the door. "Well, I, um, I'd better go. I'll talk to you later, Gabi. Just think about what I've said." Seconds later, she disappeared from view.

Jordan's nose wrinkled. "I'm so sorry. Do you think she . . . ?"

His words faded away as I nodded. "Yeah, she heard you. She definitely heard you."

"Me and my big mouth. I guess I just assumed you were alone in here. Forgive me?"

I nodded again, albeit slowly. If only I could slow the rate of my heart to the same pace. Right now it felt like it was competing in the Indy 500.

His brows unfurrowed as he gestured to the

dress forms. "Not that you're ever alone with these two present. They are your ever-faithful companions."

"True."

"And I'm pretty sure they have a 'don't ask, don't tell' policy, right?" He put his finger up in front of the male dress form and said, "Shh!" then gave me a weak smile. "See? Hem-ry's not talking."

I could tell Jordan really felt bad about what had just happened, and I sure didn't want to make things any worse by making a big deal out of it. Still, my heart kept right on racing. "His name's not Hem-ry," I managed.

"Yeah, I know." Jordan looked back at the dress form and then snapped his fingers. "I've got it!"

"What?" I asked.

"Stitch."

"Excuse me?"

"Stitch." He gave me a smug look.

"Is that a mandate or something?" I brushed a loose strand of hair behind my ear and gazed at him, more confused than ever.

A boyish grin lit Jordan's face as he pointed at the male dress form. "That's his real name, isn't it? You call him Stitch."

"Ah." I bit back a laugh, and my concerns over Nicolette faded as I stared at Jordan's twinkling eyes. "No. Not even close, sorry. Good try, though."

And just the right thing to calm my nerves at the moment.

My response didn't seem to make Jordan happy, though. His dark brows slanted in a frown, and the lines of concentration deepened under his eyes. He plopped down into the chair across from me. "I was sure I had it. It's got something to do with sewing, right?"

Hmm. "Well, yeah. Sort of."

Not that sewing was the first thing I thought of when Demetri came to mind, but whatever.

My thoughts shifted back to the sermon I'd heard on Sunday about forgiveness. Then Scarlet's story about the woman she'd held in unforgiveness resurfaced in my memory as well. Suddenly, thinking about sticking pins in Demetri—the dress form version—didn't hold as much appeal.

Shame washed over me as the truth settled in. I really just needed to forgive my boss for over-looking me and then move forward with my life. Set myself free from the proverbial prison, as it were.

"I'm going to get this, Gabi." Jordan's voice roused me from my ponderings.

"Jordan, I really don't think you need to waste your time doing that."

"No." He put his hand up. "I'm still working on it. Don't tell me. I'll figure it out. I'm really good at riddles."

Somehow I doubted he would ever figure out I'd named the dress form after my boss. I hoped not, anyway.

"Riddle-dee-dee," he said with a boyish grin.

I tried not to match his smile. Those sparkling eyes drew me in, captivating me. They made me forget about . . . well, everything else.

*Back away from the light, Gabi.*

I shifted my attention back to the female dress form. Ginger currently wore a size 14 gown in off-white—one of Demetri's more recent creations. I wasn't crazy about it, but the plus-sized brides seemed to appreciate the empire waistline. A corseted look would've suited most of them better, but I kept my opinions to myself. I'd gotten pretty good at that, actually.

Unless you counted Ginger. I shared my thoughts with her much of the time, but she kept silent on most matters. Okay, all matters.

Jordan didn't keep silent, however. He continued to chatter, rambling on about the male dress form, which he pulled out of the corner and now addressed personally.

"Happy to make your acquaintance, Stitch," he said as he extended his hand in the dress form's direction. "My name is Jordan Singer."

I tried not to chuckle. Still, how could I help it, with my nerves being in such a frazzled state today? My defenses all but melted away at his appealing smile, and before long I found myself laughing.

My reaction seemed to please Jordan. Amusement flickered in his eyes as they met mine. After a second, he turned back to the dress form, all smiles.

"Oh, what's that?" Jordan asked. "You say you're shy? Too shy to give your real name?" He glanced my way. "There's a lot of that going around, but don't you worry about it, Stitch. I'll figure this out sooner or later." He slung his arm around the dress form's shoulder.

"I told you, his name isn't Stitch," I scolded.

"Yes, well, that's just a nickname for the time being." Jordan turned the dress form around, examining him from all sides. "Honestly, he still looks like a Hem-ry to me."

I just shook my head and did my best to hide the smile that tried to creep up.

"Anyway, it's been nice meeting you, Stitch," Jordan said with a trace of laughter in his voice. "I hope to see more of you." His gaze traveled from the dress form to me as he added, "Much more," and I suddenly understood his meaning. He didn't care to see more of Stitch. He wanted to see more of me. The idea made me giddy. Or was that the effect of today's craziness?

"So . . ." His gaze shifted down to his feet, then he looked my way with a sheepish expression on his face. "I've been beating around the bush, but I really just want to come out and ask you something."

"Sure."

*As long as it doesn't involve Demetri or Nicolette, we're fine.*

He worked the toe of his boot against the floor. "I know you were too busy yesterday to grab lunch . . . "

"I'm really sorry about that. I was just . . . well, it was the Demetri thing, to be honest. Lots of things were stirring when you were here."

"Right. I get that now. And by the way, thank you for asking him to call me. He seemed pretty much himself when I went to see him at the hospital."

"I'm sure things will be back to normal soon." Not that Demetri's normal was exactly fun and games, but it would be nice to get past the "my boss is losing it" stage.

"So you weren't avoiding me?" Jordan asked.

"No. Everything was just so . . . complicated."

"Okay, I was hoping it had more to do with all of that, to be honest, because I really stopped by to see if you might like to go to dinner."

Those beautiful eyes seemed to pierce right through me, and I felt my cheeks grow warm.

"Tonight?"

"Yeah, but if you're not able to, that's okay. I'll understand. We could go tomorrow night. Or the night after."

"No, it's fine. Sounds good, actually." But then I remembered the meeting with Scarlet. "Ooo, maybe not."

His expression soured and his lips curled down in a pout. "Really?"

"Well, I'm supposed to meet Scarlet at the fabric store at 6:30 this evening. We're picking out fabrics for her wedding dress."

"But you have to eat, right? I'll just come with you to the fabric store and we can catch dinner after. If you're okay with that."

"Oh, no, no, no." I shook my head as I tried to picture this handsome reporter milling through a fabric store. "I mean, dinner sounds great, but you'll be bored out of your mind in a fabric store, trust me."

"You might be surprised." The look of interest in his eyes caught me off guard. "For your information, I'm very artsy. And like you, I've worked with fabrics."

"You have?" This certainly got my attention.

"Well, not worked with them, exactly. But I did a great article on high-end wedding fabrics last year, in fact. I could tell you anything you want to know about satins, tulles, and silks—whether we're talking local or imports. And don't even get me started on lace trims. We'll be here all night."

"Well, all right then."

I chuckled and almost missed the faint sound

of Kitty's voice from the hallway outside my room. "Hey, Gabi, you still in there?"

"Yes, I—"

"Good," she called out. "I just put the closed sign on the door. I wanted to let you know that Demetri called. You'll be happy to hear he's checking out of the hospital with a new prescription for Xanax in hand, as well as a couple of other meds he couldn't pronounce. He'll be back tomorrow, no doubt ready to rule the roost with an iron fist."

"Kitty, please st—"

"What was the deal with Nicolette?" she said, her voice getting louder now. "She sure left in a hurry. Please tell me you changed her mind and talked her into wearing the gown Demetri designed for her. Otherwise I think we might just have to medicate him further."

I released a loud groan and slapped myself on the forehead as Kitty stepped into the doorway, still ranting about the dress situation. She took one look at Jordan and looked like she might faint. For that matter, I felt a little woozy myself. I swallowed hard, pinched my eyes shut, and prayed for a miracle.

Really? Could this day get any crazier?

# 14

## Swing Time

*Either the camera will dance, or I will.*
FRED ASTAIRE

I'd seen Kitty flustered plenty of times—take the hairpiece incident, for example—but never like this. She placed her forehead against the doorjamb and began to talk to herself, rambling on and on about how life as she knew it had just come to an end.

Jordan took several quick steps in her direction and put his hand on her arm. "It's okay. I already knew about Demetri being hospitalized. Like I said, I went by to see him."

"Yes, but . . ." Kitty turned to face him, then shook her head. "You didn't know about the whole Nicolette wedding gown fiasco, and now you do. And I'm so fired."

"No you're not, because I'm not going to say anything about any of this. My article's not due to my editor for another week, so I'll just change the slant."

"Are . . . are you sure?" For the first time, the color seemed to return to her face.

"Very sure." The kindness in his voice mirrored

the expression in those gorgeous eyes of his. "So please, don't worry."

His words put me at ease right away. Kitty seemed to relax a bit too.

Still, we had one more topic to address, one sure to get her wound up all over again. I fought to swallow the lump in my throat and then spoke.

"Um, Kitty, while we're coming clean, I might as well let you know something else. Nicolette knows that Demetri's in the hospital."

"How does she . . . ?" Kitty squeezed her eyes shut. "No, I don't want to know."

"It happened exactly the same way you just told me about the dress," Jordan said. "I came through the door talking about my visit to Demetri in the hospital, not knowing that Nicolette was in here. It was totally my fault."

"When Demetri hears this, he's going to check himself back into the hospital." She dropped into my chair and began to fan herself.

"Actually, I wouldn't worry about Nicolette saying anything to him about his . . . well, his condition," I said. "She's got other things on her mind right now."

Kitty gave me a "what are you talking about?" look, but I just shrugged and reached for my sketchbook.

"That's a whole other story. I'll tell you all about it tomorrow." A glance at the clock on the wall revealed the time—5:40. "I'm supposed to meet

Scarlet at the fabric shop at 6:30 and it's on the mainland, so I've got to get out of here. You just go home and take a bubble bath and . . . just pray. God will take care of this." The words came tumbling out, and as I spoke them, I realized that I totally believed them.

Kitty still didn't look convinced, and I knew we'd have a lot to work out tomorrow, but for now I needed to hit the road. Scarlet would be waiting.

Jordan followed me out of the store and pointed to his car. "I'm parked just down the Strand. You okay to leave your car here while we're gone?"

"Sure. Maybe someone will take it." I flashed a sarcastic smile.

He opened the door on the passenger side—very gentlemanly—and I took a seat, doing my best to appear calm. With so much stirring in one day, my thoughts whirled around like fruit in a blender.

Thank goodness Jordan kept the conversation going as he drove. When he asked me to tell him about the fabric store, I dove right in, thankful for the diversion.

"Well, for one thing, the store is huge," I said. "Worth driving the distance to get there. They've got everything from everyday fabrics to high-end designer bolts in the two-hundred-dollar-a-yard range. And you should see the trims."

"Ooo, trims!" He grinned.

"We'll probably be buying some tonight." I felt

my eyes glaze over as I pictured them. "Everything a bride—or bridesmaid—could ever want to embellish her dress."

I shifted to talking about Scarlet's gown, and before long I'd opened my sketchpad. When we pulled into the parking lot at the store, Jordan turned the car off and gave my designs a closer look. He flipped from one page to the next, not saying a word.

Finally he cleared his throat. "Gabi, can I ask you a question?" He spoke to me but never looked my way. Instead, his gaze remained fixed on my sketches.

"Sure." I leaned his way, so close, in fact, that the smell of his cologne drew me in.

"You did all of these?"

"Yes."

He raked his fingers through that gorgeous hair and narrowed his gaze. "They're better than anything I've seen in Demetri's shop. In fact, they're better than most of the dresses we've featured in the magazine."

Okay, now he was teasing me. "You're just saying that."

"No I'm not." He eased the sketchbook out of my hand and gently turned to the next page.

"Don't look at that one." I groaned. "It's not done yet. I was just messing around with an idea."

"Well, keep messing. Your messing is going to end up being some bride's blessing." He chuckled.

"To be honest, I stole that line from a TV preacher. Well, not the bride part. I don't aspire to be a poet, but it just seemed to fit." Another turn of the page revealed the dress that Nicolette had fallen in love with.

From across the parking lot I caught a glimpse of Scarlet entering the store with an elderly woman at her side.

"Uh-oh." I took my sketchbook back and closed it, then tucked it into my bag.

"What's wrong?"

"Looks like Scarlet's not alone."

"Is that her grandmother?" Jordan asked as he swung his door open.

"I don't think so. I've heard for weeks about her infamous aunt Willy. I'm guessing this is her."

Jordan came around to my side of the car and opened my door. He extended his hand and I took it, not because I needed help from the car but because it felt like the right thing to do. The comfortable thing to do.

We walked into the store, and Scarlet gave me a wave, her right eyebrow elevating as she noticed Jordan. "You made it! Both of you." A little wink followed.

She wrapped me in a warm hug, and I fought the temptation to respond with, "You have no idea what I went through today before getting here!" Instead, I just said, "Yep, I made it. Ready to shop?"

"More than ready. Mama's teaching a ladies' Bible study tonight, so I've invited someone very special to help me pick out fabrics." She stepped back and nodded toward the elderly woman to her right. "Gabi and Jordan, let me introduce my aunt, Wilhelmina Lindsey."

"Wilhelmina *Neeley,*" the older woman corrected. "Scarlet seems to have forgotten my married name."

Scarlet's face turned crimson. "It's just going to take me awhile to get used to the idea, Auntie." She giggled then glanced my way. "My aunt just got married a few weeks ago. Surprised us all."

"Wait . . . Neeley?" I tried to make sense of this. "Are you related to Bella?"

"In a roundabout way," Wilhelmina answered with a smile. "I'm married to her husband's uncle Donny. We live in Splendora."

"But your name was Lindsey before?" These words came from Jordan, who seemed more than a little interested. "You were—or are— Wilhelmina Lindsey, owner of Crème de la Crème bakery in Houston?"

"The one and only." Her eyes sparkled. "You've heard of it?"

"Heard of it?" His eyes took on a dreamy expression. "It's the best bakery in the state. Maybe the whole country. I've covered a lot of bakeries for the magazine, but none like yours. Best chocolate scones I've ever tasted. Oh, and those thick macadamia nut cookie bars? Man."

Scarlet cleared her throat, and I jabbed Jordan with my elbow. He turned to Scarlet. "I mean, I hear your place is great too."

"Thanks." Scarlet sighed. "But you were right the first time. Auntie's place in Houston really is famous, and she really is the best baker in the state."

"Speaking of great bakers, we did a piece on your new chef a couple of weeks back," Jordan said as he turned back to face Wilhelmina. "He's settling in really well, from what I could see."

"Kenny?" Scarlet asked.

"Yes, that's right." Jordan nodded. "Kenny. Great guy."

I bit my lip, knowing that Scarlet and Kenny had once dated. Time to change the subject. "I guess we'd better get busy," I said as I took a couple of steps toward a bolt of beautiful white satin. "The store closes at eight, and we've got a lot to look at." I took Scarlet by the arm. "Let's start with the satins and then move to the silks, okay?"

Jordan and Wilhelmina tagged along behind us, completely wrapped up in their own conversation about the wedding biz. Well, until Scarlet and I settled on a 160-dollar-a-yard bolt of imported silk.

"I love it, Gabi, but it's way more than I can spend." Her nose wrinkled. "You know my budget."

Yes, I knew the amount of the check she'd given me on Sunday. Clearly this fabric would never work. In my dream world, maybe, but not in reality.

Wilhelmina nudged her way between us and ran arthritic fingers over the exquisite fabric. "It's lovely. I did the cake for the governor's daughter's wedding last June. Her gown was in a similar fabric, but I don't believe it was quite as nice as this." After examining it for a moment, Wilhelmina faced me. "This is my niece's big day and I want her to have the dress of her dreams, so we'll take it, no matter the cost."

"Oh, but Aunt Willy!" Scarlet's eyes filled with tears. "I mean, Aunt Wilhelmina. You don't need to do that. Gabi's design is perfect, and I'm sure the dress will turn out great, even if we go with a different fabric."

"But this is the one that makes you smile." Wilhelmina took Scarlet's hand and gave it a squeeze. "And if anyone deserves to be happy, you do." The elderly woman glanced my way. "We'll definitely take it, no arguments. Buy as many yards as you need. I'll cover the cost of the fabric. You can keep the check she's already given you to put toward your labor."

"Wow."

Wilhelmina reached inside her purse and came out with a credit card and then looked me in the eyes. "Besides, my dear, your design alone is worth more than what she's already given you. I must admit, I've never seen anything finer, and I've seen a lot of wedding gowns over the years."

My heart swelled with pride at this proclamation, and I felt a boost of confidence.

"You should see the rest of her designs." Jordan lit into a long "let's compliment Gabi until she's overwhelmed" episode, going on and on about my various sketches. Scarlet joined in, and before long her aunt was off on a tangent, telling me that I needed to open my own shop.

I managed to divert their attention to another department of the store, where we located the perfect Irish lace to complement the silk. After that I pointed out some of my favorite fabrics for the bodice, and Scarlet practically swooned. So did her aunt, who insisted we purchase anything and everything we needed to make this the loveliest dress any bride had ever worn.

After Wilhelmina paid for the materials, we walked out to the parking lot, the skies above us dusky and gray. Had we really been in the store that long?

"I'll be back on the island next Monday night," Wilhelmina said. "Any chance you'll start the gown before then? I'd love to see your progress."

"Progress?" Between now and next Monday night? I'd be lucky to have the pieces cut out by then. After all, I still had to prepare a paper pattern and then sew some sample pieces out of a less expensive cloth to fit to the dress form. Surely she realized all of that.

Or not.

"I'll swing by and check on things," she said. "Now if you all will excuse me, I'm meeting Donny at the Rossis' place for a late dinner."

Dinner! I'd almost forgotten that Jordan and I still hadn't eaten. He'd been so patient with us. Poor guy. He was probably starving.

We said our goodbyes and Scarlet headed to her car. Jordan offered to carry the bag of fabrics to the car for me. He opened my door and asked what I'd like for dinner. I'd just opened my mouth to respond when Scarlet came sprinting across the parking lot.

"Hey, Gabi, I keep forgetting to tell you something." She paused to catch her breath. "We've got some special guests coming to sing at our church next Sunday. I thought you might like to come and hear them. Maybe bring your mom and your grandmother too."

I had a hard time picturing Mimi Carmen in a Protestant church but didn't say so. "Special guests?"

"Yeah. It's a trio of ladies from Splendora. Friends of Bella's, actually. I really think you'll like them. They're very . . ." The warmth of her smile echoed in her voice. "Very special. And lots of fun."

"Wait. What are their names?" Jordan asked.

"They call themselves the Splendora Sisters, but they're not really sisters. They're just three ladies who travel around and sing together. They're great, though."

"The Splendora Sisters? I know them!" Jordan laughed and looked my way. "I covered a wedding they did a few months back. Forties swing music, stuff like that. They've got quite a following. Didn't know they did gospel music, though."

"Oh yes." Scarlet nodded. "That's their thing, really. I mean, they do weddings too, and all sorts of older music mainly, but you should hear their hymns. The harmonies are amazing."

"Sounds great." He looked at me again. "You should go, Gabi."

"You too, Jordan." Scarlet gave him a pleading look. "It'll be a lot of fun. The whole Rossi family is coming—Bella, D.J., the kids, the grandparents, the aunts, the uncles, the cousins . . ." She laughed. "Our little church will be bursting at the seams. I can't wait to see what happens when all of the Methodists, Pentecostals, Catholics, and Baptists merge."

"Now that I would pay money to see." Jordan leaned against the car and grinned.

"Thankfully you won't have to. There's no cost."

"I'd like to come," I said after thinking about it. "And I'll ask Mama and Mimi Carmen. Maybe they'll join me." Surely Mama would, anyway, based on our last conversation about church-related things.

"Hope so." She turned back toward her car. "I'm sure we'll talk before then, but either way, I'll see you there." She sprinted across the parking lot, then turned back once more. I watched as her gaze traveled from Jordan to me, then back again. "Great to see you again, Jordan," she hollered out. "At least today no one ended up covered in chocolate."

"True." Jordan laughed.

She gave us a wave and got into her car.

"It's getting late." Jordan pulled out his phone to look at the time. "We should find someplace close for dinner."

"Oh, I know. There's a place called Dixie's not far from here. It's really casual."

"I've been there lots of times. It's one of my favorites."

Before long we were seated at a small table in the quaint diner, nibbling on club sandwiches and some of the best French fries I'd had in ages.

Jordan seemed to know just how to draw the conversation out of me. I found myself bubbling over at what had just happened at the fabric store.

"I'm so excited for Scarlet. Thanks to her aunt, she's going to get her dream wedding. Or at least her dream gown. Not every girl gets that." For whatever reason, a cloud fell over me as I said those last few words.

"Dream wedding." Jordan gave me an inquisitive look. "If you could have your dream wedding, what would it be like?"

He had to go there. I pondered his question for a moment. Sadness enveloped me right away as the truth hit. I would never have my dream wedding, because there would never be a father to walk me down the aisle. There wouldn't be money for imported silk and designer lace.

Creases formed between Jordan's brows as he looked my way. "I'm sorry. Did I upset you with that question?"

"No. Every girl dreams about her wedding, especially a girl like me in the wedding biz."

"So . . ."

"With my dad out of the picture, it's just . . . complicated."

"I'm so sorry, Gabi."

He was. I could tell from the compassion in his eyes.

With a wave of my hand I dismissed his concerns. "I'll be fine. I'm sure lots of brides go through this."

"I feel sure you'll have the perfect wedding," he said. "Want to know how I know that?"

"How?"

"Because you'll be the center of attention. All eyes will be on you." He reached across the table to take my hand. "And trust me when I say that none of the guests will notice anyone else in the place."

Somehow his words reignited the joy I'd felt moments earlier. In fact, I couldn't help grinning as we finished the meal. Afterward we lingered over cups of coffee, talking about everything imaginable—our childhoods, days at the beach, sports . . . everything.

The waitress finally cleared her throat enough times that we got her meaning. She needed us to move on because her shift was coming to an end. Jordan paid the tab and opened the door for me to step outside.

As we walked toward the car, he reached for my hand. I laced my fingers through his, noticing how comfortable it felt. We took our time, walking under a starlit sky. The moon hung like a golden orb, casting its rays on us. The whole thing felt . . . magical, like something from a movie.

When we reached the car, Jordan paused. He slipped his arm around my waist and pulled me close. I felt my heart begin to race as he fingered a loose tendril of my hair. His fingertip lingered on my cheek, sending tingles down my spine. My eyes fluttered closed, and I knew—just as I'd known the Irish lace would be perfect with the imported silk—that Fred was asking Ginger to dance.

As Jordan's lips met mine, my heart responded with a resounding *yes*.

# 15

## Cheek to Cheek

Don't needle the seamstress.
AUTHOR UNKNOWN

The next few days I bounced back and forth between my work at the shop and my design for Scarlet's gown. I managed to cut out the paper pattern for her dress and was happy with it. Soon—when things slowed down—I would work up the courage to cut into those expensive fabrics.

I fended several calls from Nicolette that week but knew she deserved an answer. Soon. Still, I couldn't commit to make her dress just yet, could I? Not without time to think it through.

As I slaved away in my workroom late Friday afternoon, my thoughts shifted to Nicolette. I couldn't help but think about the design she'd selected and how perfect it would look on her. I could still see the look of joy on her face as she'd shared all of the reasons why she loved the gown in the first place.

I loved that she loved my design. Was that wrong? Under these circumstances, maybe. She was, after all, my boss's client. Or had been, anyway. To steal her away would be . . . unethical.

198

Right? Then again, didn't the bride always get what she wanted, not what others wanted for her?

"Gabriella?"

"Hmm?" I turned to face Demetri, who glared at me from the open doorway. "I'm sorry. What, Demetri?"

"I've been calling your name several times over. Vhat are you doing in here?"

I pointed at the dress I'd been hemming and pulled another straight pin from the pincushion on my wrist. "Hemming this bridesmaid dress. Isn't that what I'm supposed to be doing?"

"Yes, but you didn't answer zee question. I asked you to help Kitty at zee front desk for a few minutes vhile Lydia and Corinne assist me vith something."

"Oh, sorry." I scrambled to my feet and brushed the loose threads off my slacks. "I guess my mind was on other things. I didn't hear you."

His eyes took on a beady look, and I began to sweat under their glare. "Your mind has been on other things a lot lately. Zis vorries me."

"Nothing to worry about." I pulled my arm back, and the pincushion caught on the edge of the hem, nearly pulling Ginger down on top of me. Demetri caught her as she plummeted and set her upright again. In that moment, I had a weird flashback to an earlier mental image—one where Demetri waltzed me across the dance floor, stomping on my toes all the way.

He gestured for me to walk to the front of the store, but I could read the concern in his eyes as I passed by him. Not that I blamed him for being concerned. Lately I couldn't seem to keep my focus. How could I, with so much work left to do on Scarlet's gown? I'd given her a design she loved, sure, but implementing it was another thing altogether.

All of this wee-hours-of-the-night stuff seemed to be zapping my daytime creativity. Something had to give. I couldn't burn the candle at both ends much longer.

And this whole fiasco with Nicolette? I needed to make a decision . . . and quickly.

By the time the weekend arrived I could avoid Nicolette no longer. I called on Saturday evening to let her know that I would speak to Demetri about the possibilities of implementing the design she had suggested, and she seemed relieved to hear it. When—and how—I would talk to him, I couldn't be positive, but surely I could move forward with Nicolette's gown without too much angst from him.

Late Saturday night I told Mama and Mimi Carmen about the concert at Scarlet's church. I somehow managed to talk them into going to church with me by explaining that the Rossi family would be there. Mimi couldn't resist the idea of meeting Rosa in person.

The following morning we all made the drive to church in my car, which still gave me fits all the way. About halfway there I passed a police officer coming the other way.

*Please don't let him notice my missing side mirror!*

He didn't. The patrol car rolled right on by, and I breathed a sigh of relief.

As my car sputtered into the parking lot, I caught a glimpse of the older man who'd offered to help me the last time. The fellow headed my way, but I could tell from the slow-moving gait that he struggled with the same arthritis Mimi battled daily.

I could read the concern etched in his brow as I got out of the car. "I hope you don't think I'm just a nosy old man, but when are you going to let me take a look at this car for you?" His gaze traveled from the car to my grandmother, who struggled to get out of the passenger seat. He rushed to her side. "Here you are, lovely lady." He extended his hand and introduced himself as Daniel.

"Thank you." She took his hand, and they worked together to pull her to a standing position. Daniel then offered my grandmother the crook of his arm, and she slipped hers through it as she gazed into his eyes.

Now, I'd heard of love at first sight all of my life. Many of my brides talked about it, and I'd seen my fair share of over-the-top romance movies. But I'd never witnessed it. The sparks that flew between my grandmother and this total stranger looked like something from a Disney movie. Complete with a soundtrack.

The soundtrack turned out to be the Splendora Sisters warming up inside the church. Apparently someone had the sound turned up a bit too loud.

"I'm Daniel Real," the man said, his hold on Mimi's arm still firm.

"Carmen . . ." Her eyelashes fluttered, and she seemed to lose her ability to speak.

"Delgado." Mama spoke up from behind us. "Carmen Delgado."

"Yes, Carmen Delgado." Mimi giggled. "That's me."

Daniel led the way to the entrance of the church, and we were—as I'd predicted—greeted to death. Before long we were inside the church, where the Splendora Sisters had stopped their rehearsal and were visiting with Scarlet at the front of the sanctuary. We found seats about halfway back—quite a challenge, with the crowd and all. Daniel released his hold on my grandmother's arm and made his way to the front of the room to greet the pastor.

Mama entered our pew first, and I followed her. This left Mimi Carmen closest to the center aisle. No doubt she wanted to be able to make a clean getaway once the drums started. A minute or so later, Scarlet scurried our way, followed by the trio of women from Splendora.

When they reached our pew, they stopped. "Gabi, let me introduce you." Scarlet practically beamed as she listed their names: "Sister Twila, Sister Jolene, and Sister Bonnie Sue."

The trio of larger-than-life women greeted us with friendly waves and lots of chatter about how much they loved Mimi's colorful fan—the one with the picture of the Virgin Mary on it. We all nodded politely and tried to make conversation. Well, Mama and I tried. Mimi just stared at the buxom trio and fanned herself.

Scarlet had referred to these ladies as sisters —they were even billed as such on the marquee out front—but she had already informed me they weren't related. I might've guessed this from their appearances. Except for their size, they did not resemble one another. And the "sisters" part *definitely* didn't mean these gals hailed from a convent. Judging from the sparkly blouses and high heels, anyway. And Sister Jolene's overly teased hairdo, which put me in mind of a sixties movie I'd once seen on television.

The one who had been introduced as Twila leaned forward and gave me an inquisitive look. "My word, you're one of the prettiest girls I've ever seen. You should be in pictures."

"What?"

"Oh yes!" Bonnie Sue added, lowering her

bifocals to give me a closer look. "You look like the movie star type—those beautiful white teeth. Perfect lips . . ." She narrowed her gaze. "Those are your lips, aren't they, honey? I mean, you didn't . . ."

To my left, Mimi Carmen let out a little giggle.

"No, I-I didn't have any work done." Were they kidding me?

"Well, some women I've met have paid thousands to have beautiful lips like that," Bonnie Sue said. "So one can never be too sure these days."

"Botox is very popular," Jolene added.

"They don't use Botox, Jolene," Bonnie Sue responded. "It's collagen."

"Whatever." Jolene rolled her eyes and took to fanning herself. "That hair of yours is divine. Come over here and let me get a closer look."

Though it felt awkward, I rose and took a couple of steps toward her. "W-what about it?" I managed.

"Gorgeous! Just the right length, to your shoulders. Frames your face." She seemed mesmerized by it and reached out to fuss with it. "And that luscious black color just shimmers! How do you get it to glisten like that?"

I'd just started to tell her the brand of my conditioner when Twila interrupted. "I know! She uses Mane and Tail."

"Mane and Tail?"

"Well, sure, honey. It puts the giddyup and go in your hair—and your step!" Twila laughed and then reached to stroke my hair.

Did they really think I used horse products in my hair, or was this some kind of joke?

"And I know why you've got flawless skin too," Jolene said, reaching to touch my face. "You must use our top-secret recipe."

"No, actually, I use—"

"Olive oil and sugar." Jolene nodded. "Works like a charm for me too. See?" She took my hand to stroke her cheek with my fingers. I had to admit, it did feel soft. Then again, she was pretty wrinkly, so age might have had something to do with the softness.

"There aren't enough beauty products in the world to give me that lovely color of skin, though. Such a beautiful golden glow, like you were born with the perfect tan." Bonnie Sue gave a little pout. "Me? I'm whiter than a scoop of vanilla ice cream."

Strangely, this led to a conversation about Blue Bell, their favorite brand of ice cream, which led to one of the ladies—Twila, maybe?—talking about calories. From there they went off on a tangent about a fitness program they'd recently tried and some dieting supplements that had sent one of them to the emergency room.

I did my best to chime in, but really, what could I say? Besides, I couldn't stop thinking about their flattering comments. Beautiful, shiny hair? Gorgeous skin? White teeth? Luscious lips? Botox? Collagen? Really?

Thank goodness Scarlet took control of the conversation once again, redirecting the ladies toward Mama. The minute they found out that my mother worked as a travel agent, the conversation became fully animated. From there the chatter turned to cruises. And Europe. I noticed the sad look on Mama's face as she offered to plan an upcoming trip for them. I saw through the forced smile to the sadness underneath that said, "When? When will it be my turn? When can I go on an adventure like that?"

Then the topic shifted to the food they'd eaten on their last cruise. Mimi Carmen got involved in the chatter at this point, talking about her enchiladas and tamales. That was pretty much all she wrote. From that moment forth, my grand-mother was their best friend. On and on they went, raving about their favorite meals.

I listened in, pleased to see everyone settling in so well. Maybe this wouldn't be so rough after all.

Scarlet gestured to the group of ladies and smiled as if to say, "Aren't they getting along nicely?" I nodded. It felt good to see Mama and Mimi Carmen among people again. Both had become such homebodies.

"Do you mind if I join you ladies?"

I glanced to the center aisle to see Daniel standing there, a sheepish look on his face.

Mimi Carmen nudged me to make room. Her brusque "Scoot over, Gabriella," left little doubt in my mind where she stood on the matter. She clearly did not mind if he joined us. Welcomed it, in fact.

"I'm sorry to inconvenience you lovely ladies," he said as he pressed into the tiny spot next to Mimi. I started to scoot over a bit more to offer them more room, but Mimi squeezed my thigh with her hand to stop me.

*Ouch!*

Daniel now sat shoulder to shoulder with my grandmother, who giggled as she said, "Oh, no inconvenience at all." She waved her fan in front of her now pink cheeks.

"It's so crowded in here today," Daniel said, as much to Mama and me as to Mimi. "I usually sit in the second pew closest to the center aisle so that I can perform my duties as an usher, but someone's got my seat."

"What? Protestants have assigned seating?" Mimi mumbled something about how the Catholics would never allow that, and Daniel laughed.

The Splendora trio looked on, all grins, as this exchange took place.

Twila waved a hand toward Daniel and Mimi. "Well, I daresay you two look as cozy as two bugs in a rug."

Daniel turned all shades of red at this proclamation. Likely in an attempt to stop Twila in her tracks, he leaned forward and gave me a little wave, then said, "My offer still stands."

"He made you some sort of offer?" Mimi leaned over and whispered the words in my ear, then put her hand to her mouth. I'd just started to explain when I was interrupted.

"Do you have room for one more?" Jordan's voice sounded from the outer aisle.

I glanced at him and felt my cheeks warm as I remembered the kiss we had shared just a few nights prior. Mama, clearly in matchmaker mode, quickly scooted over and insisted that Jordan sit between us. It would be tight, what with Mimi Carmen and Daniel taking up a large portion of the pew on the other side of me, but we made it work. I couldn't help but notice that Mama looked a little out of sorts. I didn't really blame her, being surrounded by couples and all.

Not that Mimi and Daniel were a couple, but Twila was right. They certainly looked cozy together all of a sudden. I watched as my grandmother leaned across him to finish her conversation with the trio. Between the four ladies and Daniel, the conversation really took off.

From up front the band started playing the opening song, and the worship leader asked us to stand. The trio of Splendora ladies scurried up to the front pew, where they joined Scarlet's father and mother. With great flourish and fan-fare.

Mimi's eyes narrowed as she watched the band in action, her gaze now firmly locked on the bass player. "What is this, a rock and roll show?" she asked, then stuck her fingers in her ears. "I thought this was supposed to be a church."

"It *is* a church, Mimi," I said. "Trust me. Just give it a chance."

"Doesn't sound like any church I ever went to. For that matter, it doesn't look like one either. Where's the holy water? Where are the kneeling benches?"

"It's different, I'll admit, but that doesn't make it wrong," I said. I rather liked it, in fact.

Minutes later, after a couple of worship songs and announcements, the trio was introduced. So was their piano player, who turned out to be Bella's mother-in-law, Earline Neeley. Go figure. The woman—who wore a BIKERS FOR JESUS vest—played the piano with reckless abandon. Some folks were just born with special abilities, and Mrs. Neeley was one of them. Leaning forward, eyes closed, she forced the music through her fingertips. And with such speed!

"That woman has the spirit of the late, great Jerry Lee Lewis all over her," Mimi Carmen called out above the music.

This was followed by, "May he rest in peace," which my grandmother and Daniel spoke in unison. They stared at one another as if mesmerized by their timing.

The ladies sang their hearts out. Around us, a handful of folks put their hands up in the air in worship. Mimi Carmen looked a bit startled at this outward display of adoration for the Almighty, but she didn't say anything. Scarlet's father looked a wee bit nervous too. He probably wasn't used to all of the arm waving and such, but I had a feeling it would grow on him. It was certainly growing on me.

To my right, Jordan looked perfectly comfortable. Figured. Maybe he could make some sense of the Jerry Lee Lewis line for me later on. For now, he seemed content.

Sister Jolene introduced the next song—some number about God being our father. Jordan reached to take my hand.

From the pulpit, Jolene waved a finger at the audience. Looked like she was pointing it straight at me as she delivered her next line. "You can trust him, you know. He's your Daddy God."

Daddy God? A cold chill hit me as she spoke those words, and I found myself conflicted. Her impassioned speech might be just the ticket for some in attendance, but it slapped me upside the head, and not in a good way.

I shifted my position in the pew once again, my backside now uncomfortable. Was it getting hot in here? The overwhelming desire to jump and run hit me.

"Even if your earthly daddy wasn't a prince of a guy, you can still trust the ultimate Father." Jolene paused to dab her eyes. "You are his child."

Everyone else in our pew looked perfectly comfortable. Well, maybe not Mama. She gave me a little peek out of the corner of her eye as Jolene got to the part about earthly fathers. Thank goodness the music began at this point, and before I knew it the harmonies were ringing out again.

As the ladies sang a song about their Daddy God, I felt a lump well up in my throat. And when Scarlet's father followed this up with a sermon titled "God, Our Father," I couldn't seem to stop the trickle of tears that made their way down my cheeks. Did he have to go there?

Mama fished around in her purse and came out with a tissue, which she handed me. Jordan gave my hand a little squeeze. His presence brought comfort and somehow kept me from fleeing.

I'd never been so happy in all of my life for a service to come to an end. Not that I'd been to a lot of services, of course, but this one really took the cake.

Speaking of cake, the pastor invited everyone to the tiny fellowship hall for some of Scarlet's baked goods, and most everyone in attendance took him up on that offer, judging from the crowd in the foyer. I fought my way through the throng of people, Mama and Jordan at my side.

"Well, that was certainly not what I expected," Mimi Carmen said as she and Daniel followed on my heels.

"Me either," Mama called out above the crowd. "But I liked it. A lot. Especially those singers. They were really good."

We converged in the little fellowship hall and nibbled on sweets with the other guests, all of them talking over one another. I glanced around the room, now understanding why Scarlet had chosen to have her reception at Club Wed. While lovely and quaint, this room could never house two-hundred-plus guests. No way. Not with a dance floor, anyway.

Scarlet's mother approached and engaged my mom in a conversation, and before long they were as thick as thieves. Off in the distance Bella's family—probably twenty or more of them in total—visited with the Splendora Sisters, all laughter and smiles. Sister Twila held Bella's little girl, Rosa-Earline, who giggled with glee. I wanted that same sort of happy feeling to engulf me, but I couldn't get past what Jolene had said during the service.

I looked on as Bella's dad swept his grand-daughter into his arms and gave her a kiss on the forehead. My attention then shifted to D.J., who lifted Tres to his shoulders so that he could better see everyone in the crowd. All of this I watched in complete silence, my heart twisting inside me.

Jordan stood at my side, our fingers tightly laced. He appeared to be enjoying himself, if one could gauge from the expression on his face.

"They're fun to watch, aren't they."

His statement wasn't really a question—more rhetorical than anything—so I didn't dignify it with an answer. How could I, with the lump in my throat?

"Lots of great families here today," he added, then waved at Bella's uncle Laz and aunt Rosa.

"With great fathers." I sighed. "All of them."

"Sure looks like it."

"Whatever."

My one-word response apparently raised his antennae. Jordan gave me a pensive look and then led me out of the room to the church's foyer.

"You okay?" He brushed a loose hair off my face.

I shook my head and stared at the ground, unable to communicate what was going on in my heart.

"I'd love to see the Lord tear down some of those walls you've built up." He leaned close and whispered the next words. "You know, there really are a few good guys out there, Gabi. We're not all bad."

"I never said you were all bad."

"No. You didn't have to." He gestured to Daniel,

who entered the foyer with Mimi Carmen's arm linked in his. "But see what I mean? Daniel is a good man. He's helping your grandmother. And Scarlet's dad is a good man. There are still a few of us around." He shrugged.

My heart quickened as I realized I'd hurt his feelings. "I know you're right. I've lumped all men into the same bag because of my dad. And Demetri."

"You've just had a couple of lousy examples of manhood." Jordan slipped his arm around my waist and lowered his voice. "But most of us— well, those of us who have trusted in Christ—want to be great dads. I can't wait."

He'd lost me at the "trusted in Christ" line. Trusted him in a generic sense? I couldn't be sure. Seemed like he meant something more. I'd just opened my mouth to ask him about it when Bella entered the foyer with her daughter in her arms.

"We're all headed to my parents' place for lunch. Want to join us?"

"I'm not sure. I think Mimi Carmen made enchiladas."

This got an interested look from Jordan.

"She can bring them with her." Bella shifted the toddler to her other arm. "Most everyone shows up with a dish, so she'll fit right in."

"I-I'm invited?" My grandmother appeared beside me with Daniel at her side.

"Yes. You all are." Bella nodded at Daniel as well. "The more the merrier."

"I guess we could stop off at the house and pick up the enchiladas," Mama said, standing next to me.

"Please do." Bella beamed at this news. "Rosa will love that. She adores Mexican food."

Mimi flinched, and I could read the fear in her eyes. She turned my way, her words racing. "I can't let Rosa eat my food. No way."

"Of course you can!" Bella responded. "It will make her day."

"But she's a real cook," Mimi continued. "I'm just . . ."

"Your enchiladas are the best thing I ever ate." These words came from Jordan, who slipped his arm over my grandmother's shoulder. "I hope you made plenty, because I don't know if I'll touch another thing with your enchiladas there."

Mimi perked right up at this proclamation. She grinned, and Daniel joined in the conversation. "It's been years since I had homemade enchiladas," he said. "Don't get a lot of homemade anything these days. Not since my wife passed."

"May she rest in peace," Mimi and Daniel said in unison. Daniel's eyes grew moist.

"Well, you'll get nothing but homemade food if you come to the Rossis' place," Bella said. "So I hope you'll join us."

"I'd like that," Daniel said as his gaze shifted to my grandmother. "I'd like that very much."

As we walked to the car, I thought back on Jordan's words: "There really are a few good guys out there, Gabi. We're not all bad."

No, they weren't all bad. But maybe that was the part that bothered me most. With all of the good ones out there, how—and why—did I manage to get stuck with two of the worst? Demetri Markowitz *and* a deadbeat dad? C'mon. If God was really such a great Father, why couldn't he have given me a better example than those two?

Forcing those questions aside, I made up my mind to somehow get through the rest of the day.

# 16

## Night and Day

I have learned to go through life not into
it. It's like a boat. You mustn't let the water
in or you're sunk.

GINGER ROGERS

As we prepared to leave the church, Mimi Carmen
offered to ride with Daniel to give him directions
to the Rossi home. Like she'd ever been to the
Rossi home before. Seriously?

Daniel didn't seem to mind one little bit, if one
could judge from the look on his face. The two of
them headed off to his car, all flirtatious smiles.

Jordan asked me to ride with him, but I couldn't
very well leave Mama alone, so I told him we
could meet there. He didn't seem to mind.

Mama and I stopped off at the house to pick
up the enchiladas, then made the drive to the
Rossis'. I did my best to regroup and put the
sermon behind me. No point in dragging my
mother down just because I happened to be overwhelmed. Still, she seemed to pick up on my
silence.

"You okay over there?" she asked as I fidgeted
with the volume on the radio.

"Hmm? Oh, yeah." I released a slow breath and hoped she would let it go.

"Kind of a hard morning?" she asked.

I shrugged. Thank goodness she didn't have time to say much more, because I turned the car onto Broadway and we arrived at our destination just a minute later. I'd been to Club Wed many times, but never inside the Rossi home next door. The old Victorian was nearly as lovely as the wedding facility, with its oversized veranda and manicured lawn. To think Bella had grown up here. Lucky girl.

With a great dad, no less.

Sister Jolene's words hit me again like a cruel slap across the face, but I pushed them away.

*God. Father. Good.* Really?

I reached for the pan of enchiladas and carried them to the front steps, where Bella's aunt Rosa snatched them from my hand. "These look amazing!"

Mimi Carmen, who stood on the veranda next to Daniel, offered to give Rosa the recipe, and seconds later the women disappeared into the house.

Mama and I walked up the steps to the veranda, where Bella and D.J. greeted us, along with approximately a hundred of their closest relatives, many under the age of ten. Okay, maybe not a hundred, but close. Wow. Was every Sunday dinner like this? If so, where did they seat everyone? At the wedding facility next door?

Mama seemed mesmerized with the beautiful house. As we stepped into the foyer, she gasped and then raved over the intricately carved woodwork. Bella's mother offered to show her around the home, and she disappeared seconds later, completely swept away by her surroundings.

With everyone talking, I barely made out Jordan's voice. When he tapped me on the shoulder, I jumped.

"Whoa. Didn't mean to scare you there." The warmth of his smile echoed in his voice.

My heart rate skipped to double time. "I'm okay." Gesturing to the house, I did my best to calm down. "Isn't this amazing?"

"Yes. I've always loved these old Victorians. Plan to live in one myself one day."

"You do?"

"Yep. I've had my eye on a place about a half mile from here. It's just gone into foreclosure. If the price is right, I might just make an offer."

"Wow." This definitely made an impression. "I'd love to see it someday."

"I hope you will." He leaned over and gave me a little kiss on the cheek. "I definitely hope you will. Maybe you can even help me decorate. I hear you're great with fabrics and such. Maybe I'll hire you to make the curtains." A playful smile followed his words.

"Will there be mice involved?" I asked. "Because I could really use the help."

That got a laugh out of him.

We found ourselves caught up in conversation with several of Bella's siblings moments later. Jordan and Armando really hit it off, and I enjoyed my conversation with D.J.'s brother Bubba and his wife Jenna. Well, for a moment, anyway. Turned out Bubba had to tend to something on the grill. But Jenna stayed around and I discovered she was just my kind of girl.

I enjoyed her company so much that I ended up seated next to her at lunch. And as for how all of the people found a seat at this soiree, I observed the family setting up tables all the way out the dining room and down the foyer. They put the older kids at a bit of a distance, but the little ones, like Bella's daughter, Rosa-Earline, stayed nearby. I'd never seen so many high chairs and booster seats. The family must own stock in a baby supply store.

I'd also never seen so much food. Wow. An eclectic mix greeted me: grilled chicken and brisket from Bubba, and lasagna, fettuccini, and Caesar salad from Rosa, along with the most beautiful garlic twists I'd ever seen. Three kinds of pizza from Uncle Laz, and Mimi's enchiladas. Oh, and a gorgeous Italian cream cake from Scarlet, who rushed in the door seconds after we sat down.

Mimi Carmen and Daniel both looked like they'd died and gone to heaven. After Bella's father blessed the food, the feasting began. The clinking of silverware, coupled with the chatter and the oohing and aahing over the food, took precedence. I couldn't help but hone in on Jordan's social skills. He managed to make easy conversation with all of the guys, especially D.J. and Armando, while still including me.

Rosa took a big helping of Mimi's enchiladas, and a blissful look came over her. "Carmen, these are the best enchiladas I've ever eaten in my life. One of these days you have to come over and show me your secret."

"Thank you, I would love that." My grand-mother's cheeks flushed pink. "It means a lot, coming from a food expert like you."

"Food expert, my eye. Just because I have a television show doesn't mean I'm an expert. I just love to cook for the family."

"Ooo, me too. It brings me such joy." Mimi Carmen slipped into Spanish, and before long the women were fully engaged in a lively conversation—in Spanish, Italian, and English. Fascinating. They seemed to make sense of it all. By the time they finished, Rosa had invited my grandmother to appear on her show in an upcoming episode.

"I-I don't know if I could." Mimi Carmen's eyes flooded. "I'm not exactly . . ." She pointed at her round midsection. "Television material."

"And I am?" Rosa laughed as she gestured to her ample physique and graying hair. "That's what makes it so perfect. We're two real women, women who love to feed our families. And we care more about good quality homemade food, so . . . so there." She slipped an arm around Mimi Carmen's shoulders. "Besides, the important thing here isn't how we look, it's how we bless others with our cooking."

"She's definitely a blessing. That's for sure." These words came from Jordan, who swallowed another bite of the enchiladas and added, "Mmm."

"I say you go for it, Mimi Carmen." I gave her an encouraging smile. "Maybe you'll become a big TV star too."

"*Big* being the key word." She giggled and patted her belly. "Well, maybe I will. Let me think about it, okay?"

Rosa waved her hand and filled her fork with more enchiladas. "Don't think too long. Laz and I need to incorporate more guests. Ever since his heart attack . . ." She paused and her eyes filled with tears. "Anyway, we're slowing down, and that's a good thing."

At this point the Splendora trio began to share about their upcoming gigs, and the conversation shifted. I watched as Jolene carried on about an offer they'd had to travel to Italy, and once again

I saw sadness in my mother's eyes as she offered to arrange the trip.

Bella shifted my attention to a quiet woman across the table. "Gabi, did you meet my sister-in-law Marcella? She runs Patti-Lou's Petals."

"Oh, wow. I had no idea." With a nod of my head I acknowledged her. "We've ordered from you several times. My boss loves to send his brides flowers."

"Your boss has more than one bride?" Marcella gave me a curious look until Bella explained who my boss happened to be. Then her eyes widened. "Ah. Demetri Markowitz. A name I know well."

She hesitated at this point and I laughed. "It's okay. I can only imagine your impression of him. Probably similar to my own."

"Well, let's just say he's very picky." She rolled her eyes.

"Tell me about it."

Marcella shared a detailed story of Demetri's last visit to her shop, and I groaned. Apparently my boss had quite the reputation, and not just among brides and alterations specialists.

"I know his type," Marcella said. "But that's okay. I won't have to deal with it much longer. I hope to be selling the shop soon."

"Really?" This got a shocked look from Bella's parents, who ceased their conversation at the opposite end of the table to hear her explanation.

"Yeah. The boys are growing up and they need

us now. And you know how busy little Anna keeps me. She's a handful." She directed the next part to me. "Our oldest is in sports and our second son is active in theater—at the Grand Opera Society, in fact. He's got quite a gift."

I couldn't imagine a young boy having the courage to stand on the stage and sing, but apparently courage ran deep in this family. So did talent.

"I feel like I'm missing out on everything," Marcella added.

"So what will happen to the florist shop?" Bella asked.

"I'm hoping someone will make me an offer on it." She shrugged. "I've been thinking of asking Alex Rigas if he knows someone."

"Alex Rigas?" Bella looked surprised. "The guy whose family owns the nursery in Splendora?"

"Yes." Marcella nodded. "They've been in the business for years and have the best flowers in the state. He's bound to know someone who might be interested."

"Well, yes, but someone outside of the family?" Bella's mother looked astonished by this news. So did her father, in fact.

"Sure, why not? Getting someone new on board will give the place a fresh face. It really needs that."

"I hardly know what to think." Bella's father still looked shocked by this news.

"You've done such a great job with the flowers, but I completely understand." Bella looked my way and sighed. "It's always such a dilemma when you have children."

"I stayed home with my babies, and they all turned out well." Bella's mother looked at Armando, who was seated to her right, and then slapped him on the back of the head. "Well, most of them."

This got a laugh out of most in attendance.

When the meal ended, most of the kids headed outside to play. All but the little ones, who went upstairs to nap. The older folks—including Rosa, Laz, Mimi, and Daniel—retired to the living room. My mother offered to help Bella's mother in the kitchen. The menfolk, as Bella's father called them, headed out to look at the vegetable garden in the backyard.

I found myself alone at the table with Bella, Scarlet, and the Splendora Sisters. Bella decided this would be a good time to sing my praises to the ladies, who seemed intrigued with my life as an alterations specialist. With a wave of my hand I dismissed the idea that I led a glamorous life.

"It's anything but," I said, laughing. "Trust me."

"I still think she should do her own dress designs," Scarlet said. "That's her real gift."

I tried to shush her, but she would not be shushed.

"Well, why don't you do that full-time, honey?" Twila asked.

Great.

I shrugged and chose my words with care. "I've joked a lot about coming out of the closet."

Jolene's right eyebrow elevated slightly. "Beg your pardon?"

Bella laughed so hard that she made a funny snorting sound. Before long Scarlet joined her. The trio of ladies still looked perplexed.

"I mean, I feel like I've been hiding this big secret, afraid people would find out what I'm up to after the rest of the world goes to bed at night."

Ack! That certainly didn't come out right.

"Sounds like we need to pray for you, honey. God can deliver you from that life if you want him to." Twila's smile radiated both playfulness and a hint of concern.

Bella got control of herself. "Ladies, it's not what you're thinking. Gabi here is afraid to let her boss find out that she secretly designs wedding dresses. At night. When everyone else is sleeping."

"Afraid?" Bonnie Sue looked astonished at this news. "Why afraid?"

"Are you a beginner?" Twila asked. "Is that it? You're not sure of yourself?"

"I'm sure you'll get better with time," Jolene said. "That's always how it is. Practice makes perfect. Take our singing, for instance."

She went into a lengthy story about how their little—er, big—singing trio started out as novices but developed over time. She lost me when she got to the story about one of the ladies falling in love with a cruise director on a ship. What that had to do with singing, I couldn't say. And what it had to do with my dress designs was a bigger mystery still.

"Oh, it's not that, Jolene," Bella said when the story drew to a close. "Gabi here is a brilliant dress designer."

"The best," Scarlet added. "Light-years better than that guy she works for."

"Well, what's your holdup then?" Twila gave me a pensive look.

Before I could respond, Bonnie Sue chimed in. "Ooo, I'd love to see your designs. When can we do that?"

I knew my sketchpad was in the car but didn't offer up that information. Unfortunately, Scarlet knew me well enough to figure it out. She asked for my keys and returned from my car moments later with my prized possession in hand.

From the moment the women saw my designs, they gushed. And gushed. And gushed some more. Their opinions differed on which one was the best, but they all agreed I had talent. Their kind words really built me up.

I finally took the sketchpad back and thanked them for the high praise.

"Give honor where honor is due," Jolene said. "That's what the Bible says. And you definitely deserve it, girl."

"Yes, you do." Twila wiggled her index finger in my face. "But it's more than praise we need to give you. I'm ready to reach into my pocketbook right now."

"Pocketbook?" This really threw me.

"Yes! You've got to become our personal seamstress. Can you make dresses in plus sizes?"

"Of course," I said. "But what do you need dresses for?"

"Well, for one thing, we're going to be performing at Dickens on the Strand again this year, and we'll need Victorian dresses. Those aren't so far removed from wedding gowns, right?"

"Right." I nodded.

This led to a lengthy discussion about their singing schedule, which somehow led Bella back to the song they'd performed this morning. The one about God being our Father. Great. Just what I needed.

Still, with the confident chatter coming from these ladies and all the praise for my designs, I almost found myself believing I could rise above the pain of the past and start fresh today.

Almost.

# 17
## Second Chorus

The higher up you go, the more mistakes you are allowed. Right at the top, if you make enough of them, it's considered to be your style.

FRED ASTAIRE

We wrapped up our conversation with the Splendora Sisters, and the trio of ladies headed to the living room to join the others.

Bella took me by the arm and led me out to the veranda, away from the crowd. "You're upset about something today."

"I-I am?"

"You are." Her nose wrinkled. "Was it the stuff Jolene was talking about in church? About fathers, I mean?"

I'd never been very good at lying. Why start now?

"I guess. It just stinks not to have a great dad. Doesn't seem fair."

"You're right. It's not fair. You of all people deserved an idyllic childhood. You're the sweetest person I know."

"Then you need to get to know me better. I'm not that sweet."

"Please." She gazed intently into my eyes. "But you know what? I really believe God is going to give you a husband who will be a great dad to your kids. I know it won't exactly make up for what you've missed in your life, but it will be a great way to start a legacy. A godly legacy. And that's worth far more than any other gift you could pass on."

I shrugged, unable to speak over the lump in my throat.

"It's obvious your life hasn't been easy. I know you and your mom and grandma have had a rough time."

I managed a nod and swiped at my misty eyes with the back of my hand. She had to go there, didn't she?

A look of genuine compassion flooded Bella's eyes. "You've worked hard, and God will reward that. The poster in your office says it all, Gabi. The only way to enjoy anything in this life is to earn it first."

"I know, but . . ." My words drifted off. Seemed like I'd worked extra hard. Without a dad to fill in the gap.

"When things are handed to you on a silver platter—when you do nothing to earn them—you don't appreciate them. Sure, some people seem to have all the luck. Things seem to come to them more easily. But just because they appear to have it all doesn't mean they appreciate what they have."

"I guess."

She pointed at the house. "My family came to America from Italy, but I still remember the stories of how hard life was back then. Just getting the food to feed all the kids was difficult. My dad and my uncle worked so hard to build Parma John's and the wedding facility. I've worked hard too, and—"

I never let her finish. "See? That's the difference between us. You had a father, for one thing. And he got the business rolling for you. You're successful, Bella. But it doesn't hurt that you've had the support of your dad and your uncle."

Ugh. Had I really said those words out loud?

I pinched my eyes shut and muttered, "I'm sorry. I shouldn't have said that."

"It's okay. I totally understand. And you're right. I did have a leg up because my parents started the wedding facility then passed it off to me." She paused and her eyes filled with tears. "It's still hard, Gabi. I work a lot of hours and don't get to be with my kids as much as I'd like. That's why I sympathize with Marcella for wanting to sell the flower shop. But I'm not ready to give up my life as a wedding planner either, so I have to find a balance in all of it. God fills in the gap. And as for any success we've had with Club Wed, well, that's the Lord's doing, not mine, trust me."

"You've built something great here, Bella. I . . . I want that. I want to be successful, and I don't want to have to ride on any man's coattails."

"A man like Demetri, you mean?"

"Right."

"Well then, define success. You want what he has? A shop? Lots of money? Material possessions? Or do you really just want to get to do the one thing you love, surrounded by people you love?"

"That's it." The sigh that followed on my end was louder than I'd planned. "I want to do what I love. And having the people I love—my family, you, Scarlet, Hannah—all cheering me on."

"Then ask God for that. But still be prepared to work hard. It doesn't get any easier, no matter how long you're at it. And remember that true success isn't about how much you earn in a year or how many times you get a write-up in *Texas Bride* magazine. It's measured in the heart. In the soul, really."

For a moment, neither of us said a word. We watched as the guys—Jordan, D.J., and the others—played basketball in the driveway nearby. The sound of the children's voices rang out as they played tag in the yard. And I could hear people laughing and talking inside the house. But I could tell, based on the expression on her face, that I'd lost Bella to her thoughts.

"What do you want to leave behind when you're gone, Gabi?" she finally asked. "Besides a lot of beautiful dresses, I mean."

I pushed aside my emotions and managed to squeak out a response. "Never really thought about it."

"I think about it all the time. The wedding facility will stand for years—maybe hundreds of years, if God allows—but it will eventually crumble. And all of the dresses you design will last for years too, but not forever. There's really only one thing that lasts forever, Gabi."

"What do you mean?"

"I mean your relationship with your real Father. It can last forever if you accept his invitation to the ball."

Now she'd lost me entirely. "The ball?"

"Speaking symbolically here." A tiny smile tipped up the edges of Bella's lips. "He's extended a special invitation to you, Gabi, whether you know it or not."

"He has?"

"Yes." She nodded and her eyes pooled. "I'm talking about the very best sort of happily ever after you could ever imagine. But it all hinges on one thing—you have to accept."

"Accept . . . the invitation?"

"Accept the one who offers it." We sat down, and in the gentlest way, she shared a story about a Father who loved so much that he gave his only Son . . . for me.

I'd been stirred to tears many times in my life, but not like I was in that moment. For whatever reason, it all made sense to me now. God the Father. The invitation to dance, not just for now but . . . forever. That silly Cinderella story really *was* a Bible tale. Who knew?

Bella offered to pray with me, and before long I was whispering the sweetest prayer of my life —accepting my own personal engraved invitation to the ball.

Mama joined us on the veranda just as we wrapped up the prayer. "There you are, Gabriella." I could read the concern in her eyes as she watched Bella give me a big hug. "Are you all right?"

"I am." A little sniffle followed.

"You sure?"

"Yes." I smiled and reached to take her hand. "I'll tell you all about it on the way home."

"That's why I came to get you," she said. "Mimi Carmen has fallen asleep on the sofa. It's rather . . . embarrassing."

Bella chuckled. "No doubt Rosa and Laz are asleep as well. If not, they will be soon. That's a Sunday afternoon ritual around here. Most of the family naps."

"Still, I think we'd better get her home," Mama said. "Daniel looks pretty weary, and he still has to drive himself home."

"True."

We walked into the living room, where we found almost every person sleeping—Rosa, Laz,

Mimi, and the three Splendora ladies. Only Daniel remained awake, but he looked pretty groggy.

"That's what love looks like when you get to be their age," Bella said and giggled. "One day that will be D.J. and me."

"Today." D.J.'s voice sounded from the door. "I'm wiped out, Bella. Let's get these kids home so we can take a nap."

"All right, babe." She walked over to him and gave him the sweetest kiss on the cheek, her eyes lit by love. Together they headed off to gather the kids.

Mama tapped Mimi Carmen on the shoulder. She didn't budge, so I called her name. She jerked awake like a jack-in-the-box springing free from its confines, sputtering the whole way.

Until she saw Daniel, who looked on with a smile. Then she slapped herself on the forehead and groaned. "Well, there I go making a goober of myself."

"Not at all." He extended a hand to assist her.

With his help, she made it off the sofa, and we convinced her the time had come to go home. Bella's mother gave us back the enchilada dish, now sparkling clean, and we walked across the grand foyer, out the front door, and onto the veranda, prepared to say our goodbyes.

I hated for this day to end, but I didn't regret a moment of it, not even Jolene's passionate words this morning. They made more sense to me now.

Thinking of them reminded me that I needed to say goodbye to Jordan as well. If I could find him, anyway.

Daniel trudged along behind us to the door, and I could tell he looked exhausted. Scarlet must've picked up on that too. She leaned my way.

"Daniel lives right around the corner from me," she whispered. "So I'll follow him home to make sure he gets there okay." After a moment's pause, she added, "He's an amazing person, Gabi. I've known him for years. He and his wife were my Sunday school teachers during a very vulnerable time in my life. Since she passed away, he's been so . . . lonely. But he's a good man."

As soon as she spoke the words "good man," I expected to flinch. To feel some sort of reaction. Strange. The words didn't hurt like they had this morning. Not at all.

At that very moment, Jordan rounded the side of the house, basketball in hand. He looked my way and the most gorgeous smile lit his face. Scarlet must've noticed, because she nudged me. "Something's going on there. I know it."

I shushed her as he walked our way. Yes, something was going on between us, no doubt about that. But this wasn't the time or the place to talk about it.

Jordan met us on the veranda and joined in the goodbyes, then reached for my hand and gave it a squeeze. "I know we didn't have much time together, just the two of us," he said. "But it still felt like it. Great family day."

I couldn't have put it better myself.

We thanked Bella's family for a wonderful afternoon and made our way down the front steps. When we got to our cars, Bella came tearing my way, holding little Rosa-Earline, who was still half asleep.

"I'm so happy for you," she whispered. "Truly happy."

"Happy for what?" Scarlet asked.

"She's going to the ball." Bella giggled.

Scarlet looked genuinely perplexed. I put my hand on her arm and smiled. "I'll call you later," I promised. "But it's good. All good."

"Ah, the world is a happy place! I can't wait to hear it!" Scarlet turned toward her car, then looked back at me, her eyes growing large. "Ooo, Gabi. I almost forgot."

"What?"

"Aunt Willy's coming into town tomorrow night, remember?" Scarlet's nose wrinkled at this statement. "She called me this morning to remind me. I know you've been working on the pattern, and I don't want to pressure you, but it would be great if we had something to show her after all the money she's spent." Scarlet's eyes took on a pleading look, and she reached to grab my hand.

"I . . . I'll do my best, but no promises, okay? I've got the pattern cut and the sample pieces started, but the actual dress is a long way from being complete."

"Oh, I know. I think she just wants to catch the vision."

*Catch the vision.* Interesting choice of words. After everything that had happened today, I felt as if I'd caught the vision. God had big things ahead for me, I just knew it. And maybe, just maybe, if I kept my eyes on the prize—whatever that happened to be—I could watch that vision unfold in front of me. In the meantime, I would put my nose to the grindstone and work on Scarlet's dress when I got home. Really, with her squeezing the life out of my hand like that, what else could I do?

# 10

## Let's Face the Music and Dance

All the girls I ever danced with thought they couldn't do it, but of course they could. So they always cried. All except Ginger. No, no, Ginger never cried.

FRED ASTAIRE

I arrived home from Bella's house ready to dive into my work. With Mama and Mimi both napping, the house stayed eerily quiet. Fidgeting around on the radio, I finally came across a station that had music similar to what I'd heard in Scarlet's church. Not the Splendora Sisters' gospel style. More like the songs the band played. Might take some getting used to, but hearing about God's love while working on a wedding dress seemed appropriate.

Mimi called out to me around seven o'clock to say that she'd warmed up some leftovers. I swallowed down a few bites of food, barely tasting them, and then headed back to my sewing room.

"How's it coming in there?" Mama asked as she stopped by before going to bed. "Looks like you've got a little sewing done."

239

"I've sewn the sample pieces together, and you can see the design of the dress now. But I haven't cut into the actual fabric yet." A little yawn escaped. "Scarlet's aunt is coming to see the progress tomorrow, but she's just going to have to catch the vision with this fabric, not the real thing." I paused. "Unless I change my mind and decide to cut some of the pieces out tonight. I haven't decided for sure yet."

"She paid for the fabric?" Mama asked. "Isn't that what you said?"

"Yes, and it was awfully expensive." Glancing over at the yardage, which I'd laid out on the guest bed, I shook my head. "I can't even imagine being able to afford a dress this costly."

"I have a feeling you'll have the dreamiest wedding dress of all, Gabriella." Mama walked into the room and gave me a little kiss on the forehead. "A real Cinderella gown, straight from a fairy tale. One fit for a royal ball."

I found myself smiling. Little did she know that I'd spent the afternoon talking to Bella about that very thing. So I told her. I shared the whole story—including the part where I'd prayed to ask Jesus into my heart.

"Bella said it was like accepting an invitation to the ball," I explained. "I get it now. The King was asking me to dance."

Mama's eyes misted over. "I'm so glad, Gabi," she said. "It just seems so . . . fitting." A little shrug followed. "I haven't thought much about God things for years, but I have to admit, this whole day really stirred my heart."

"Mine too."

"Given me a lot to think about." Mama slipped her hand over her mouth to cover a yawn. "Wore me out, though."

"Me too." My yawn echoed hers.

"Don't stay up too late, sweet girl," Mama said. "You need your beauty sleep."

I nodded but wasn't sure I could keep that promise. We said our good nights and she headed off to bed. I could hear Mimi Carmen snoring in the next room. Nothing unusual there. Still, I felt compelled to turn up the radio a bit to cover the noise. Then I dove back in, determined to get as much done as I could before going to bed.

Off in the distance, the hallway clock struck the hour. Eleven? Twelve? I'd lost count. Whenever I got in the zone, time didn't matter. All I could see, think, hear, or smell was the project in front of me. At the present, that project was the bodice of Scarlet's wedding dress. The sample pieces came together nicely. I made the decision to cut into the expensive fabric and prayed all the while as I tried to keep my hand steady on the scissors.

So far, so good. The cut pieces looked great. So great, in fact, that I decided to keep moving forward. I worked until my back ached, beading the most intricate design I'd ever attempted. In my mind's eye, I could see it so clearly. But the beading process seemed to take more time than I'd anticipated, both frustrating me and propelling me to work harder than ever, no matter the hour.

Somewhere around two in the morning I stopped for a potty break. Though my body ached to be put to bed, I could not still my thoughts long enough to give the idea serious consideration. All that mattered was the beading project I'd started. One thing could be said of Gabi Delgado—she finished what she started, no matter how long it took or how many calories it burned.

I finally gave up around 4:30, my now bleary vision presenting a problem. Somehow I staggered to my bed, tumbling in before setting my alarm. Surely I would wake up on time. I always did.

Only, I didn't. Not this time. When I rolled over in the bed, my body stiff and sore, streams of sunlight poured in through the slatted blinds. I had that weird out-of-body experience where I thought—hoped, really—I was dreaming all of this. Reaching for the alarm clock, I did my best not to panic. Until I saw the time, at which point I went into full-blown freak-out mode.

Demetri would kill me. KILL me. After firing me, of course. Why today, of all days? The poor man was still battling frazzled nerves after his hospitalization.

My cell phone rang and I grasped it, my breaths

coming a little shorter when I saw Demetri's phone number. No longer able to put off the inevitable, I answered with a hesitant "Hello?"

"Gabi, you had better be lying on zee side of zee road bleeding."

"E-excuse me?"

"Please tell me something catastrophic has happened. I can't imagine any other reason vhy you would go mee-sing on such an important day."

"Important day? No, I don't really have that much on my plate today, Demetri. In fact, I—"

"Nicolette called, and she's coming back in for a private consultation. She said it vas urgent and insisted you be here."

*Oh. No!*

"She'll be here in twenty-five minutes and—"

"I'll be there, I promise. I'm sorry, Demetri. I really am. I—"

*What to say, what to say?*

Fortunately—or unfortunately—I didn't have to say anything. Mimi Carmen did it for me. She appeared in my doorway, eyes wide, rambling in Spanish about how I'd overslept, about how she'd worried herself to death pacing the living room, afraid to open my door for fear she would find a dead body inside.

Demetri heard every word, but I couldn't be sure he was able to handle the translation from Spanish to English. Ending the call, I flew out of bed, assured Mimi I was fine, dressed while brushing my teeth, and pulled my hair back into a loose bun. Hopefully the wrinkles in my cheek from the pillowcase would fade before I got to the shop.

They didn't.

"Vhat happened to your face?" Demetri's gaze narrowed as he took several quick steps toward me once I entered the shop.

"Oh, I . . ." My purse slid off my shoulder and clunked to the floor. I reached down to pick it up. "Nothing that I know of."

The Dynamic Duo passed by me on their way to the front of the store. Lydia paused to stare at me, then whispered something unintelligible to Corinne.

"You look like something zee cat dragged in," Demetri hissed under his breath as he passed by. "Vash away zee dark circles under your eyes vith a strong cup of coffee and head to your office so zat Nicolette doesn't notice." He shook a frantic finger in my face. "I've been beside myself, Gabi."

Great. That would make two of him.

"I'm only fifteen minutes late," I said. "I'll stay after and make up the time, no problem."

"Yes, you vill. In the meantime, do something about your face. Nicolette vill be here soon." He turned on his heels and marched across the shop toward his office.

I raced to my workroom and stared at my reflection in the full-length mirror. Okay, so I had a few wrinkles from my pillowcase. Big deal. And yeah, the mascara on my right eye dribbled down onto the skin below. That was an easy fix.

Grabbing a tissue, I went to work. Just as I managed to make the mascara mess even worse, Kitty's voice sounded from the doorway. "Are you okay, Gabi?"

"Hmm?" I nodded. "Yeah. Fine. Wish I'd had time to stop for coffee, though."

"I can make some. Don't mind a bit." She paused and I could read the concern in her eyes. "You sure you're okay? You don't look well."

I tried to force back the little yawn that threatened to escape but could not. "F-fine."

"You sick?" She tilted her head to the right and gave me a closer look, much like a doctor would give a patient.

"No, no." I shook my head and felt my cheeks warm. "Just . . . busy."

"Well, I'll have a talk with Demetri. He must really be overworking you for you to come dragging in here looking threadbare." She grinned. "Threadbare. Ha. Not sure where that came from." Her expression shifted to one of concern. "Still, he's got you going around the clock, and it's obvious you're not in any shape to keep working at this pace."

I felt a little wave of panic. "No, please don't say anything to Demetri. This time it's not his fault."

He had no idea I stayed up half the night working on designs for other people, now did he? A niggling of guilt crept up my spine. In spite of my feelings of angst toward Demetri, I owed him a good day's work. He paid me to do a professional job, and I couldn't let my nighttime escapades—if one could call them that—distract me from the work I actually got paid for. Not any longer.

"I really hope you're all right, Gabi," Kitty said. "Because Nicolette is on her way in. She's going to talk to Demetri about her dress. Only problem is, none of us seems to know which dress she's referring to, the one he made for her or something else entirely. So I think—"

Kitty never had time to finish the sentence. The door swung wide and Nicolette entered. She pulled off her sunglasses, crossed her arms over her ample chest, and glanced at me. "Gabi! Good. You're here." She grabbed me and whispered in my ear, "I decided we should tell him together. This is going to be so much fun!"

"But I never really agreed to—"

"I can't thank you enough for agreeing to make my dress." She giggled, now the carefree, giddy bride once more. "Quite a relief, I tell you. For a while there I thought I might just have to fly off

246

to New York or Paris for my gown. But you've saved the day!"

At this point Kitty shot out the door in what appeared to be a panic. Seconds later Demetri rushed into the room, the fakest smile I'd ever seen plastered across his face. Nicolette swooped over to give him a hug. Demetri, not the hugging sort, took her hand and kissed it.

"And how is my favorite customer?" he asked, his voice a little too rehearsed.

"Lovely, now that this wonderful talent of yours has saved the day."

I cringed as she used the word *talent,* and all the more when I saw him flinch. Demetri had called me many things, but never that. Material girl, sure. Alterations expert, maybe. But . . . talent?

Nicolette offered a broad smile and sashayed over to the dress form, all aflutter. "I'll be the belle of the ball on my wedding day, and all because of *Gabriella Delgado's* luscious design." She used her hands to frame the words, as if seeing my name on a marquee or something.

"Is zat so?" Demetri crossed his arms and looked at me, his expression none too friendly. Then he turned back to our giddy bride, speaking through clenched teeth. "Nicolette, *dah*-ling, come vith me to my office."

"No, let's stay here," she said, turning back to give me a little wink. "It makes sense to be in

Gabi's work space, anyway." She glanced at my desk and then gave me a funny look. "I don't see your sketchbook, though. Did you bring it? I'm dying to show Demetri that design."

"Design?" He looked back and forth between us, and I had another of those weird out-of-body experiences. Maybe I was still dreaming all of this. Sure. I would wake up and this would all be a silly nightmare.

Or not.

"Gabi, vhat is she referring to?" Demetri's penetrating glare seared my conscience, and I shifted my gaze to the floor.

I bent my head forward and studied my hands, which were, ironically, folded in prayer. "I, well . . ." I shook my head and looked back up, preparing myself for whatever came next.

"I'm really sad that you don't have the sketch with you." Nicolette's smile faded.

Great. Now I had two people upset with me.

"I guess we'll just have to work around that. We have so much to discuss." She clasped her hands together, pure delight on her face. Demetri, on the other hand, did not look so delighted. In fact, he looked as if he needed a blood pressure tablet, and the sooner the better.

"Oh, but first let me tell you about my honeymoon plans!" Nicolette said. "Peter has booked the most marvelous little over-the-water hotel in Bora Bora!"

Thank goodness her jovial mood kept Demetri from blowing his top. His "Yes, please tell us" was phony-baloney but shifted the conversation in a different direction, which gave me a moment's reprieve. Nicolette seemed thrilled to ramble on about her upcoming trip to Bora Bora.

Then again, what girl wouldn't be thrilled to receive the news that she would be honeymooning in paradise? I could hardly imagine spending thousands of dollars a day on a honeymoon, but apparently she could. She chatted on and on about the luxury hotel she and her soon-to-be husband would be staying at. Turned out several Hollywood types had stayed there. Go figure.

Only when she turned her conversation away from the honeymoon did she speak the words I'd been dreading all along. Her impassioned "I've chosen Gabi's design for my wedding dress!" caused Demetri to gasp and reach for his heart.

And me? It caused me to feel like the room was spinning.

As Nicolette carried on and on, filling Demetri in on every wonderful, terrible detail of the "perfect gown straight from heaven" that she'd chosen from my sketchbook, I knew my time at Haute Couture Bridal had drawn to a fateful end. From the mortified expression on my boss's face, he was planning my demise as Nicolette spoke. No doubt I would get the boot the moment she left the store—if not before.

When she paused for breath, he cleared his throat. "Nicolette, just to clarify, you vill not be wearing the gown I made for you?"

"No." She shook her head. "I simply can't walk down the aisle in that dress, Demetri. I thought I made that clear before. It's not a good fit for my big day. It's really more of a party dress, I think. Not what I envisioned making my entrance in."

"I see."

Only, I could tell he did not. He listened, jaw clenched, lips tight, as she told him once again how talented I was, how I had designed a dress that suited her to a T.

Demetri simply nodded. Oh boy. Was he gonna kill me or what?

When she wrapped up her end of the conversation, he responded with one line: "You vill have the dress of your dreams," and then told her that he had to cut the meeting short. No doubt he needed to run to the break room to stick his head in the oven.

Not that we had an oven.

Nicolette yammered on all the way to the front door, where she gave me a little wave, offered a joyous "Thank you so much! You've made this bride so happy!" and then sauntered out the door.

As Demetri turned to face me, I saw my life flash before my eyes. Well, not my whole life, actually. Just tiny snippets of it. I didn't really have time for the elongated version, because my boss came barreling my way. I darted to my right, thinking he might take me down. Instead, he stopped, put his hand on a mannequin's arm to steady himself, and appeared to be counting. In Russian.

After a couple of minutes, he released a slow breath and gave me a brusque nod. "So, zat's it zen? Zis is vhat I get for all I've done for you?"

"Demetri, please let me explain."

A wild-eyed look came over him, and he spoke through clenched teeth. "Explain how you stole one of my designs and called it your own?"

"W-what?" Was he kidding?

"Explain how you talked one of my brides into using it under false pretenses?"

"Demetri, no! I would never do that. Please give me the benefit of the doubt here. It's the least you can do."

"Zee very least. Not zat I owe you zat, you . . . you . . . traitor!"

"The truth is, I design wedding gowns too. I-I always have."

"Puh-*leeze*." He rolled his eyes. "Where are zeese sketches she refers to? I have no doubt you've copied one of my designs and called it your own. When I have zee proof, you vill not only lose your job, you vill find yourself on zee end of a lawsuit."

"This is ridiculous!" Anger welled up inside me, and I felt as if I would cry. "How can you accuse me of this with hardly any explanation? You know me better than that."

"Obviously I don't know you at all. I never even knew you vere a so-called designer."

So-called? Ugh!

"It's true, Demetri. I've wanted to talk to you about this for ages. And for your information, I didn't show Nicolette my designs. She found my sketchpad and—"

"Gabi, just go." With a wave of his hand he dismissed me.

"Go? Where?"

"Wherever liars and traitors go." He gestured toward the door. "I vill be here phoning my lawyer. You can expect a call."

Shivers ran down my spine at that announcement.

"I can find another material girl, no problem. Zay are a dime a dozen."

"Exactly." I pressed my balled-up fists against my waist and faced him head-on. "Material girls *are* a dime a dozen. But girls like me, girls who excel at wedding dress design—we're harder to come by. Much harder, actually. You go ahead and call an attorney, Demetri. When you see my sketches—which are nothing like anything you've ever designed—you will know in an instant that my designs are my own. So there!"

Courage grabbed hold of me in that moment. Underneath Demetri's ever-present glare, I held my head high and marched back to my office, where I packed up my things, including my dress forms, and lugged them one by one out to the car. Kitty and the Dynamic Duo looked on, their wide-eyed stares now boring holes through me.

Sure, I'd left before. And I'd come back at his bidding. But this time . . . no, this time would be different. There wouldn't be any returning to the scene of the crime. For while I'd envisioned myself hard-pressed under Demetri's thumb, unable to fend for myself, I now realized the opposite was true.

He wasn't the boss of me.

And that suddenly felt mighty good.

# 19

## I Won't Dance

Part of the joy of dancing is conversation. Trouble is, some men can't talk and dance at the same time.

GINGER ROGERS

One good thing about leaving my job at nine o'clock in the morning—it meant I had the rest of the day free to work on Scarlet's dress. When I arrived home, I bared my soul to Mimi, who pacified me with chocolate. Truffles, to be precise. Oddly, she didn't look worried about my lack of income. In fact, judging from the carefree expression on her face, she didn't seem particularly troubled about anything.

Before settling in to work, I telephoned Mama and gave her the news. I could tell she had her concerns, but she offered nothing but sympathy. After that I decided to call Jordan to fill him in. I hated to interrupt his workday, but I knew I couldn't make it through the rest of the morning without telling him. He answered on the third ring, sounding a little breathless.

"Hey, Gabi, I was just thinking about you." His cheerful tone served as a direct contrast to my somber mood.

"Hey," I managed.

"You calling from work?" he asked. Before I could answer, he added, "I'm at the gym. On the treadmill, actually." That explained the breathlessness.

Well, no point in beating around the bush. Might as well come out with it.

"I . . . I got fired this morning."

"What? Again?" He laughed but then grew serious. "I'm sorry, Gabi. You mean, for real?"

"Yeah, for real."

"What happened? Wait, hang on. I need to get off the treadmill."

"That's pretty much what I did. Well, the proverbial treadmill, I mean." I gave a weak laugh.

I spent the next few minutes filling him in. With a knot the size of a golf ball in my throat, I choked out, "I can't go back. I mean, even if Demetri begs, I really can't go back this time."

"Good for you. Hold your ground, girl. You don't need him anyway."

This prompted a "how in the world am I going to survive?" outpouring from me.

Jordan listened in silence but had his say at the end. "I don't have all of those answers, Gabi, but I know someone who does. Have you prayed about it?"

A lengthy pause followed. "I . . . haven't. But I will."

"Good. Because no one can really tell you

what to do. But I'm sure the Lord has a plan, and I'm convinced it doesn't include going back into that little closet and working with Ginger and . . . Hem-ry."

"I told you, he's not Hem-ry."

"Right, right. Stitch?"

"No." I sighed. Time to come clean. "His name is Demetri."

"Right. I know your boss's name is Demetri."

"No. The male dress form. I named him Demetri because I enjoy sticking pins in him." I groaned as I realized how awful that sounded as I spoke it aloud.

Jordan busted out with a laugh so loud that I had to pull the phone away from my ear for a moment. "That's the funniest thing I've ever heard," he said once he calmed down. "Seriously."

"Not really that funny, actually. I keep thinking that I need to forgive him, and I try, but every time I do, he pulls another stunt and I'm back to being mad at him again."

"Oh, trust me, you'll have plenty of people in your life willing to annoy you daily. Ask me how I know." He paused. "But I still think it's for the best that you're out from under Demetri's thumb. You didn't need to be there. You've crossed out of Egypt and into the Promised Land, Gabi. It's scary, sure, but God's got your back. And I know he has a plan. Just promise me you won't let him sucker you in one more time."

"What do you mean?"

"I mean, if he offers you your job again, you won't take it. Don't go back to Egypt. To slavery."

"Oh, I won't, trust me."

"Good. Remember this day. Circle it on the calendar so you never forget the day you stepped into the water. And leave behind some stones in the river to remind yourself not to go back."

"Stones?"

"Yes. Pretty sure I remember this story because of the tie to my name. The Israelites left twelve stones in the Jordan River as a reminder of what God had done when he stopped the flow of the water so that they could pass over. Kind of a cool way to put the past in the past."

"So, you want me to find a river and drop some stones in it?" Maybe the Gulf of Mexico would do instead.

"No." His voice grew more serious. "I want you to rename the dress form. Call him Hem-ry or Stitch or Fred, but don't ever call him Demetri again. Let go of the past, Gabi. Forgive and move on."

*Forgive and move on.*

Those words propelled me long after I ended the call with Jordan. As I fidgeted with the beautiful front panel of Scarlet's gown, working and reworking the beading design until I had it just right, I pondered his words.

*Don't go back to Egypt.*

I should embroider that on a sampler and hang it on my wall. Then, if and when the moment of temptation came, I wouldn't go back. I would look at the words and remind myself that my current unemployed life, no matter how scary, was the Promised Land. Well, the outskirts of the Promised Land, anyway. I could trust God with my future.

Passion to work on Scarlet's dress now fueled me. I pinned the paper pattern to the expensive fabric and observed the cut-out pieces. I knew I wouldn't be able to get much of the sewing done before Scarlet and her aunt arrived at 6:30, but I did manage to make considerable progress on the bodice.

All the while, I prayed. In fact, I filled God's ears—not with complaints but with heartfelt ponderings, good and bad. This one-on-one time brought an energy I hadn't known. The songs on the radio helped too, even steadying my trembling hands as I worked.

When I didn't pause for lunch, Mimi brought me a tray with a sandwich and apple slices. "You need to keep up your strength," she scolded.

"I know, but I'm working against a deadline. Scarlet is coming this evening with her aunt."

Mimi responded in Spanish, something about how life was for the living. She disappeared into the other room, but I thought I heard her talking to someone on the phone, so I rose and tiptoed out into the hallway, curiosity getting the better of me. Mimi rarely called anyone these days. But judging from the lilt in her voice, she seemed to be having a grand time talking on the phone today.

I strained to make out her words. Only when I heard her speak the name Daniel did I realize who was on the other end of the line. Wow. I didn't mean to listen in but just couldn't help myself. Her girlish giggles totally threw me.

I'd just turned to head back to my workroom when she ended her call. She came walking out into the hallway, singing a happy tune in Spanish. Until she saw me. Then her cheeks turned a lovely amber hue.

"Oh, Gabi. There you are. I thought you were working."

"I took a break."

"Ah. Yes." Her nose wrinkled and she fussed with a framed picture on the wall, straightening it. Only, it was already straight, so she actually made it crooked. "Did you . . . I mean, I was on the phone."

"So I heard." I gave her a knowing look.

"Well, it's time for my show." She headed into the living room, and I followed on her heels, unwilling to let this go. I watched as she took a seat in her recliner and then fidgeted with the remote. Seconds later the TV popped on. Mimi adjusted the channel until it landed on *Doña Bárbara*. As the familiar theme song played, she settled back against the chair and seemed to relax.

"I'm glad you're making friends at the church, Mimi," I said over the music. "Really glad."

She watched the screen for a moment. When she turned my way, I noticed her eyes were filled with tears.

"Are you okay?" I asked.

"It's just . . . my story." Her words in Spanish were laced with emotion. She gestured to the television.

"What about it?" I asked.

An outdoor scene filled the screen—a lovely woman walked alongside a stream with a handsome man at her side. The man swept her into his arms and gave her a kiss.

"It's not real, I know," Mimi said, "but the characters have become almost like family to me." A sheepish look came over her. "It's silly, I guess. But I feel like I know them. It's not healthy, I suppose."

"Oh, I don't know. Lots of women get addicted to these shows, Mimi."

"Still, I think I really miss having a big family and lots of friends around. I don't talk about it much, but being a homebody isn't much fun, especially in my . . . condition."

"You should get out more. Do more."

"That's what I've decided. I'm not saying I'm giving up my show." She cringed. "Not sure I'm ready for that. But I need to start interacting with more real people."

"People like Rosa? And Laz?"

She grinned. "Yes, all of the Rossis are wonderful. And Scarlet's mama too. I talked to her about her work at the bakery, and it turns out we have a lot in common." Mimi muted the television as a commercial came on. "I have a handful of friends at my church, but we're not as close as we used to be. You'd be surprised how many can't even go anymore because they're not able to get around."

Her words made me sad, but I didn't know how to respond in a way that would make her feel better about the situation.

"I think maybe I'll try out that new church for a while," she said, then turned the volume up a notch. "It's different."

"Really? You liked it?"

"Still can't quite get used to the music, but the people are so friendly." Her cheeks turned pink. "Very welcoming."

"Mimi, are you trying to tell me something?"

"No, no." She shook her head. "Well, maybe. I mean, I'm old, but I haven't completely given up on the idea of falling in love again. Your grandfather, God rest his soul, was the most wonderful man I've ever known. But he's been gone for over twenty years. Maybe it's time I . . ."

"What?" I asked, unable to hide my grin.

"Well, maybe I need to open myself up to the possibilities, that's all."

My thoughts shifted back to Daniel, how he'd helped her out of the car. Offered her his arm. There really were some good men left, just like Jordan had said.

"And another thing." She released a sigh. "I have to start taking better care of myself." She pointed to her ample midsection. "It's getting harder and harder to get around. I don't think I can go on living like this, carrying around all of these excess pounds. I don't know how I'm going to do it, but I have to get in shape. Otherwise I won't be here to hold my great-grandchildren in these tubby arms of mine."

I thought to argue the point but didn't want to change her mind. The weight loss idea was a good one, and she'd never mentioned it before.

Suddenly I remembered something. "I saw in the church bulletin that Scarlet is going to be starting some sort of weight loss group at the church when she gets back from her honeymoon. Might be fun."

"Maybe." She shrugged. "Or maybe I'll join a gym. Take up racquetball." She pretended to swing a racket and then laughed. "The hardest part of all will be watching what I eat. I love my food."

At this statement, she remembered that she needed to thaw out a pot roast for tonight's dinner.

I reminded her that Scarlet and her aunt would be coming by, and she nodded.

"That's fine. It's big enough for all of us."

She headed to the kitchen, and moments later I heard pots and pans rattling. Her story continued to play on the television, but with the volume so low I couldn't make it out. Not that I needed to. There was no point in getting swallowed up by a fictional world when some very real people needed my attention.

With that in mind, I headed to my workroom to dive back in to Scarlet's dress.

# 20

## Funny Face

From the manner in which a woman draws her thread at every stitch of her needlework, any other woman can surmise her thoughts.

HONORE DE BALZAC

In late afternoon I finished the bodice of Scarlet's dress. After that I connected the skirt pieces and then pinned them to the top. By the time Scarlet and her aunt arrived at 6:30, I had the beginnings of what I felt sure would be a lovely gown with a fairy-tale feel to it.

Bella surprised me by showing up a few minutes later. She greeted the ladies and then dove into a story about what a rough day she'd had. I didn't bother to interrupt to tell them I'd been fired. Didn't have to. Mimi Carmen took care of that for me.

We talked for a bit about my situation, but I eventually turned the conversation back to the bride-to-be, who deserved the attention. I led the ladies into my workroom, and Scarlet squealed with glee when she saw the dress for the first time. Tears sprang to her eyes, in fact, a sure sign that

I was on the right track with the gown's design.

"Oh, Gabi, I don't know how you've done it, but you have. You absolutely have. It's just what I saw in my head."

"The fabric is just how I thought it would be too," Wilhelmina added. "Absolutely lovely. It looks so rich."

*It is rich.*

Bella stood in front of the dress form, examining my beadwork. She turned to give me a curious look. "Gabi, did you do this by hand?"

"Yes."

"All of it? I mean, the fabric didn't come beaded . . . at all? It's your design? Your creation?"

"Right. I did it all. I created a little scroll-like design and just sewed them on by hand."

"It must have worn you out." She clucked her tongue in motherly fashion.

I didn't tell her that I'd stayed up half the night working on it. Neither did I mention that I'd overslept this morning as a result of the exhaustion.

Scarlet's excitement had her bouncing up and down now. "Can I try it on?"

"Well, it's not really at a point yet where you can tell much. The middle part is just pinned together, and there's no zipper yet or anything. And all of the edges are raw. No hem, nothing like that."

"I know, but it doesn't matter. Please?" She assumed the begging pose, hands clasped together in front of her. "If I get jabbed with a pin, it'll be so worth it. I won't say a word, I promise."

"Okay, okay."

With Bella's help, I got the dress from its pedestal and slipped it over Scarlet's head. I took several clips and closed up the opening in the back where the zipper would be placed. Then I stepped back for a look. Wow. Sure, I still had a lot of work to do, but so far so good. Seeing it on Scarlet made me want to do a little jig.

She stood a little straighter and gazed at her reflection in the mirror, a lone tear now trickling down her cheek.

"Don't you like it?" I asked.

"Like it? I love it. Absolutely, without a doubt, love, love, love it!"

"I think it's going to be perfect when it's done," Bella said. "I can just envision Scarlet walking down the aisle in this glorious skirt. There's just the right amount of volume to be princess-like but not over-the-top."

"Every eye in the place will be on you, honey." Wilhelmina's eyes misted over.

"They're right. It's wonderful." Scarlet took my hand and gave it a squeeze. "Best of all, I don't look overly inflated. That was my biggest fear."

"Overly inflated?" Bella's brow wrinkled. "What do you mean?"

"You would never understand, Bella." Scarlet

turned and the skirt made a lovely swishing sound. "You're what—a size 2?"

"Puh-leeze." Bella groaned. "Before kids, maybe."

"Anyway, you're teeny-tiny. And I'm sure you looked amazing in your wedding dress. But let's just say that white isn't the most slimming color, so I've been dreading wearing bolts and bolts of white fabric lopped around my body."

"Hardly bolts and bolts," I argued. "And I'm trying not to be offended at that 'lopped around my body' comment. I hope you think more of my work than that."

Scarlet laughed. "Okay, okay, you're right. My apologies." She stared at her reflection and then did a twirl. "I'm past all of my fears now that I've seen myself in the dress. I don't know how you've done it, Gabi, but you've made me look like I have a waist."

I could explain exactly how I'd done it, of course. I'd strategized the best design for her body type and come up with the perfect gown to emphasize the smaller waistline. The fuller skirt made the waist seem even smaller. The bead-work on the bodice drew the eye up, again showing off the narrower midsection. Beadwork I'd spent hours doing and had almost lost my job over.

Bella gave Scarlet a motherly look. "Silly girl, you do have a waist." She stood back, arms crossed, an admiring look on her face. "And it's getting smaller every day."

"Not on purpose, really," Scarlet said, then giggled. "I mean, I'm eating better and have been working myself to death, so I have lost quite a few pounds. But it's not all diet and exercise. This corset thingy is doing its work, holding everything in place."

"Blame the corset if you like, but I've noticed a definite difference in you over the past few weeks, and it's not just the glow of being in love."

"Thank you for saying that." Scarlet reached out to give Bella's hand a squeeze. "I wish I could say it came from working out at the gym or running laps or something. Truth is, I'm putting in a lot of hours at the bakery, so I don't really have time to think about food right now."

"Surrounded on every side by baked goods?" Bella shook her head. "I don't know how you do it. I put on three pounds every time I walk through the door of your bakery." She went off on a tangent about sticky buns, which led to a funny conversation about hip size.

As Bella and Scarlet gabbed, I pinned and tucked, trying to envision how I could take in the waistline another inch or so without destroying the beading I'd worked so hard on. Bella hadn't exaggerated—Scarlet's waist had definitely trimmed down. I should be celebrating alongside them, but I found myself calculating the extra hours it would take to downsize the dress in all the right places.

I looked at Scarlet's reflection in the mirror just in time to see her running her fingertips over the beading. She shook her head and sighed—a contented, blissful sigh. "I'm the happiest girl on the island."

In that moment, nothing else mattered. Not the number of hours I'd worked. Not the lecture from Demetri when I'd arrived late. Not the loss of my day job. Not the backache from stooping over with needle and thread in hand. Nothing. Only the look of joy on the bride-to-be's face. For that one instant, the exhaustion faded away, replaced by an inner zeal. All that remained was the absolute conviction that I was doing exactly what the Lord had called me to do . . . and I'd never been happier.

Scarlet's gaze shifted to me, and she grinned. "Gabi, I want to ask a favor."

"Sure. Anything."

"I want you to be one of my bridesmaids."

"Really?" Wow.

"Well, sure. I love that we're getting to be such good friends. Bonding over dresses and cakes and all things weddings. You know?"

"I do. And . . . I'd be honored."

My mind reeled that she would ask me to join the wedding party. I didn't know when I'd ever been more flattered. It looked like the dress design business might turn out to be about more

269

than dresses. Maybe it had more to do with relationships.

When we put the gown back on the dress form, Wilhelmina circled it, examining it from every side. She didn't say anything for a moment. When she did speak, her words surprised me. "Gabi, I like this dress so much that I think I need to design a cake to match it."

"A matching cake?"

"Yes. I love how you've done the ruffled skirt. The layering is exquisite, not like anything I've ever seen before. That would make a lovely bottom tier for the cake. And the princess-cut waistline is to die for. I see a layer with that design implement too. The beadwork on the bodice . . ." She picked up the fabric panel that I'd spent hours beading in the night. "It's the most beautiful thing I've ever laid eyes on."

"Really?"

"Really. And I think I can duplicate it, at least to some extent, on the upper-middle layers of the cake. Do you mind if I photograph this? That way I'll get it just right. No guesswork."

"Of course I don't mind." Was she kidding? Just the opposite!

"Tell you what I'm going to do." Wilhelmina reached into her purse and came out with a tiny camera, which she used to snap photos from several angles. "I'll take lots of pictures of the cake when it's done and call it the 'Gabriella.' All of the cakes in my shop are named after various women I've met in my journey, so it just fits."

"But I'm not a bride," I argued.

She countered with, "Yet," and then followed that with, "Someday."

"I keep telling her that," Bella said. "Someday her prince will come."

"*Someday* is highly overrated," I said. Still, I couldn't get past what Wilhelmina had said. "Are you really planning to use my wedding dress as a design for the cake?"

"I am. Maybe Scarlet will be the first in a long line of brides to have a cake with this design at her wedding. You never know. I can picture this being quite a popular cake design, if I duplicate what you have going on here." She pointed to the lovely, long *V* at the waistline of the dress.

"Oh?"

"Yes, this is wonderful. I can see it all in my imagination now." Her gaze shifted to my wall. "Speaking of having an imagination, I notice you have a lot of Fred and Ginger pictures."

"Yes, I'm a huge fan."

"I've always loved them too."

"You have?" An arched eyebrow indicated Scarlet's humorous surprise at this news. "You never told me, Aunt Willy."

"There hasn't been much time for dancing in my life, but if I ever found the time, I'd want to be led around the dance floor by Fred or someone just like him—with his style, his grace, his great moves."

This got a laugh—make that a snort—out of Bella.

"Fred Astaire is amazing," I said. "But I'm more impressed with Ginger. She got overlooked a lot, I think, which makes me want to root for her even more."

"You think?" Wilhelmina looked startled by this. "You do know she won an award for best actress, don't you?"

"She did?" Somehow that fact had eluded me. "I guess I didn't know it."

"Years ago. I was just a girl myself at the time. She won for a movie called *Kitty Foyle*."

"Strange. I don't remember that one."

"That's because it *wasn't* one of the ones with Fred Astaire." Wilhelmina gave me a knowing look as if this should all make sense. "Do you see my point?"

"Not really," I admitted.

"She made it to stardom on her own, in a film that didn't include him. In her own right she was a terrific actress, even without the guy on her arm. But she's best known for her movies with Fred, which didn't win the big awards. So even though she didn't technically need him to be successful, it was their on-screen romance that stood the test of time."

Interesting.

"This whole conversation reminds me of what we talked about when we were all together before." Scarlet turned to her aunt. "Bella says that Gabi has a Cinderella complex."

I groaned and fought the temptation to slug Scarlet on the arm. Why did she have to go there?

"Well, that's fascinating." The fine lines on Wilhelmina's forehead became more prominent. "You do realize that Ginger Rogers was in the made-for-TV version of *Cinderella*, don't you?"

"No." How I'd missed that, I couldn't be sure. "What part did she play?"

"Kind of an obscure one," Wilhelmina said. "She was actually the queen. Mother of Prince Charming."

"Fascinating."

"Of course, this was after she'd aged a bit. But I find it very ironic, don't you?"

"Yes, do you think someone's trying to tell you something here, Gabi?" Scarlet asked.

"That I should go into television?" I smiled weakly.

"No, goofy." She slugged me on the arm now. Though she'd meant it to be a joke, it actually kind of hurt. Just my arm, not my feelings. "I'm just saying that maybe the Lord is trying to open your eyes—and your heart—to the idea that it's time to get beyond the Cinderella complex. You're not meant to hide in a closet, working. It's time to let your little light shine, girl!"

Somehow the mention of hiding in a closet provoked a conversation about a new pair of shoes that Bella had just purchased, which somehow led to a comment from Wilhelmina about her recent trip to the podiatrist, which, strangely, inspired Scarlet to give me a passionate speech about how God had the perfect fella out there for me, one with a glass slipper in his back pocket.

Mimi Carmen walked in right as the words *glass slipper* were spoken and went off on a tangent about a new pair of house slippers that she'd seen at Walmart, which she hoped to get for her birthday. And that's pretty much where the conversation about my Cinderella complex came to an end. Thank goodness.

After a few minutes, my grandmother snapped her fingers. "I just remembered why I came in here. The pot roast and vegetables are done." The next line she directed at me. "Your mama is due home from work any minute. Let's not tell her just yet that you lost your job."

"Too late, Mimi. I called her this morning."

She groaned as we followed her into the kitchen. Mama showed up moments later, and Mimi served up heaping portions of the luscious beef stew with its bright orange carrots, celery, onions, and lots of potatoes.

We'd no sooner taken our seats at the table when my cell phone rang. Glancing down, I saw an unfamiliar number. Well, unfamiliar at first. After a moment, I recognized it.

"I'd better take this. It's Nicolette."

Mimi nodded, and Scarlet offered up a rushed "I'll be praying. It'll be okay, Gabi."

I answered as I shot out of the room, heading for the privacy of my bedroom. "Hello?"

"Gabi, I'm glad I caught you. There's something I want to say."

"You want to say you're sorry?"

Nicolette seemed taken aback by this. "No, I want to say that I've come up with the perfect solution regarding the wedding dress debacle."

"You have?"

"Yes. I've decided that I will wear the gown Demetri designed."

Waves of relief flooded over me, and I felt like I could breathe for the first time all day. "Oh, Nicolette, thank you! This makes my day!"

"I'll wear the gown Demetri designed to my reception." She chuckled. "What do you think of that?"

"I'm not sure I understand."

"It's simple, Gabi. I'll wear the gown that you're making to my ceremony, and I'll wear his gown to the reception. That way, when the story releases in *Texas Bride*, it will be true that I wore Demetri's gown on my wedding day and he won't be humiliated. Better still, I won't have wasted my daddy's money. This was all his idea, you see." She laughed. "Who knows. Maybe Demetri will even give you your job back when I tell him. Stranger things have happened."

I thought about Jordan's admonition to stay out of Egypt. "No, I don't think I'll be going back, even if he offers." Still, I did have to wonder how he would respond to Nicolette's idea.

"Demetri told me that he threatened you with a lawsuit. Did you sign some sort of noncompete clause with him or something?"

"No. Never."

"Then you have nothing to worry about. Besides, I've already told him that I'll tell all of my friends at the Junior League to stay as far away from him as possible if he goes through with his threats. I think it scared him witless."

*He doesn't have far to go, then.*

I chastened myself for such an unkind thought.

"Thank you for your support, Nicolette. If everything works out like you say, I would love to make your dress."

"Then I will be the happiest bride on the island."

She shared a couple more thoughts and then we ended the call, agreeing to meet up at the fabric store the day after tomorrow. Wow, had this day ever brought some interesting challenges . . . and opportunities. From out of nowhere, I had work appearing at my door.

Looked like I had two wedding dresses to make, and both in a hurry!

# 21

## I'll Be Hard to Handle

No one can have everything. Because for every dream dreamed there arises another dream. For every hope hoped there emerges another hope.

GINGER ROGERS

I worked late into the night, long after Scarlet and the other ladies left. Mama and Mimi Carmen shuffled off to bed, stopping by my room to scold me for working too hard, as always.

"All work and no play makes Jack a dull boy," Mimi said, then waggled her finger at me. "Get some sleep tonight, sweet girl."

"I will." And I did. I tumbled into the bed in the spare bedroom around midnight, with visions of wedding gowns dancing through my head and whispered prayers thanking God for his goodness on my lips.

I awoke in the wee hours of the night with the eerie feeling that someone had come into the room. A shadow in the corner caught me off guard, and I gasped. A lifelike form hovered in the stillness, dark and creepy—the curve of a woman's body.

I couldn't say a word—fear knotted itself in my throat. My heart rate doubled and I found myself breathless. But then my eyes grew accustomed to the dark and I made out the image with clearer vision.

One of the dress forms.

*That's all, Gabi. Just dress forms. They're not real.*

It took a moment for my heart rate to slow and the blood to stop pounding in my ears. At this point I decided I'd had enough, so I got up and went to my own room, where I crawled into bed and slept like a log.

I had planned to sleep in, which made sense after staying up so late two nights in a row. So when my cell phone rang at 8:15, I could hardly make sense of the sound. I glanced down to see the words *Haute Couture* on the screen and groaned aloud.

I answered on the third ring but didn't try to cover up the exhaustion in my voice this time.

"Gabi, you're late. Zis is not acceptable."

Demetri. Really?

"No, Demetri. I'm not late. You fired me. I won't be back."

"But Nicolette phoned and explained the whole thing. You are forgiven, Gabi. Don't make me say it twice."

"I'm forgiven?"

"Yes. And Genevieve Villiamson vill be here at

nine for her fitting, remember? You've already met vith her once and—"

"Let one of the Fab Five cover it." I sat up in bed, my head still fuzzy. "I won't be there, Demetri."

"But you've already vorked vith Genevieve and know her preferences. I really think you should—"

"Demetri, stop right there." I couldn't believe my boldness to interrupt him, but the words tumbled forth like leaves on an autumn wind. "This whole hiring/firing relationship of ours just isn't working for me." I couldn't believe those words had come out of me. Imagine! Mousy little me, speaking up for myself. I began to shiver as my nerves kicked in, so I pulled the covers up to my shoulders.

"V-vhat did you say, Gabi?" His strained words came out slowly.

"This on-again, off-again relationship of ours is tougher than a rocky marriage. And I haven't done anything to deserve it, to be honest. Yesterday you accused me of many things—none of them true, by the way—and today you do an about-face and act as if it never happened. I just can't live like that. It's not healthy."

"But—"

A jolt of courage propelled me to speak my mind again. "So, as much as it pains me to say this, I want a divorce."

"A vhat?" I could imagine the veins popping out

on his forehead above those perfectly sculpted brows as he spoke.

"A divorce. A parting of the ways."

"But—"

"No buts, Demetri. You have a lovely shop and create lovely designs with the help of five lovely women, but I need a different kind of lovely in my life. I think I'll stick with what I do best."

"Alterations and mending?"

"No. Designing wedding gowns. The very thing I was created to do. So go fetch Doria. She will know what to do when Genevieve arrives. And for once, Demetri, calm down. Situations like these are better handled when you're not so worked up. It's better for your health, and it's better for those you work with."

He went silent and I wondered if he would speak again. His words, "You're really not coming back zis time?" threw me a little. I heard the pain in his voice.

"I'm not. But you're going to be okay, I promise. Go. Get. Doria."

We ended the call, and I could almost envision him staggering across the shop to the studio out back. Doria would happily take on the project with Genevieve. She had been instrumental in creating the gown in the first place and would know just what to do.

I rose from the bed and made my way to the kitchen, where Mama was preparing to leave for work. She carried on about the trip she was arranging for the Splendora Sisters, and I soon found myself dreaming of cruises and Italy. From the look in Mama's eyes, she was dreaming too.

Mimi Carmen, on the other hand, was in an unusual frame of mind. After eating an apple and a boiled egg, she announced that she would be in her room, putting on her most comfortable slacks so that she could take a walk around the neighborhood.

*Really? You're going for a walk?*

"Want to go with me, Gabi?" she asked, a twinkle in her eyes. "All work and no play—"

"Makes Jack a dull boy." I spoke the words along with her and then nodded. "Sure. I'll go for a walk."

And so we walked. If one could call moving down the sidewalk with Mimi Carmen a true walk. Mostly we talked about everything under the sun—our hopes, dreams, goals . . . everything. Girl talk. I couldn't remember the last time I'd enjoyed her company like this.

I offered to take her out to lunch at Parma John's, enticing her with the idea of a salad. Really, I didn't need to be spending the money, being unemployed and all, but I couldn't resist the temptation to see Scarlet and hear more about her aunt's take on the gown.

When we arrived at Parma John's, the smell of pizza accosted us. I thought my grandmother would fall off the dieting wagon pronto, but she amazed me by ordering a salad with light Italian dressing.

Minutes later Bella entered with her daughter in her arms. She saw me and gave a little wave.

"Well, howdy, stranger. Long time, no see."

"Who do we have here?" Mimi Carmen reached out to snag the toddler from Bella. "It's that lovely little doll I met on Sunday." She took the little one in her arms and began to talk in baby talk.

Bella took one look at Mimi and said, "You're hired!"

"I'm—what?"

Bella plopped down at the table. "D.J. and I both work full-time. Mama is so busy at the Grand Opera Society right now, and you know Rosa—she and Laz film several episodes of their show a week. Poor Rosa-Earline. She gets tossed around from person to person."

"You're saying you need someone to take her full-time?" I asked.

"No, but it would be great to have another option when everyone else is busy." She gave my grandmother a pleading look. "What do you think, Mimi Carmen?"

I smiled as she called my grandmother the name I'd given her as a child.

"I think Rosa-Earline and I will have a lovely time together." Mimi rose and headed off to the jukebox to show the toddler her favorite tunes. Bella leaned forward on her elbows and gazed at me. "Well, that's one prayer answered."

"Speaking of prayer, I've been doing more of it."

"Perfect. So what do you think will happen with your day job? I mean, I know he let you go, but . . ." She shrugged. "He's done that before, and it doesn't always stick."

"Yeah. Only, this time it's sticking." I filled her in on the details of my phone call with Demetri, and she put her hands down on the table.

"Good, Gabi. Stick to your guns. You don't need Demetri."

"I don't?"

"No. And if he doesn't shape up and start treating people better, I'm going to stop recommending him to my brides."

Ack. I swallowed hard at that idea. Wasn't it enough that Demetri was already angry with me? He would never forgive me if I turned Bella against him.

"Here's what I want you to do," Bella said. "Do you have all of your sketches?"

"You mean all of the ones I've ever done?"

"Ever done, ever started, ever thought about doing."

"Well, that's the problem. Some of them are on the backs of napkins, some are in sketchbooks, some are on slips of loose paper."

"Doesn't matter. You need to compile them. Make sense of them. Create a portfolio of sorts. And since we're talking about this, I might as well go ahead and let you know what I'm thinking about the future of Club Wed." The most delightful look lit up her face. "You know how you're always talking about Demetri's Fab Five? Well, I've decided to create my own."

"Your own . . . what? Designers?"

"Well, sort of. My own inner circle of friends in the wedding biz. Ladies who spend their days and their nights eating, sleeping, and breathing wedding-related things." She glanced up and smiled as Scarlet joined us. "Like wedding cakes."

"What did I miss?" Scarlet pulled up a chair and sat down.

"Talking about wedding vendors," Bella said. "I was just about to tell Gabi there's really only one place on the island for truly great cakes. No one can top yours, Scarlet."

"Why, thank you." Scarlet's cheeks turned the prettiest shade of pink. "The same is true with wedding photos. Hannah and Drew are at the top of my list." Bella glanced my way. "And the same can be said about wedding gowns. Gorgeous, over-the-moon, to-die-for wedding gowns that would have any bride swooning and any father of the bride ready to pull out his pocketbook and write a hefty check."

"Well, amen to that." But I still didn't completely understand her point. Seemed like she was leading up to some sort of big announcement.

"So, here's my plan. You ladies"—Bella pointed

back and forth between Scarlet and me—"are going to be my very own Fab Five."

"But there are only three of us," Scarlet said as she took a seat. "Counting Hannah, I mean."

"I know, I know, but you get my point. You're going to be my most recommended. When people have come to me looking for wedding pros, you've always been the first on my list. The first photographer. The first baker. The first dress designer. I've posted a list of my preferred vendors on my website, and you're at the top, all of you." She turned my way to speak directly to me. "Actually, I'm just adding you today. But I'll need details. Contact info. That kind of thing."

My heart rate skipped to double time. She'd flattered me beyond belief, but Demetri wouldn't be as flattered if he found out. In fact, he would probably do everything in his power to put an end to my career in a hurry.

Still, the idea that Bella Neeley would consider me one of her inner circle almost left me giddy. Only God opened doors like that. I had to acknowledge that I couldn't have accomplished this on my own.

"Anyway, I've always done a good job of recommending the best in the biz," Bella said. "But I want to do more. Here's my idea." She shifted in her seat. "My parents and I have been talking about this for quite a while, actually. We want to expand Club Wed."

"Expand?" I thought about the old Victorian home and tried to figure out how they would go about it. Every square inch was spoken for.

"We're talking about moving an interior wall near the front, just off the foyer, to call our Vendors Square. We'll display your gowns there, Gabi. And some faux wedding cakes, Scarlet. You're always bringing samples by, so why not put them there? And we'll hang several wedding photos that Hannah and Drew have taken. Oh, and flowers. We'll always have fresh flowers from Marcella's store." Bella's nose wrinkled. "Only, she's going to be passing the store to someone else soon. Not sure how that will work."

"Still, it's a great idea." Scarlet clasped her hands together. "I love it, Bella."

"Thanks. We'll also promote my brother-in-law's catering service. Bubba makes the best barbecue in the world."

"That's five!" I said. "Me, Scarlet, Hannah, Marcella, and Bubba."

"It might become six. I think I'll give a nod to Parma John's." She gestured to the restaurant. "Uncle Laz and my brothers still enjoy catering when they have the time. Who knows where this will go. I just want to spend more time promoting people in the wedding business. This is a tough gig, and you all deserve to do well. Before long it might be a Terrific Ten or an Easygoing Eleven."

"Easygoing Eleven?" Scarlet let out an unladylike snort. "Not a very fitting description of most of us on the list. What about Energetic Eleven? Or maybe Eager Eleven?"

"Nah, *eager* makes us sound too . . . eager." I shrugged.

"Okay then, what about the Exhilarating Eleven? Or maybe"—she snapped her fingers—"the *Evangelical* Eleven! That's perfect! We're all Christians, after all."

Bella slapped herself on the forehead. "If you keep this up, I'm going to start calling you the *Exasperating* Eleven."

This got a laugh out of all of us.

"Ooo, I know," I said after a moment's thought. "What about the Elegant Eleven?"

"Perfect." Bella gave me an admiring look. "But who knows how many vendors we'll end up with when all is said and done. The point is, you'll always be one of the top vendors on my list. All of you."

I hardly knew how to thank her. Scarlet didn't seem to have any trouble. She jumped up and threw her arms around Bella's neck. "You're going to be the best sister-in-law ever!"

"Thank you. And best of all, we'll work out a plan where we offer brides the option of ordering your products directly from Club Wed, which means you guys could come and go as you please from our facility. If you could handle that with whatever else you've got going."

"I can handle it," I said with a smile. "Trust me."

"Me too." Scarlet's nose wrinkled. "Well, I think I can. I do have a honeymoon to go on first." Her cheeks flamed pink and she laughed.

"Ooo, I just thought of more folks to add to the list," Bella said. "The Splendora Sisters. They're the best wedding singers around. Their forties tunes are amazing." She grinned, obviously happy with her choice. "And the band! We have connections to an amazing swing band. Their leader is a personal friend of the family."

"So how will this work?" I asked.

"A lot of brides come to me with vendors already chosen. I would never presume to convince them to change their minds. But a lot of them come in completely clueless and ask for my recommendations. I used to just hand them a list of several possibilities. But why not offer them one-stop shopping?"

"I love it!" Scarlet let out a little squeal.

"I have a lot of other things on my mind too," Bella said. "D.J. and I have been talking about opening a Club Wed up in Splendora."

"Where's that, again?" I asked.

"It's a little town north of Houston by about an hour. D.J. is from Splendora. His uncle runs a truck stop there."

"And you're going to run the facility there too?" I asked. "How will that work?"

"Well, not at the truck stop, silly. I'm thinking

about building a little wedding chapel in the woods."

"Remember, Aunt Willy lives there now too," Scarlet said. "And she has a lot of experience with brides, so she'll be a big help."

"Oh, that's right."

Bella shrugged. "Just thinking about the possibilities. In my mind's eye, I see a sweet little chapel—sort of a town-and-country feel. The simplicity of the country with the convenience of an in-town wedding. I've spent hours sketching out my ideas. And I've got the perfect location in mind, if I can get it for the right price. It's on the prettiest woodsy street called Hill and Dale. I can picture it now."

"Wow."

"I know." Bella sighed. "I'm such a dreamer. Would you believe I've even given thought to planning destination weddings?"

"Destination weddings?"

"Sure. For instance, a bride came to me recently, asking if I would coordinate her wedding in Saint Thomas."

"Saint Thomas!" I could almost feel the sand between my toes now.

"I know, right?" Bella grinned. "I told her I would think about it but didn't give a firm answer. Not sure about the logistics. But this particular bride needed more than a coordinator. She wanted someone to design the dresses with a tropical flair—the wedding gown and the brides-maids dresses, I mean."

After talking with Bella, I felt absolutely dizzy. Her ideas, though wonderful, overwhelmed me on a thousand levels. When I pondered her destination wedding idea, I couldn't help but think of Mama, how she'd longed to travel.

Suddenly, I gasped. "Bella. My mother's a travel agent."

"Ooo, that's right." She clamped a hand over her mouth and then pulled it away. "Do you think she would be interested in helping me if I ever decided to do the destination wedding thing?"

"She would probably flip." My heart soared as I thought about my mother getting a chance to spread her wings a little.

"Well, one thing at a time." Bella reached to squeeze my hand. "I'm going to give you an assignment. We've got to get your business up and running. You'll need a name, and you'll have to file for a business license with the state." She went into a lengthy explanation of all I would need to do but lost me somewhere after the words *sales tax*.

We ended our lunch a few minutes later, but I thought about Bella's comments all the way back to the house. When Mimi and I arrived home, I scoured the web for business models. Read every article on how to grow a company from the ground up.

After several hours, I felt stiff and sore from sitting hunched over the computer so long, yet invigorated for the task ahead. Bella was right. If I worked hard enough, I could achieve my dreams. Didn't Ginger Rogers practice for hours on end? Sure she did. If she could land on her feet, so could I. I wouldn't do it in sparkling dance shoes with Fred Astaire on my arm, but I would prove my worth. No doubt about it.

I came from a long line of hardworking women, after all. Mimi Carmen had spent thirty years at the phone company before retiring. Mama worked harder than almost anyone I knew, though you couldn't judge it from her paycheck.

Maybe that was the point: the size of the check was not a true reflection of the workload. Pity those poor men who slaved away in the south Texas heat digging ditches and doing electrical work. If I felt so much angst about not working my way up the corporate ladder, how did they feel? And many of them had large families—lots of mouths to feed. Me? I just had Mama and Mimi Carmen, and we were managing okay.

Mostly.

But my situation would get better now. I knew in my gut—in my spirit, as Bella would say. Yes, my situation would improve, and I would get to do the thing I was put on this earth to do—design gowns for brides.

# 22

## You'll Never Get Rich

*Why didn't you tell me I was in love with you?*

FRED ASTAIRE

Later that same afternoon Jordan called to say he needed to swing by my place to drop something off. With him being so secretive and all, I could hardly imagine what it might be. So when he showed up with a copy of his completed article, I had to smile.

"I want you to read it before I turn it in." He beamed, obviously proud of himself.

"But . . . how did you manage to cover the information about Nicolette's gown when we're not sure how all of that is going to turn out?"

"I told you I'd give the whole piece a different slant, and I did. Read it, Gabi."

And so I did. I took a seat on the living room sofa and read every glorious word. I paused when I reached the part where he talked about the role that alterations specialists play in the implementation of a bride's wedding dress. And I couldn't help but smile when I came to the part where he mentioned the dress forms. But I lost my breath when he described the fact that Nicolette planned to wear both dresses on her big day.

"How did you know?" I asked.

"She called me last night to fill me in. I think it's the best possible solution, don't you?" Jordan leaned back against the sofa.

"As long as Demetri calls off his lawyers, yes."

"He's just bluffing, Gabi. Besides, this decision on Nicolette's part means I'm free to promote both you and Demetri in the article."

"He will still be angry to see my name listed."

"That's too bad. He'll have to get over it." Jordan shrugged. "Who knows? Maybe one day he'll play nice. There's really not room for too much animosity in the wedding business, after all. Paths eventually cross . . . and cross again."

"True. I'm just so relieved that you mentioned Haute Couture by name and raved about Demetri's designs." Relief flooded over me. "Hopefully that will pacify him for now."

"I'm sure it will."

"I had a great talk with Bella today," I added. "And I have so much to tell you, but I'm swamped with work. Scarlet's coming by tomorrow after church to try on her gown, and I've been thinking a lot about Nicolette's dress. I didn't make the connection before, but both weddings are on the same weekend."

"Oh, wow. My heart goes out to you." He looked genuinely concerned at this news.

"Yeah, tell me about it." I rose and began to pace the living room. "Scarlet is getting married on the first Saturday in October, and Nicolette is getting married the night before. A Friday night wedding. Both are at Club Wed."

"I feel for Bella too. I'm sure this happens a lot." Jordan stood and took a few steps in my direction.

"Me too. I really don't know how she does it."

"She has a team," Jordan said. "That's the answer. You've got to be surrounded by people who will support you. Help you. People who know the business."

"Oh, that's what Bella and I were talking about." I took a seat once more and spent the next several minutes filling him in on the conversation I'd had with Bella and Scarlet over lunch.

"Now that's the best news I've heard all day," he said. "If you've got Bella and her family on your team, then you're good to go. You don't need Demetri anyway."

"That's what she said. I guess I'm reaching the point where I really need to stop giving him such a hold on my life."

"What do you mean?"

"Nearly every decision I've made over the past few years has been with him in mind. If I've been Cinderella, then he's been the evil stepmother."

"Meaning?"

"Meaning, I've made every decision wondering

if he would flip out." I paused and thought about it. "I can't imagine what it will be like not to have to worry about that anymore."

"Pretty freeing, I would say."

"A lot of things are freeing now," I said. "And that's a good thing."

"A very good thing. The only thing that's not free is your time, and I'm a little bummed about that. I was hoping to take you out to an early dinner tonight. Maybe spend the afternoon together before going to a restaurant."

"Aw, I'm sorry. But you're welcome to hang out with me while I work and then stay for dinner. Mimi Carmen's got tamales started in the kitchen."

"I'd love that. Tamales sound great."

"Well, FYI, she's having someone over for dinner tonight. It's a big secret, but I've got it figured out."

"Are you telling me she has a date?" When I nodded, he lowered his voice to say, "Daniel?"

"Yep. He's coming by at seven. But in the meantime, prepare yourself for some noise. We've got a toddler in the house."

"A toddler?"

"Bella's little girl, Rosa-Earline. Mimi calls her Rosie. She's in the kitchen in her little . . . whatever you call that thing she sits in. She'll be here until 6:30. Bella's got an appointment this afternoon and didn't have anyone to watch her. Mimi is in her element, I think."

"And your mother? How's she taking it?"

"Mama's at work. Those Splendora Sisters are keeping her busy these days. Apparently they've got quite a few scheduling issues for their upcoming tour."

"I can't even imagine touring with them, can you?" He tilted his head back and laughed. "The hair spray alone would be my undoing. A man could choke to death with that much spray in the air. Put a hole in the ozone layer."

We had a good laugh at that image. Still, I couldn't help but think that my mother would fit right in with those gals and their eccentricities. They would be good for her.

"You need some help with Nicolette's dress?" Jordan's words interrupted my thoughts.

"You have no idea. Do you mind?"

He shook his head. "I told you, I'm a whiz with fabrics. Just live and learn from the master."

Turned out his cutting skills were really good. He said it had something to do with clipping all of his articles from the pages of various magazines and newspapers over the years. Regardless, I led him to my sewing room and put him to work on the pattern pieces. He kept me in stitches—laughing—as we worked side by side. The after-noon passed, and I found myself cocooned in a sweet sort of contentment I'd never felt while working. Certainly not while working for Demetri.

Jordan spent much of the afternoon in a state of playful bantering, doing anything he could to make me smile. Oh, how I loved hanging out with him. Did he realize how much?

"Where did you come from?" I asked at one point.

He glanced up from the pattern pieces to answer. "New York. My whole family's from Long Island."

"No. Where did you *come* from? As in, what planet? What fairy tale? You're not like any other guy I've known."

This got a panicked look from him. "I hope that's a good thing. I'm all guy, trust me. Don't let that earlier comment about laces and trims fool you."

"Ha! I don't mean it like that. I'm just saying that you're so good at talking to me about, well, all sorts of things. You make me really . . . comfortable."

"It's a gift. What can I say? Besides, I love spending time with you, doing . . ." He gestured to the fabrics scattered around the room. "This."

"You're serious?"

"Yes. It's the best date I've ever been on. One I'll never forget."

"You've got to be kidding." I brushed a loose hair out of my face and stared at him to see if he was joking. "Cutting out pattern pieces is the best date you've been on?"

"It is." Jordan walked my way, pattern pieces floating through the air and landing on the hardwood floor. When he reached for my hand, I gave it willingly, then allowed myself to be swept into his arms. Jordan pressed a couple of tiny kisses onto the end of my nose. "It's perfect because you're here."

"I think I get it now," I whispered. "Why Ginger was so comfortable in Fred's arms."

"Oh?" Jordan's lips traveled up my cheek. "Why is that?"

"They were a perfect fit."

"A perfect fit, eh?"

Tilting my head back, I peered at his face—that gorgeous, sweet expression, half playful, half serious. I leaned lightly into him, tipping my face toward his. As his lips met mine, I was lost in the beauty of the moment. When the kiss ended, we lingered in one another's arms.

"So, let's get to the bottom of this," Jordan said after a few seconds of blissful silence.

"This . . . what?"

He pointed to the poster on my wall. "Your fascination with Ginger Rogers. Where did it come from, anyway?"

"Ah." I paused, not sure if I really wanted to explain. "I don't have many great memories of my dad," I said after a bit of awkward silence. "But I do have a pretty vivid memory of him taking me to the old Marquee Theater when I was a kid to see a Fred Astaire–Ginger Rogers movie. *Top Hat*, I think."

"I always loved that movie."

"Me too. Might sound weird, but remembering that my dad actually cared enough about me to take me to the theater to see them dance on the big screen has brought me some comfort." I shrugged. "I know it's crazy, but maybe I feel like Fred and Ginger link me to my dad in some way."

"Have you thought about trying to get in touch with him?" Jordan's expression reflected gentle understanding and concern.

"Oh, I hear from him a couple of times a year. Usually when he's had too much to drink or wants me to invest in one of his many network marketing schemes." A little sigh worked its way out. "It's silly to think that a movie—or an actor— could take me back to a pleasant childhood memory, but Fred and Ginger just have that power."

"Well, let God use that memory of your dad— the one in the theater—to heal you from whatever pain you might have to struggle through related to your dad. And remember, God's a much better dancing partner."

"Yes, but does he have the keys to the Marquee Theater?" I quirked a brow.

"He has the keys to the kingdom. I would imagine the Marquee Theater would be small potatoes in comparison."

"True, true." Though I really had no clue what the whole "keys to the kingdom" comment meant. Still, I could picture God standing there with a huge ring of keys in his hand.

Keys.

The sermon about forgiveness surfaced again, and I thought about Scarlet's comment about forgiving my father. Setting him—and myself—free from prison.

Weird.

"Anyway, I'm glad you explained the Ginger and Fred thing to me." Jordan's words interrupted my thoughts. "And you're right. They were the perfect fit. Comfortable. But . . ." He traced my cheek with his fingertip. "If we're being perfectly honest, on the inside I'm a nervous wreck when I'm around you."

"You are?" This certainly took me by surprise.

"Mm-hmm." He brushed his lips against my cheek. "You know that feeling you get when you're cutting into a brand-new yard of expensive fabric?"

I nodded but couldn't speak, what with the tingles running all the way from my head to my toes.

"Well, that's the same feeling I get when I'm thinking about kissing you. I'm so excited I can hardly wait. But I'm also a little scared."

"Of what?" My words came out as a whisper.

"Of messing things up. Of moving too fast. Of scaring you away."

"You're not going to scare me away, Jordan," I said. I wanted to add, "So shut up and kiss me already," but I didn't have to. His lips met mine for the most passionate kiss yet.

I remained in his arms, my heart thumping as never before. Well, until Mimi Carmen cleared her throat behind us. "Sorry, folks, but there's a little girl crying in the living room and I can't get her to calm down."

I felt my cheeks grow warm, so I took a step back and turned to her as if nothing were out of the ordinary. "Give her to Jordan," I said and winked at him. "He has a gift with toddlers."

Turned out he did have a gift with toddlers. Little Rosie was all smiles after just a couple of minutes in his welcoming arms. By the time Bella arrived at 6:30, her daughter and Jordan were both sleeping soundly on the couch, with Mimi Carmen watching her prerecorded show from the recliner. While putting on . . . makeup? No way! Mimi rarely wore the stuff. But sure enough, I caught her in the act of dabbing on lipstick and powder-ing her cheeks. She shoved the makeup bag into the seat and rose when Bella entered the room.

Bella took one look at the snoozing duo on the sofa and grinned. "What have we here?" she asked.

I brushed a loose hair from my face and smiled. "He has a gift with small children, apparently."

"And he's sharing it with us." Bella smiled as she gazed down at the two of them. "That's very generous."

She lifted Rosa-Earline from Jordan's arms, and he stirred. One eye opened to a slit, and the most delicious smile lit his face. "I was teaching her how to rest," he said. "She's a fast learner."

"Mm-hmm." Bella nuzzled her daughter's cheek against hers. "I hope she didn't rest so long that she stays up all night."

"Nah. We've only been sleeping . . ." He glanced at the clock on the wall. "Two hours?" At this revelation he looked panicked.

"It's okay," I said. "I got a lot done while you were sleeping."

We spent the next few minutes chatting with Bella. She left around 6:45, just as Mama came in the door from work. Daniel arrived about five minutes after that. Not that he managed to get a word in edgewise. Turned out Mama was in a talkative mood, having spent the afternoon with the Splendora Sisters.

"They're going to have the trip of a lifetime," she explained. "I booked it today."

We gathered in our little dining room around the table, which came alive with conversation. Daniel and Mimi discussed the music at church, offering their opinions on contemporary music. Jordan tried to chime in a time or two but happened to be on the opposing team, since he enjoyed the drums and all. Mama was like Switzerland—she remained neutral. Well, either that or she was enjoying her tamales.

When we finished eating, Mimi headed into the kitchen to fetch the tres leches cake.

Jordan cleared his throat. "I have an announcement to make."

"An announcement?" Mama's eyes lit up, and I knew she expected him to drop to one knee right then and there. Instead, he took my hand and gave it a squeeze. "I've signed us up to take dancing lessons."

"Say what?" I must've misunderstood.

"Ballroom." A masculine laugh followed. "And yes, I'm serious. I've been thinking about your fascination with Fred and Ginger and decided that I needed to get inspired."

"But I told you . . . I have two left feet."

"Maybe Ginger did at one time too." He continued to hold my hand. "Gabi, when you want something bad enough, you work hard to get it. I'm . . ." His cheeks flushed. "I'm trying to woo you, okay?"

"Well, if that isn't the sweetest thing ever," Mimi said as she entered the room with the cake in hand. "Just remember, Prince Charming, she turns into a pumpkin at midnight."

This got a laugh out of Daniel, who rose to help Mimi put the cake down.

"Doubtful." Jordan gave me a funny look.

"Though I'm trying to imagine what you'd look like in bright orange. As round as a ball."

"On the ballroom dance floor? Pretty comedic. And I'm going to be as round as a ball if I keep eating like this."

"Me too." He rubbed his belly and laughed.

"But I'll take your dance lessons. Just let me know when we start, okay?"

"The class starts in mid-November. You'll have these two wedding dresses behind you by then."

"Okay, okay." I grabbed the knife and cut a slice of the cake. "Better go ahead and get some shin guards now, though. And some steel-toed boots to protect your feet."

"Duly noted. I shall shop tomorrow. Oh, and by the way, the reason I've signed us up to take ballroom lessons is because we're going to be in the audience when *Dancing with the Stars* comes to Galveston in December. They're on tour, and you-know-who is making a guest appearance."

"B-B-Brock Benson?" My mother dropped her fork, and it clattered to the table.

"Yep. He and Cheryl Burke are dancing together, and we'll be the first in line to see them. I have connections, being in the publishing biz and all." He squared his shoulders. "I got us tickets." Jordan gestured to the group at the table. "Actually, I got a handful of tickets, so I think we're all good to go, if that sounds all right with you ladies."

The squeals that followed were deafening. Daniel didn't appear to know who Brock Benson was, so I explained. "He's a big superstar. He starred in several pirate movies."

"I haven't been to a movie theater since 2002 when my wife passed." Daniel took a bite of his cake.

"We'll have to remedy that," Mimi said. "Trust me, we see every movie that Brock Benson makes."

She didn't bother to mention that we usually rented them instead of going to the theater. These days fitting in the seat at the movie theater presented a challenge for Mimi. Then again, if she kept eating like she did tonight—only one tamale and a teensy-tiny sliver of cake—a trip to the movies might not be out of the question before long.

"Brock came to the island last Christmas for Dickens on the Strand," Jordan explained. "He was the grand marshal of the parade. They tried to get him to come back this year, but he's too busy. His wife just had a baby."

"Oh, I had no idea."

"Brock has been nominated for an Academy Award, and his wife will need a new dress, one that will be seen by thousands of people. What do you think?"

"Are you serious?"

"Sure am. I have no doubt Bella could arrange it. Just say the word."

"I-I would be honored."

"Think of the thousands—no, millions—of people who will see it. Perfect promotion for your business."

I thought about his words as we nibbled on our cake. Man. What was up with all of the lucky breaks lately? I'd caught a thousand lucky stars. First Scarlet's aunt decided to name a cake after me. Then Bella agreed to put me at the top of her vendors list. Now Brock Benson's wife might wear one of my gowns on television? How did I get to be so lucky?

Then again, maybe it had nothing to do with luck. Maybe it had a little something to do with prayer. I'd been doing a lot of praying lately.

When we finished our cake and coffee, I offered to do the dishes so that Mimi and Daniel could have some time together in the living room. Mama seemed content to slip off to her room to read a book. Jordan tagged along on my heels to the kitchen, where he helped load the dishwasher. Just as I closed the door, he took the dishcloth from my hands and set it on the counter.

"Is everything okay?" I asked.

"Mm-hmm. It is now. I've just been dying to kiss you ever since you agreed to take ballroom lessons with me." He pressed a tiny kiss onto the tip of my nose.

"I still can't believe you did that."

"I can't either, to be honest. Very out of

character for me. But when I'm around you, I just lose all control of my senses." Another kiss followed, this one on my cheek. "You make me do things I wouldn't ordinarily do, Gabi. I'm starting to think you've cast some sort of spell on me."

I was pretty sure it was the other way around, but didn't say so. Instead, I grinned and said, "It's my fairy godmother. That's what I pay her to do."

"Then she's mighty good at it. You might want to give her a raise."

I'd just started to explain that I couldn't possibly do that now that I didn't have a job, but I never had the chance. Jordan slipped his arms around my waist and drew me closer. My arms instinctively wrapped around his neck, and I leaned into him as he gave me a kiss I wouldn't soon forget.

In that moment, I thought back to what he'd said earlier: "Best date ever!"

Right now, with the handsomest fella on Galveston Island sweeping me off my feet, I had to agree.

# 23

## Lady in the Dark

Ginger Rogers was, as a partner, a faithful reflection of everything that Astaire intended. She could even shed her own light.

ARLENE CROCE

The next few weeks sped by at whirlwind pace. Somewhere between the designing, cutting, sewing, and fitting, I managed to sneak in some precious time with Jordan. I also met with Bella to get the ball rolling on the new Vendors Square at Club Wed. Already the calls were pouring in from brides looking for one-of-a-kind specialty dresses. Looked like my dance card was filling up rapidly.

On the weekend before Scarlet's wedding, Bella threw a party for the bridesmaids. A slumber party, no less. On a personal level, I had a lot to celebrate—the successful completion of Scarlet's dress and the paycheck I'd received upon finishing Nicolette's gown as well. Getting those two dresses behind me had changed my entire perspective on life. Now I had the confidence to move forward with my line: Gabriella's.

Not tonight, however. No, tonight was all about partying with the girls.

"Aunt Rosa and Uncle Laz are in New York filming an episode with Bobby Flay," Bella explained as we arrived at the Rossi home. "So we've got their suite upstairs to ourselves."

She was wrong about that. We'd no sooner eaten our pizza and settled in to play a game when Rosa and Laz entered the foyer, yawning.

"Aunt Rosa?" Bella rushed to meet her. "I thought you weren't coming back until tomorrow afternoon."

"I know, I know." Rosa groaned. "But Bobby has the flu, so they're postponing until week after next."

"I'm beat." Laz yawned again and headed up the stairs. "You girls don't make too much noise. This old man needs his beauty sleep."

We spent the next ten minutes clearing our stuff out of their suite and moving it across the hall to one of the smaller bedrooms. I couldn't quite figure out how the four of us—Bella, Hannah, Scarlet, and me—were going to sleep in one bed, but surely Bella had a plan.

Turned out she had a plan for our entertainment that night as well.

"We're going to play a game." She pulled out a little bowl filled with slips of paper. "Twenty Questions."

"Twenty Questions?" Scarlet wrinkled her nose. "I don't like the sound of that."

"Yes." Bella situated the bowl in the middle of

the bed, and we all gathered around it. "I've got twenty questions written down on slips of paper. When it's your turn, you reach in the bowl and grab one, then open it and answer the question. They're fun. And perfectly safe."

"Are you sure?" Scarlet did not look convinced.

"Very sure. I'll even go first, to show you." Bella reached into the bowl and came out with a slip of paper. After opening it, she read the words aloud. "What was the name of the first movie you ever remember seeing?" Her face lit in a smile. "You guys remember the old Marquee Theater off Rosenberg?"

At once, the story I'd told Jordan about my father taking me to the theater to see *Top Hat* resurfaced.

"That place hasn't been open in years," Hannah said.

"I went there once," I said and then shrugged. No point in sharing any more than that.

"Me too," Bella said. "When I was a little girl."

"Same here."

"Wouldn't it be funny if it turned out to be the same night?" She laughed. "I'm trying to remember the name of the movie Aunt Rosa took me to see. I just remember it had Frank Sinatra in it." After a moment, she snapped her fingers. "Ooo, I know. *Anchors Aweigh*."

"I went with my . . ." *No, Gabi. Don't mention*

310

*your father tonight.* "I went to see *Top Hat*, a Fred Astaire and Ginger Rogers movie."

"Well, duh." Scarlet chuckled. "You're crazy about them."

"Always have been. I used to dance around my bedroom and pretend to be like Ginger. Never really had a real gown, but I did have a ruffled slip that made a pretty good dance dress."

"So you never took dance lessons?" Bella asked.

"No. I keep telling everyone I have two left feet."

Bella rolled her eyes. "Please. I'm sure you could learn."

"I don't know." I shrugged. "Maybe."

"I remember my first movie." Scarlet lit into a lengthy story about her favorite old Lucille Ball movie—something about a trailer. I didn't hear much, though. My thoughts remained on the image of my father dancing with me at that theater. Why did this keep coming up?

In the middle of Scarlet's impassioned story about Lucille Ball, she stopped and glanced at Hannah, who looked ill.

"Ugh. Sorry. I guess the pizza isn't settling so well on my stomach," Hannah said. "I haven't been feeling so great lately."

Bella gave her a suspicious look. "What do you mean?"

"Not sure. But all day long I've been queasy. Can't seem to shake it."

"Mm-hmm."

Hannah reached for the bowl, clearly wanting to change the subject. "Let's move on, shall we?" She opened a piece of paper and read, "What's your biggest pet peeve?" After a moment, she said, "I guess my biggest pet peeve is having people crowd in around me. Must be the photographer in me. I like my space."

"How's that working out for you now that you and Drew are married?" Scarlet asked.

Hannah's cheeks flushed the prettiest shade of pink. "Oh, I don't mind Drew being close. He doesn't count."

"Mm-hmm. Thought so." Scarlet turned to face me. "What about you, Gabi?"

"I hate the smell of nail polish, especially in confined areas. I guess you could call that a pet peeve."

"So I'm assuming you don't spend a lot of time at the nail salon?" Hannah laughed.

"No. I'd probably run screaming from the room, to be honest."

"Where did this nail polish fetish begin?" Scarlet asked. "I sense a story here."

"Alyssa Fairfield."

"Who's that?" Hannah's brow wrinkled.

"You mean you haven't heard of Houston's former Miss Teen USA? She came to Demetri for a wedding dress, which he designed. Next thing you know, she's mine."

"Meaning? She needed alterations?"

"The whole dress pretty much had to be made over to her specifications." I shuddered at the memory. "But nothing I did satisfied her. The girl drove me out of my ever-lovin' mind. She sat behind me and watched my every move. While talking about me on her cell phone to some friend of hers . . . and not in a good way."

"As if you couldn't hear her?"

"Yeah. But the worst—the absolute worst—was the nail polish. She apparently had some sort of fixation with her nails. The woman changed her polish every single day, and usually in my little alterations room. I can't tell you how many shades of pink I heard about over those three weeks. I think the smell must've affected her ability to reason correctly. Mine too, actually. The longer I worked on her dress, the loopier I got. And she was downright unreasonable."

"What about you, Scarlet?" Bella asked.

"I can't stand the taste of fondant," Scarlet said. "That's my pet peeve. All of the bakers use it to decorate, and the cakes look great, but they taste icky."

"My pet peeve is people who interrupt," Bella said. "They really get on my—"

"Next question." Scarlet laughed and then grabbed another slip from the bowl. "Favorite reality star."

"Ooo, pick me, pick me!" Hannah raised her

hand. "Derek Hough. *Dancing with the Stars*." For a minute there, she looked like she might swoon.

Until Scarlet slapped her on the arm. "You're married."

"I may be married, but I'm not blind. Besides, Drew knows about my fascination with Derek. He also knows that I plan to be on *Dancing with the Stars* one day myself."

"You're a ballroom dancer?" I asked.

"Nah." She waved a hand and chuckled. "But a girl can dream, can't she? Besides, I'd be willing to learn if Derek would choose me for his partner."

"Well, speaking of *Dancing with the Stars* . . ." I thought back to Jordan's recent announcement. "Jordan and I are going to be in the audience when they come to town in a couple of months."

"Me too!" Hannah laughed. "I wouldn't miss it for the world. In fact, I was one of the first to get my tickets."

This led to a conversation about Bella and some of the others going to a live shooting of *Dancing with the Stars* in Hollywood.

I turned to Scarlet, more curious than anything. "Who's your favorite reality star?"

"Hmm." Her eyes narrowed to slits. "That would be a toss-up between Duff on *Ace of Cakes* and Buddy Valastro on *Cake Boss*."

"Never heard of either," I admitted.

"Are you serious?" She appeared shocked at this

admission. *"Ace of Cakes* and *Cake Boss*? Don't you watch the food shows, girl?"

"Nope. Not much, anyway. Only when Mimi has them playing on the TV, but even then I don't pay attention." Now, if she'd asked if I watched *Project Runway* or *Say Yes to the Dress*, I could've given her a better answer.

I reached for the bowl. "My turn." I pulled a slip of paper out and smiled as I read the words. "Ooo, this is a good one. Name your biggest supporter."

Bella laughed and then said, "Spanx." She slapped her knee. "Kidding, kidding! But I am a girl who likes her Lycra. Wouldn't leave home without it, especially after having two kids. Things just aren't where they used to be." She got control of herself and looked at me. "Sorry, it was your turn, Gabi. You answer the question."

"I think you guys are my biggest supporters. You've all been great to me. So encouraging. And Mimi Carmen and Mama too." A long pause followed as I thought of the one person who, in recent weeks, had proven to be a huge support in my life. "And Jordan."

"He's a great guy, Gabi," Bella said. "I like him a lot."

"Me too." I felt my cheeks warm as I said the words.

"My biggest supporter would have to be Drew," Hannah said, her hand moving to her stomach. "But my parents are great too. My dad is a typical

Irishman through and through. Very dedicated to his family but a little on the stubborn side."

"Maybe I'm the only PK on the planet who would answer this way, but I'd have to go with my dad too." Scarlet's eyes grew misty.

"PK?" I asked. "What's that?"

"Preacher's kid," Hannah and Scarlet said in unison.

"You're clearly not up on the latest church lingo," Hannah said. "We'll have to remedy that." She went off on a tangent about church-related chatter, but my thoughts were elsewhere. They'd lost me back on the conversation about their fathers. Must be nice to have a dad support you like that.

Bella reached into the bowl and opened another slip of paper. "Most romantic moment." A giggle followed. "I, um, well, I'm not sure I can share that publicly."

We'd just started to press her on the matter when the sound of a man's voice raised in song filled the air.

"Do you hear . . . singing?" Bella rose and walked to the window. "Doesn't sound like it's coming from downstairs. Not inside, anyway."

"I hear it too." Scarlet joined her at the window. Together they opened it and the song grew louder.

"Maybe Drew's up to his tricks again," Hannah said as she rose from the bed and walked to the window. "He wasn't thrilled when I told him I wanted to spend the night here. This might be his way to get me back home again."

"Typical honeymooner." Bella laughed.

"Doesn't sound like him, though." Hannah leaned out the open window. "Nope. I don't know who that is."

I pressed into the space next to her and gazed out into the shadows, the sound of the tenor voice clearer than ever at this point. Down below, on the far side of the lawn, I could see a man's shadow. His voice, now familiar, captivated me.

"Wait a minute. That's Jordan." Scarlet turned my way. "Did you tell him you were going to be here tonight?"

"Sure, but I didn't think anything of it." I leaned forward to double-check. "Yeah, that's definitely him. I can tell by the broad shoulders. Mmm. Quite a lovely shadow, I don't mind saying."

His sweet love song filled the air. I couldn't make out all of the words to the unfamiliar tune but managed to get "night and day, day and night" out of it. When the song ended, he called out to me. "Gabriella Delgado, your presence is requested on the front lawn."

I leaned out the window and did my best to shush him. "You're going to wake up the whole Rossi family," I said. "It's after midnight."

"Yes, and we all know what happens to you at

midnight. That's why I came when I did, to see if you really turn into a cinder girl."

From the window next to mine, Rosa's voice rang out. "What's up with all of the singing out here? Don't you know the old people are trying to sleep?"

This was followed by "Can't a fella get any rest?" from Laz.

"Better go down, Gabi," Bella said. "I don't think Prince Charming's going to wait all night."

I rushed down the stairs and opened the front door of her house, still astounded to see Jordan at this hour. "What are you doing here?"

"Oh, just needed to see my girl." He took hold of my hand and led me to the swing on the veranda.

"At midnight?" I asked as I took the spot next to him.

"Yep. Hope you don't mind the interruption."

"I never mind when it's you."

"Great line, Gabi!" Scarlet's voice rang out from the window above, and for the first time I realized we weren't exactly alone.

Now Aunt Rosa chimed in. "Would you mind speaking up? The old folks are hard of hearing, and we're not getting all of this."

Laz's words, "Let them have their privacy," were followed by the closing of a window.

Jordan laughed. "I had an interview at the Galleria in Houston today and saw something in

318

one of the stores that I thought you might like. Couldn't wait to give it to you." He pulled out a box and passed it to me. "Open it."

I unwrapped the paper and opened the little box to find the most intricate glass Cinderella carriage inside. I'd never seen anything so beautiful. Must have cost him a fortune too, based on the Swarovski tag. "Jordan . . ." I hardly knew what to say. The unexpected gift took my breath away.

"Do you like it?" he asked.

"Like it? I love it." I turned the delicate piece around to examine it from the back.

"Did you say love?"

"Yes. It's perfect."

He paused, and I could sense that he was struggling for words. "Well, um . . . speaking of love . . ."

Love? Were we speaking of love?

As his eyes met mine, I felt a surge of emotion. I placed the little carriage back in its box. When Jordan whispered the words, "I love you," I realized the true reason for his visit. He hadn't just come to whisk me off to the ball in a crystal carriage. He'd come to share his heart with me.

What was a girl to do? When a fella says, "I love you," there's really only one way to respond. My whispered "I love you too" was followed by the sweetest kiss we'd ever shared.

Well, sweet until Scarlet hollered out, "Woo-hoo!" from the upstairs window.

I heard the click of a window from Rosa and Laz's room, and before long an unfamiliar song played over us.

"Is that Frank Sinatra?" Jordan asked after a moment.

"Sounds like it."

I'd never heard that particular song before, but the words "dancing in the dark" caught my attention.

"I'm pretty sure someone is giving us instructions to dance." Jordan reached for my hand, and I rose and let him lead me across the veranda and down the front steps onto the walkway. From there, the moonlight hovered overhead, a lovely orb in the sky, offering the perfect ambience. Jordan pulled me into his arms and kissed me soundly before leading me in a dance I wouldn't soon forget.

Okay, so I had two left feet, but who cared?

Obviously not Prince Charming. He swept me away on a lovely cloud, the sweet croonings of Frank Sinatra floating down around us. From up above, my support team—stronger than any Lycra product—oohed and aahed, chiming in from time to time with their thoughts on how we were doing. As the song carried on, my friends disappeared from view, but they returned as the song came to an end. I looked up and had to laugh.

"Do you see that?" I nudged Jordan, who glanced up as well.

Bella, Scarlet, and Hannah all held scorecards in their hands. I could barely make out the scores at first, with the light from the bedroom shining behind the ladies and not in front, but finally realized the scores ranged from a 9.5 to a perfect 10.

I had to give the moment a ten as well. Maybe even an eleven. And as soon as Jordan stopped kissing me, I would let him know.

# 24

## Royal Wedding

When two people love each other, they don't look at each other; they look in the same direction.

GINGER ROGERS

The days before "wedding weekend" were filled with ups and downs. I fended off calls from Demetri, who was still anxious about Nicolette's gown choice, and I took calls from new brides anxious to see my sketches. On Tuesday I met with a petite blonde from Houston to discuss a Hawaiian-themed gown, and on Thursday I took measurements for a bride in her golden years who was marrying again after years of being widowed.

By the time Friday arrived, I could hardly wait to see Nicolette and Scarlet walk the aisle in their respective gowns. I arrived at Club Wed about twenty minutes before Nicolette's ceremony and stopped by the bride's room. I found her inside with her bridesmaids, putting finishing touches on her makeup. She turned, and I gasped as I saw her in the dress with her hair upswept and a flawless makeup job.

"Oh, Nicolette."

"Gabi!" She hiked the skirt and barreled my way in a very unladylike fashion. "It's perfect. You're perfect. You've made my day . . ." She giggled. "Perfect!"

"I'm glad you like it."

"Like it? I love it. Oh, and so does Ashley. Have you met my friend Ashley?" She took me by the hand and pulled me across the room to meet a gorgeous young woman with red hair.

"Ashley, this is her! This is Gabi. The one who made my dress."

Ashley grabbed my hand and squealed. "Oh, thank God! I'm so glad you're here. I have to get your card. I just got engaged, and I'm getting married in January. It's going to be the sweetest winter wedding you ever saw. Think snowflakes. Big, beautiful snowflakes!"

She rambled on about her big day, but Nicolette interrupted. "Show her your ring, Ashley!"

As the lovely redhead extended her hand, I glanced down and saw the most exquisite diamond I'd ever laid eyes on. "Wow."

"It's gorgeous." Ashley released an exaggerated sigh. "And the more I stare at it, the more I think my idea for a dress is perfect!"

"Oh?"

"Yes. I want my gown to have a similar feel to the diamonds in my ring." Her nose wrinkled, and for the first time I noticed her freckles. "Does that make sense? I mean, I don't want a diamond dress, but lots of sparkle would be good." She squeezed my hand. "Do you do lots of sparkle? Oh, and the cut of the diamond—did you notice that? All of the different facets put off different colors. Now, I'm not asking for a colorful wedding dress or anything like that, but maybe interesting cuts in the fabric? Different angles? That way the light could pick up the nuances. Am I making any sense at all?"

Before I could answer, Nicolette chimed in. "Ashley, Gabi is a whiz. She can do anything you ask. You should see her sketchbook—it's loaded with the most creative dresses you ever saw. But get her quick, honey, before someone steals her time. She's getting busier every day now that her designs are featured at Club Wed."

"Okay." Ashley nodded. "Well, I'll call you Monday then." She lowered her voice. "Before that Kandy Jamison finds out about you. She just got engaged too. Oh, and Meredith O'Henry. They're going to beat me to the punch if I'm not fast on my feet, and we can't let that happen."

"I guess it's the season for engagements," I said.

"I guess." Ashley grinned. "I just know that Bella has recommended you, and she says that any bride would be lucky to have you."

"Oh, well, Bella's awfully sweet." Embarrassment flooded over me.

"No, she's just awfully honest." Bella's voice

sounded from behind me. "But we can talk about that later. Nicolette, it's time to make that once-in-a-lifetime walk down the aisle. Are you ready?"

All of the girls in the room let out collective squeals, and I backed away from them into the safety of the hallway. Minutes later I watched as Nicolette walked down the aisle. She looked like a million bucks, and judging from the smile on her daddy's face, he felt like she was worth it.

Afterward I looked on with the other guests as Nicolette entered the beautifully decorated reception hall wearing Demetri's gown. She looked lovely, and I took pride in the fact that I'd revamped the top of it to accommodate her . . . well, her changes.

The following morning I woke up early to head to wedding number two. As lovely as Nicolette's had been, I knew it wouldn't compare to this one, because the bride happened to be a dear friend.

As I contemplated our relationship, I realized that God had done something extra special between the two of us over the past few weeks. We'd bonded, and not just over a dress. Our hours at church had been life changing. My current bridesmaid status answered any lingering questions about that.

I decided to wait until I arrived at Scarlet's church to get dressed. I met up with my friends in the tiny office—aka the bride's room—and we dove in, ready to get this party started. Donning my new dress, I stared at my reflection in the mirror.

"You look beautiful," Bella said as she stepped into place alongside me. "And in case I haven't mentioned it a thousand times before, you did a great job on these bridesmaid dresses."

"Yeah, I usually hate bridesmaid dresses," Hannah said as she joined us. "But these are amazing."

"It's the fall colors. I think they work." Indeed, as I stared at our reflections—Bella in a deep purple, Hannah in wine, and me in a shimmering golden-brown—I thought we looked pretty spiffy.

Not as spiffy as the bride, though. When Scarlet finished with her makeup and hair, she donned the princess gown, and we all gasped in unison.

"Oh, Gabi." Scarlet fanned her face, no doubt to keep the tears from coming. "It's exactly what I've dreamed of from the time I was a little girl. It's like you saw inside my head to the picture I'd painted there. How do you do that?"

I couldn't answer the question, really. Mostly I just listened to my brides as they shared their hearts and then leaned on God to do the rest.

God.

Interesting how much I found myself thinking about—and talking to—him these days. In fact, I could hardly remember my life before that awesome day when Bella sat with me on the veranda to talk about the real Prince Charming asking me to dance.

This, of course, made me think of Jordan. I could hardly wait to see him.

But I must wait. I had a wedding to attend. No, not just to attend—to participate in.

Less than an hour later I walked down the aisle carrying a bouquet of fall flowers prepared by Bella's sister-in-law and joined the other ladies at the front of the church. Out in the crowd I caught a glimpse of the Rossi family. Bella's mother was awash in tears. No doubt. This was her son's big day, after all.

My gaze traveled to Mimi Carmen and Mama, who were seated next to Daniel. In the row behind them, the Splendora Sisters squirmed and fussed, trying to get a better look. I couldn't help but notice the buxom trio was fully decked out in glitter and sequins.

Finally the moment arrived. The back doors of the sanctuary opened, and the bride entered on her father's arm. A gasp went up as Scarlet made her way down the aisle in that glorious dress. She looked like a picture in a magazine, a princess ready to meet her prince at the altar.

Glancing over at Armando, I noticed the tears in his eyes. He wasn't the only one. As Scarlet's father reached the front of the church, he switched to his pastoral role, and I noticed he sounded a little choked up. Thank goodness this improved as the ceremony carried on, and he managed to get control of himself in time to ask the couple to share their vows. As they spoke their rehearsed lines, Scarlet and Armando gazed into one another's eyes, pure joy radiating.

I knew that kind of joy. I'd discovered it myself.

As much as I hated to look away from the bride and groom, I had to find Jordan. Ah, there he was, right behind Sister Twila's large hat. He leaned to his right to meet my gaze, and we both smiled. In that moment, unspoken words traveled between us—a thousand "I love yous" followed by promises to go on loving for years to come. I read all of this and more in his eyes.

The ceremony ended with a longer-than-usual kiss from the bride and groom, which got a laugh out of the audience. After the ceremony, Hannah's hubby, Drew, snagged several photos of the wedding party, and then we headed off to Club Wed for the reception. At one point Hannah had to leave the room in a hurry. I had a sneaking suspicion she still didn't feel well.

When I arrived at the wedding facility, I buzzed through the reception hall, amazed at how quickly Bella's team had transformed the room. Whereas last night's high-society theme took my breath away, today's table linens and centerpieces transported me right off to a fairy-tale wonderland. Magical, really, and perfect for light-and-breezy Scarlet, who deserved the very best.

I stopped at the cake table and gasped as I laid eyes on the Gabriella cake design for the first time. Now, I'd seen a lot of cakes in my day, being in the wedding biz and all, but nothing had ever come close to this wonder. Five beautifully balanced tiers showed off every single aspect of the wedding gown I'd created, only in cake form.

Wilhelmina stood behind the table, giving instructions to a team of girls from her bakery who had come to cut and serve the beautiful cake. It seemed like a travesty to cut into it, though!

"How did you do that?" I asked. "It's remarkable."

"Oh, I didn't do anything," she said with a wave of her hand. "It's all you, Gabi. It's your design in sugar."

"Wow."

It felt a little strange, honestly, standing there looking at something that I had created, made over again in another form. Flattering. Off in the distance I heard D.J. Neeley's voice ring out, welcoming the bride and groom as Mr. and Mrs. Armando and Scarlet Rossi.

Scarlet Rossi.

The very words made my heart sing.

Apparently the Rossis were pretty excited about this announcement too. They released a collective shout, and cheers rang out in Italian all across the room. The bride and groom had their first dance, and then they traded partners—

Armando danced with his mother while Scarlet danced with her dad.

I tried not to let my emotions get control of me as I watched Scarlet move across the dance floor in her daddy's arms. Still, I had to look away. Thank goodness when I turned around I found Jordan standing behind me. He slipped his arms around my waist and drew me close, whispering, "You look beautiful" in my ear.

I managed a quiet "Thank you" and nuzzled close.

When the dances ended, Scarlet came rushing my way. "Oh, Gabi, you saw it? The cake? It's perfect, just like my dress. I couldn't have asked for anything more glorious."

"So you don't mind that your old auntie made the cake instead of you?" Wilhelmina asked. "For a while I thought you might be upset that I offered."

"Of course not!" Scarlet laughed. "What bride wants to make her own wedding cake? Are you kidding me? I've been like a chicken with my head cut off. I could barely function these past two days. If not for Mama running the shop for me, I don't know what I would have done."

She carried on until D.J. made the announcement, "Dinner is served." From that moment until the time the reception ended, I enjoyed what Bella called "bridesmaid bliss"—the pure joy that comes with celebrating a friend's special day.

During the meal I kept a watchful eye on Hannah, who still didn't look well. I noticed that Bella kept looking her way too. And Drew—still in photographer mode—appeared to be hovering. Very, very suspicious.

The reception ended on a high note, with the happy couple pulling away in his overly decorated car. I stuck around to help clean the reception hall, but my aching feet finally convinced me I should go home. I said my goodbyes to all of my friends and gave Jordan a kiss to tide us over until our next meeting.

When I left Club Wed, I made the drive down Broadway, taking note of the setting sun in the distance. I turned onto a side street and ended up driving past the old Marquee Theater.

I slowed the car as I passed by. Poor old building. It had certainly seen better days. Felt a lot like the relationship with my dad—alive and thriving one minute, withered the next. My car sputtered and threatened to stall, so I quickly pressed my foot on the accelerator and made up my mind to get past my feelings regarding him.

As I drove, however, another feeling came over me, one I couldn't explain. I thought about the sermon Scarlet's dad had preached on forgiveness. It simply wouldn't leave me alone.

Something made me turn the car around, and before long I found myself in the parking lot of the theater. I turned the car off and clutched the keys in my hand as I stared at the ticket booth. Faded posters of several old movies lined the front wall, and I gazed at them, trying to read the print.

My eyes drifted closed, and I could see myself again, just like I'd seen Scarlet today, floating around the dance floor in her father's arms. My daddy held me tight and twirled me around and around in the front of the theater long after the other moviegoers had gone.

In that moment, with the memories flooding over me, tears flowed. Tears for a little girl whose daddy decided to end the dance too soon, and tears for a father who missed out on his daughter's life.

What happened next could only be explained as a God moment. The tears dried up, and with the twilight skies hovering over me, new hope set in—hope that tomorrow could be different from yesterday, not just with my business, not just with my love life, but with the one secret chamber of my heart that I'd kept locked up all these years. I alone held the key to unlock this prison door, and today was the day to set not only myself free but someone else as well.

I scrambled around inside my purse until I came out with my cell phone. Finding the right number in my address book was tricky, seeing as how I rarely, if ever, used it. And punching the number took courage never before required. Still, with the phone now pressed to my ear, I anticipated what God would do with my courageous act.

When my father answered, it took me a moment to speak. The word "Dad?" came out a little squeaky.

"Gabriella." He spoke my name with fluid motion, the *l*'s rolling off his tongue. "Long time, no see."

I could've said the same thing but didn't.

"How's my girl?"

Ugh. The temptation to end the call right there grabbed hold of me, but I worked through it. "I'm doing okay. Are you busy?"

"No, just watching an old movie on TV."

Ironic.

"I, well, I just wanted to . . . to talk."

A moment's pause on his end almost proved to be my undoing. Until he responded with, "I'd like that, Gabriella. I really would."

In that moment, I looked down at the car keys in my hand and made a decision. I would unlock the prison door . . . and I wouldn't look back.

# 25

# Smoke Gets in Your Eyes

I'm just a hoofer with a spare set of tails.
FRED ASTAIRE

The Monday after the wedding weekend ended, I received a call from Bella, who asked me to come to Club Wed for a vendors meeting. When I arrived at three o'clock, I found that Hannah had already arrived and was helping Bella work on the area. Minutes later I joined them, ready to add another dress to my collection.

I hung the gown on the dress form and stepped back, thrilled with the result. The whole room shimmered, a vast sea of Austrian crystals and intricate beadwork. Several feet away Hannah worked on her area, putting up photos of Nicolette's wedding. She paused and a panicked look crossed her face, then she bolted from the room.

"Is she okay?"

"I hope so." Bella followed after her.

They returned a few minutes later. Hannah still looked pale but seemed more composed. She drew a couple of deep breaths and then went back to work on her photographs. Seconds later, she turned back to face us and blurted out, "We're having a baby!"

I'd known this moment was coming. Had imagined how she might convey the news. Still, the way she delivered it caught me off guard.

Delivered. Ha!

Hannah's announcement prompted a squeal from Bella. The squeal caused Guido, the parrot, to let out a shriek from the foyer, where he sat in his cage.

Laughter bubbled up as I realized how many times I'd suspected as much. "I knew it, Hannah!" I said.

"We found out on Saturday morning, just before the wedding. I mean, I'd suspected for a few days but didn't want to take the test. We've only been married a few months, and, well . . ." Her face turned a lovely shade of pink. "I was worried about what people would say. And we wanted to tell our families first."

"Pooh on what people would say." With a wave of her hand Bella dismissed any concerns on that matter. "It's none of their business. I've known girls who got pregnant on their wedding night."

"True, but there's a lot to think about when you start adding babies to the mix. I mean, it'll change everything at our studio. Thank goodness Drew and I work together. I can pretty much set my hours. So I suppose we can go back and forth, doing photo shoots and taking care of the baby."

"Of course you can," Bella said. "It's going to work out seamlessly. Okay, maybe not seamlessly, but it'll all be fine in the end. Ask me how I know."

I started to say, "How do you know?" just to tease her, but decided against it.

"Did you tell Scarlet?" Bella asked. "She's gonna flip."

"Yes." Hannah giggled. "I couldn't help myself. I told her right after the ceremony. She cried. In a good way, I mean."

"So when you ran out during the photo session after the ceremony—"

"Morning sickness. I was terrified I might lose my cookies during the ceremony. Thank God I didn't."

"Thank God is right." Bella's eyes welled with tears. "I'm thanking him for a lot of things today. For your little blessing. For Scarlet's new life with Armando. For Armando's turnaround over the past year. For all of the wonderful people God has brought into my family's life. Mostly, though, I'm thankful that he gives me the strength to do the things he's called me to do, even when I'm worn out."

This led to a discussion about the marathon wedding weekend she had just lived through, and that led us back to a discussion about the vendors. Moments later, Hannah started looking a little green around the gills. She put her hand to her mouth and shot out of the room without so much as a word.

"Don't worry, she'll be okay." Bella shook her head. "I remember that nauseous-all-the-time stage. It's awful. But she'll be over it soon."

"Sure hope so," I said.

At that very moment someone hollered out a cheery "Yoo-hoo!"

I turned to see the Splendora Sisters entering the room, talking a mile a minute. Then I realized they weren't alone.

"Mama?"

"Hi, Gabi." My mother took a seat and opened a notepad.

"What's going on?" I asked.

"Oh, I asked your mama to join us," Bella said. "Her travel agency has been booking lots of honeymoons for my brides, so it only makes sense. We'll start promoting the company along with the other vendors. And remember how I told you that I was giving thought to offering destination weddings?"

"Right."

"You're the one who suggested I contact your mother to help with that."

My heart swelled with pride that she had carried through and chosen Mama. What a blessing! "Bella, that's great," I managed. "Totally great."

"Maybe not so great." Mama's nose wrinkled, and I could see the concern etched in her brow.

"I have something I need to tell all of you that might change Bella's plan a little." She turned to face me. "Gabi, you know I've always longed to travel."

"Right."

"Well, what if I told you that I've been given an opportunity to do that . . . and it's not going to cost me a penny?"

"What do you mean? How? Where?"

"It's our fault!" Sister Jolene said. A ripple of laughter followed.

"Yes, blame it on us," Sister Twila added.

"We called your mama for help with our tour, you see," Sister Bonnie Sue chimed in. "Bella's family in Italy wants us to come over there the week after Thanksgiving to sing. They've arranged several events from one end of the country to the other. But the travel arrangements were giving us grief, so we asked for your mother's help."

"Italy?" My thoughts tumbled madly. "Mama, are you saying that you're—"

"She's coming with us!" the Splendora trio interrupted in perfect unison.

Mama's cheeks flamed red. "It's true, honey. You see, the ladies are accustomed to traveling, but they're all going to be overwhelmed with their singing engagements."

"Of course, but Mama, I'm not sure what this has to do with you."

"We need an assistant." Twila leaned down to

glance at the photos Hannah had placed in her area of the room. "And she's perfect!"

"I've worked the travel industry for years," Mama said. "So I know how to advise them. I know the best B&Bs, the best hotels, and the best modes of transportation. And I'm able to go as their tour guide."

"I can't believe it, Mama. You're finally getting to travel. And to Italy of all places!" Wonder of wonders!

"Not just Italy." Her eyes shone with obvious excitement. "There's more."

"What?"

"Our good friend Gordy is a bandleader," Jolene said. "A forties swing band, to be precise. The band is working on a cruise ship starting in January. Gordy has asked our trio to perform three gigs a week."

"Sounds like fun," Bella said.

"My travel agency has connections with the cruise line," Mama explained. "When I booked the passage for so many people, I was told that I could have a room for free."

"For free?" My mind reeled. "Where are you cruising?"

"In January and February we'll be in the western Caribbean, sailing out of Galveston, so I'll be in and out of port every week." She pinched my cheeks. "I'll be here to see you and then set sail again."

"January and February? Two months?" I wanted to ask how Mimi Carmen had taken this news but didn't dare.

"After that I believe we go to Saint Thomas." She shook her head. "No, I think that's Saint Croix. Anyway, we'll be in the eastern Caribbean in March and April."

"Wait." I put my hand up in the air to stop her. "You're telling me that you're leaving in a few weeks to go to Italy, then you're going to be on a cruise ship for four months?"

"Actually, longer than that. Because it turns out the band has been asked to do an Alaskan cruise, which starts in early July and runs through September. But don't you see, honey? I'll be home in May and June. We can spend that time together." She paused and her expression of joy faded. "We will have to discuss this with Mimi, of course. Do you think she'll try to talk me out of it?"

"I don't know, Mama. She's bound to miss you. But I'm working from home now, so at least I'll be there."

"That's exactly what we told her." Jolene clapped her hands together.

"I won't exactly be leaving her behind," Mama said. "I can bring Mimi along on the first cruise as my roomie. Or the second. Whichever one she prefers—the western Caribbean or the eastern. It'll be the trip of a lifetime for her."

340

"Wow."

"Then again, she's fallen so in love with Rosa-Earline that I doubt she'll want to be away for long." Mama chuckled. "But I might be able to convince her."

This started a lengthy conversation from Bella about her daughter's first steps, and before long the Splendora ladies were carrying on about how fast children grow up. We eventually got back to the business of talking about the Vendors Square and spent some time getting the room set up. Then we set plans in motion for another meeting next month.

As we rose to leave, I gave Mama a hug before she headed back to the travel agency. "I still can't believe it, Mama. This is an amazing opportunity, and you totally deserve it."

"I don't know if I deserve it, but I'm certainly grateful for it." Little creases appeared around her eyes. "But I have had some concerns."

"Oh?"

"Yes. Are you upset with me, Gabi? I want you to be honest."

"No, I'm not upset. I'm so happy that you're finally going to get to travel. Just surprised. And I hope Mimi takes the news well."

Mama chuckled. "Are you kidding? She can't see straight since Daniel started hanging around so much. You'll have to keep an eye on those two while I'm away, Gabi. Silly lovebirds."

Mama disappeared out the front door with the Splendora ladies still talking a mile a minute.

As they headed down the front steps, I noticed a familiar car pulling up in the driveway and my breath caught in my throat. I turned to face Bella.

"D-Demetri?"

She nodded and put her hand on my arm, likely in an attempt to calm me down. "Yes, Demetri. Stick with me here, Gabi. What I'm about to do is for your own good."

# 26

## The Band Wagon

The hardest job kids face today is learning good manners without seeing any.

FRED ASTAIRE

"Demetri!" Bella called out my former boss's name as he climbed out of his expensive car and headed our way.

I noticed his usual stylish attire. The expensive suit. The perfectly styled hair. The confident stride as he walked across the pathway from the driveway to the veranda.

"Bella, dah-ling." He extended a hand in an overly gracious manner but paused about midway into the greeting when he noticed I was standing beside her. "Oh." Just one word, but he pulled his hand back as he said it.

"Demetri, glad you could come. I know what a busy man you are." Bella gestured for him to enter, and we all walked into the foyer of Club Wed.

"Yes, vell, I got your message zat you needed to see me. If I had known—" He never finished the sentence. Instead, he turned to look inside the Vendors Square, his gaze landing on the beautiful gown I'd just put on display. He must've also noticed the various sketches I'd framed and hung, because he took several steps toward the room.

After giving it all a thorough look, he turned back to face us. "Vhat is zis?"

"Ah." Bella smiled. "Well, this is the Vendors Square area I told you about. You can see that my preferred vendors—like Gabi here—have already begun promoting their products."

"I see zat."

"What do you think of her designs?" Bella asked. "Lovely, aren't they?"

I felt my breath catch in my throat. Of all the questions to ask one of the leading designers in the state.

"Zay are fine." He seemed to dismiss them, turning to look at Hannah's photographs instead. After a moment, he turned back to face us. "Bella, I am a busy man. Please don't vaste my time. Is zis little get-together some sort of ploy to convince me to take Gabi back?"

"No, I don't want my job back." I put my hand up to stop him before he humiliated either of us. "That's not what this is about."

"Not at all," Bella said with a wave of her hand. "Not at all."

"Zen vhat?"

"I will not work for you, Demetri," I said. "To be honest, I was so unhappy in that little room doing alterations. I'm much more suited to designing my own gowns." I sighed. "And I don't need a team to sew them for me. I love that part too. Basically, I just love the whole process."

"Zen what is zee purpose of zis interruption to my day?" He looked down his nose at me.

Bella squared her shoulders. "She's saying that she will not work *for* you, but she's perfectly willing to work *with* you."

*I am?*

Before he could say a word, Bella put a hand up to silence him. "She's not asking to be a partner. Not yet, anyway. But the idea of you featuring her designs at Haute Couture Bridal would be fine for now." She flashed a winning smile.

"I vill die before zat happens. Already my attorneys are vorking on zee papers to . . ." His words fizzled off.

"They're working on nothing, because there's nothing to work on." Bella chuckled and patted him on the arm. "Be reasonable, Demetri. You are a designer, yes, but your boutique sells gowns designed by others as well as your own."

"Zis is true, but—"

"And you only carry the finest. You're known across the island for that."

"Across zee state." He stood a bit straighter at this comment.

"Across zee—the—state." She smiled. "So it makes sense for you to carry Gabi's designs in your store. They're going to be famous, you know.

I wish you could have heard all of the guests at the wedding this past weekend, going on and on."

"Nicolette's vedding?" His jaw clenched.

"Well, Nicolette's two gowns got rave reviews too, but I'm referring to Scarlet Lindsey, now Scarlet Rossi. Do you know her?"

"I do not."

"Oh, you should get to know her. She's my new sister-in-law and a very influential woman in the wedding business. She runs Let Them Eat Cake."

"Ah yes. I've been zere. Great sticky buns."

"Yes. Well, Scarlet's aunt is Wilhelmina Lindsey—er, Neeley. Do you know her?"

"Of course. Everyone in zee industry knows zat name."

From out in the foyer the parrot let out a sound like a machine gun going off, and Demetri nearly came out of his skin. I bit back a laugh and refocused on Bella.

"Well, you might be interested to know that Wilhelmina recently designed a special cake to coordinate with one of Gabi's designs," Bella said. "And that cake is going to be prominently featured in *Texas Bride* magazine, along with a link to Gabi's website."

"You . . . you have a vebsite?" He stared at me as if he couldn't quite believe all of this.

To be honest, I couldn't quite believe it myself. It all still felt like a dream, one that I might wake up from. "I do now," I managed. Still, I couldn't stop thinking about what Bella had said about the photo appearing in *Texas Bride*. When did that happen?

"My web designer has done a fabulous job creating a site for her," Bella said. In the next room, the bird began to warble "Amazing Grace." In multiple keys. "Which reminds me, some of the links on your Haute Couture site need to be updated. In fact, the whole site could use an overhaul. It's looking a little outdated, Demetri, and outdated is never a good thing in the wedding business."

He seemed perplexed by her words. In fact, he seemed perplexed by the whole thing.

"So, what do you say?" Bella's tone exuded confidence. "We're not asking for a favor here. Far from it. You can see that Gabi doesn't need you. She will do just fine on her own, whether you carry her designs or not."

"With Bella's help," I threw in.

"And with the help of the other wedding vendors on the island. But there's strength in numbers. Do you want to let this fresh, young designer have some floor space in your shop, or do we take this offer to Premiere Bridal on the mainland?"

He blanched as she mentioned Haute Couture's primary competitor. "Zis is a travesty. You have painted me into zee corner!"

"I'll admit, it's a big decision." Bella's lips

turned up in a smile. "But how fun to be billed as the designer who discovered Gabriella Delgado. I have no doubt those words will come in handy for you someday. After the media picks up on her successes, I mean. But of course that's totally up to you. No pressure." With a wave of her hand she appeared to play down the situation. I had the feeling, though, that she was playing him. Like a violin.

And he appeared to be considering it. Go figure.

Bella's words flattered me. They also terrified me on some level. Did she really think I would one day be that well known? Frightening thought.

For a moment, I remembered what it felt like to be holed up in that tiny little alterations room. Safe. Snug. Hidden away from the masses. No fears. Well, other than the fear that Demetri would take my head off at any moment.

I contrasted that with the idea of being in the limelight in front of adoring fans. Ack. Could I really do this?

Guido took to singing "Ninety-Nine Bottles of Beer on the Wall." This got a strange look from Demetri but lifted the tension in the room briefly.

"Even if I did agree to do zis, it vould be impossible," he said, just as Guido got to ninety-seven bottles of beer on the wall. "I have no room in my store for a new line."

"You do." Bella fussed with one of my framed

sketches on the wall, straightening it a bit. Not that it needed to be straightened. "The answer is quite simple, really. Take the wall down between the store and the current alterations closet. Er, room."

"Take zee vall down?"

"Yes. Just make that area part of the store, a little nook of sorts. The Gabriella collection will fit nicely, I think." Bella spoke with firm conviction, as if she had decided the whole thing. "Of course, the collection is growing as we speak, but I feel sure you can accommodate a handful of the gowns. When they're complete, I mean. Right now Gabi is in creative mode."

"I understand zat. But I need an alterations area," Demetri said after a few moments. "I can't possibly give up zat space."

"There's plenty of room in the studio for alterations," Bella said with another wave of her hand. "And to be honest, the Fab Five could— should—handle the alterations anyway. Don't you think? I mean, they implement your designs. Why not alter them?"

He paced the tiny space, pausing to look once again at the gown I'd put on the display. "Zis, I never thought of."

"It will save you money in the long run," I said. "If you don't have to pay someone to do altera- tions, I mean."

"Yes, but vill one of zee ladies lower herself to

such a task?" He clucked his tongue. "Zis is zee question."

"The answer is yes. Because altering a gown is just part of the overall picture," I said. "It goes with the territory."

Still, I could only imagine the look on Beatrix's face when Demetri told her that she would be responsible to raise a hem or take in a waistline. No doubt she would flip. Say it was beneath her.

"To your vay of thinking, maybe." He raked his hands through his practically perfect hair, messing it up a bit. "Zay may not agree."

"We all make compromises, Demetri."

*Trust me. I've compromised. And compromised. And compromised.*

"I vill think on zeese things and let you know." He looked away from the gown and faced Bella. "Just out of curiosity, veech of Nicolette's gowns did you like zee best?"

"Well, I really couldn't say." Bella's expression never changed as she spoke. "You see, I was so busy doing what I do best—caring for my bride and her family—that I didn't pay much attention to what she was wearing."

My former boss blanched at this.

"We all play our role, Demetri," Bella said. "You do your thing, I do mine. But in the end, the opinion that really matters isn't mine or yours. It's the bride's. She's the one we have in mind from the beginning, and she's the one we hope to please in the end. So I suppose, to answer your question, I'd have to say both, because Nicolette looked radiantly happy at both the ceremony and the reception."

"Ah." Demetri gave a tight-lipped smile. "I suppose you are right."

"You know I'm right. But we can talk more about this when we meet to discuss the addition of Gabi's line to your store. In the meantime, thank you for stopping by."

I'd never heard anyone dismiss Demetri as if he were just an ordinary, normal human being before. Usually folks bowed down at his feet. But as Bella returned to tidying up the room, leaving him to find his way to the door, it became evident to me that she saw him not as some sort of hero to be worshiped but as a fellow professional in the wedding biz.

And now she saw me that way too. Well, maybe not exactly like she saw Demetri, but she saw me as a pro.

Bella and I had a good, long laugh after Demetri headed off on his way, then she gushed about what a creative soul I was, how my designs flowed like water.

For whatever reason, her words sent me reeling back in time to that day on the beach. I could feel the early morning breeze rippling through my hair. I could hear the waves as they lapped the shore. I could sense the wonder as I reached for my sketchbook to quickly capture an idea so it wouldn't flit away.

In that moment, something hit me from out of the blue. "God created." I spoke the words aloud, though I hadn't meant to.

"Yes, he did," Bella responded. "Birds? Fish? Earth?"

"No, I mean, God is in the business of creating . . . and so am I."

"True." Bella grinned. "That's why I said you're a creative soul, Gabi. One of the best I've seen, by the way, but I might be a little biased." She winked and reached over to pick up one of Hannah's photos that had fallen.

"Thank you. I just never put it together before. God spoke some words and the whole earth came to be. Ideas flit through my brain and I scratch them down on paper, and then they come to be. It's just weird. I never really thought of it as creating before."

"Well, go back and read the creation story. Maybe he has something he wants to show you."

Later that night, while nuzzled under the covers, I opened the Bible app on my phone to the first chapter of Genesis. I read the story of creation, waiting for the Lord to zap me with some sort of supernatural message that I hadn't picked up on before.

Instead, a little nudge took place in my heart

when I reached the verse about how the Spirit of God moved over the waters during creation.

"That's it." I pinched my eyes shut and thought back to the day at the beach. Though I couldn't put it into words at the time, that's exactly what I'd felt—the Spirit of God moving across my creation. That's why the sketch for Scarlet's dress had come pouring out of me, not because of any talent on my part but because the Holy Spirit was moving across my creation—in this case, the sketch.

I read the verse again and again, realizing the significance of this. If what the Lord was showing me was true, I could ask him to stir in me in this way every time I sat down to create something. Every time I needed to come up with a design, a sketch, a plan for a particular bride-to-be.

When God created, he made something out of nothing. My creations were made of fabric, thread, and beads. But when his Spirit breathed on that fabric, that thread, those beads, they came together to bring pleasure to his creation.

I'd never been one to write things down, but I grabbed an empty journal from the bedside table and scribbled as fast as I could. Better get it all down before I forgot. Then I closed my eyes and prayed about God's plans—for my life, my business, my family, my friendships.

Afterward I turned off the lamp and rolled over, peaceful and filled with joy.

No sooner did my head touch the pillow, however, than an idea hit. A God-breathed idea, as Scarlet would call it.

My new bride, Ashley, needed a dress for her winter wonderland wedding. I hadn't given it a lot of thought. Other than a rushed telephone conversation and a small deposit check, she hadn't really given me much to go on. Oh, but the ideas now flowed like water.

I sat up in bed, snapped on the lamp, and grabbed my sketchpad and artist's pencil, ready to get to work once more. As I scribbled and scratched a dazzling design onto the page, that wonderful cocoon-like feeling enveloped me, just as it had that day at the beach. I could sense —literally sense—the hand of God. With that hand guiding mine, we crafted a thing of beauty.

# 27

## Blue Skies

I have no desire to prove anything by it. I have never used it as an outlet or a means of expressing myself. I just dance.

FRED ASTAIRE

The month of October was spent meeting with new brides and sketching nearly a dozen dress designs. I spent a lot of time at the beach with my artist's pencil in hand. At least until the weather grew chilly. At that point I purchased a small drafting table and put it in my sewing room at the house. I set it in front of the window so that I could see outside and be inspired by nature. Crazy how much work I could get done when I had something lovely to look at. Not that looking at the house across the street was particularly inspiring, but seeing out beyond my own little world helped. A lot.

Demetri softened in his approach to me, and by early November, with Bella's help, I'd set up a small display of gowns in Haute Couture in the spot where my closet-like work space had once been. This act was greeted with a few glares from the Fab Five. Well, all but Doria, who congratulated me and told me how proud she was.

Kitty raved over the gowns, gushing over every ruffle and crystal like a proud grandmother. By the week before Thanksgiving, we were back to normal where Haute Couture was concerned. Okay, maybe not normal, exactly, but close. I only saw Demetri on occasion, usually at some function involving the other vendors or while crossing paths at Parma John's, where Jordan and I spent much of our time. Kitty took care of most of my business dealings with the shop, and Bella helped me with my clientele, offering sage advice and all the encouragement a girl could ever need. When she wasn't up to her eyeballs in brides, anyway.

The Saturday after I set up my new display at the bridal store, I received a call from Jordan. The call came late morning, just after I had swung by Scarlet's bakery to pick up a cake for Mimi, who wanted to surprise Daniel for his birthday.

"I'm excited about our date tonight," Jordan said.

"Me too." I shifted the phone to my other ear and pointed through the glass case at a beautiful chocolate cake, perfect for Mimi and Daniel's night out. "I have an afternoon wedding, but I'll be back at the house by five. Mama's getting ready for Italy and Mimi Carmen has a date. I'm picking up a cake right now, but it's for the two of them. She's got some sort of special dinner planned for Daniel's birthday."

"Another date with Daniel, eh?" Jordan chuckled. "They're quite an item these days."

"Oh yes, they're two peas in a pod."

"Well, this might sound selfish, but I'm glad she's busy because I want you all to myself. I've got a special night planned, so prepare yourself to be wowed."

"Oh?"

"Yes. No questions, though. Okay?"

"Okay. But what do I wear? Casual? Dressy? What?"

"Wear the dress that's on display at Club Wed."

"The floor-length gown? Ivory? The one with the feathers?" Was he kidding?

"That's the one."

"But that's a wedding dress." Maybe people wouldn't realize it because it was vintage. "Why so fancy? Where are you taking me? This must be some date."

"Don't ask any questions, oh curious one. Just wear the dress and put on your dancing shoes."

Ah. I got it now. The ballroom dance classes he'd signed us up for must be starting. But why risk wearing such a fancy gown to a lesson? I started to tell him that I thought it might be too risky but decided against it. If Fred wanted Ginger to dress in her finest, Ginger would dress in her finest.

"Yes, sir." I fought the temptation to salute. He must have something up his sleeve.

I thought about it as I took care of my bride's needs that afternoon. I pondered it as I showered and dressed for our date. I speculated, curiosity growing, as I fixed my hair in a Ginger-like upsweep. I chewed on it awhile as I put on my makeup, paying careful attention to the way I fixed my eye shadow and perfectly lined my lips. I wanted to get it just right—sort of a Ginger-ish effect to sweep my Fred off his feet.

Just the idea made me giggle. Well, that, and trying to picture Jordan as Fred Astaire in the first place. Other than that night in the moonlight, I'd never even seen him dance. Still, he had all of the other qualities that made a movie hero great, didn't he? Kindness, a joyful nature, a strong relationship with God. Yep. And it didn't hurt that he was knock-you-down gorgeous.

Wowza. I just thought he'd looked gorgeous before. When he showed up in a full tuxedo complete with tails, I almost lost my breath.

"Oh. My. Goodness." I dragged him into the house and called for Mama and Mimi Carmen to come have a look.

My grandmother let out a little whistle when she saw Jordan's getup. "Well now, if you aren't the cat's meow! Haven't seen a tux and tails like that since . . ." She laughed. "Well, since I was a girl, really. That's the real deal you're wearing there."

"Yep. Sure is." He spun around and sent the tails flying.

Mama chuckled and asked him to turn around again, more slowly this time, so she could have a closer look at the tails.

"I'm sorry, I know it's probably not appropriate for a woman my age to look at a man's backside," she said. "But those tails are divine."

"All the girls tell me that." Jordan laughed and I punched him in the arm.

"These clothes take me back to the old days, when men were men and ladies were . . ." Mimi pointed to my dress. "Well, ladies dressed like that."

"And movies were clean and safe and filled with great song and dance numbers." Mama began to whistle a little song and then skittered off to find her camera. Soon we were being photographed. From every conceivable angle, no less.

After nearly a dozen photos, Jordan glanced at his watch and then took me by the hand. "Ladies, I'd love to stay and chat, but we have special plans tonight. Our carriage awaits."

"Where are you going?" my mother asked.

He put his finger to his lips. "I'm not telling. It's a surprise."

"Must be a doozy of a surprise then." Mimi Carmen released a sigh and a blissful look came over her. "This is what every woman, young and old, longs for—a fella to show up at her door, dressed like this, ready to take her out for a night on the town." Her face lit up as she said, "Ooo, that reminds me! Daniel will be here shortly to pick me up. Thanks for the cake, Gabi."

"You're welcome." I gave her a little kiss on the cheek and whispered, "Have a great night, Mimi. Hope it's filled with romance."

She blushed and then took off down the hall, carrying on in Spanish about some character on her soap opera falling in love. I didn't catch all of it, but I had to smile.

"We're off to the ball." Jordan offered me the crook of his arm and I took it, feeling very much like a princess as he glided me out the front door.

My neighbor, Mrs. McGillicuddy, looked up from her front porch and whistled as she saw us heading down the walkway in front of my house. "Well, aren't we something! Who are you two supposed to be?"

"Just ourselves," I hollered back. And it felt mighty good to be myself on the arm of the man I loved.

The man I loved.

Oh, how those words made my heart sing. In fact, it sang so loudly that I found myself humming along. The song intensified as we climbed into Jordan's car.

We only drove for about five minutes, headed straight into the business district, when Jordan pulled the car into a parking lot. Strange. No great restaurants around here. None that I could remember. Only the old Marquee Theater, but little else to stir a girl's fancy.

"Is this right?" I asked, looking around.

"Right as rain."

He climbed out of the car and walked around to my side, then opened my door for me. I got out and let him lead me across the street to the front of the Marquee. An usher straight from the Hollywood golden years greeted us at the entrance, bowing low as if we were important guests. "Pleasure to have you with us, Mr. Singer. Miss Delgado."

I jabbed Jordan with my elbow. "How does he know our names?" I whispered.

"I have no idea." Jordan's eyes glistened with merriment. "Seriously, Gabi, just play along with me here, okay?"

"O-okay."

Stepping inside the lobby was just like stepping back in time. Chandeliers hung overhead, casting the most romantic glow over the spacious lobby. Wall sconces, intricately designed, graced the walls.

I had forgotten how lovely this place was and how it made me feel. "I've stepped back into an old movie." I knew my words sounded breathless, but I didn't care. Who could breathe on a night such as this?

"Exactly," Jordan said as he placed his hand on my back and led me to the concessions area. "That's the idea."

The young man behind the counter was dressed

in perfect attire for his job—creased slacks and a freshly pressed jacket over a white shirt, complete with a little black bow tie. We ordered a bucket of popcorn, which sizzled and popped in the popcorn maker moments later. Jordan then requested a Diet Coke. The fellow never flinched, though I whispered, "They didn't have diet drinks in the olden days."

"Hey, work with me here." Jordan gave me a wink that melted my heart.

The same usher who had welcomed us at the front door awaited us when we arrived at the door to the theater. "Enjoy your movie, folks," he said, then pulled the door open.

We stepped inside the old theater, and my heart sailed backwards in time. I was a little girl climbing the carpeted steps to the balcony with my hand tightly clutching my father's.

Forcing the image aside, I squinted to better see the room. I could make out the large screen down front. An old black-and-white movie played on the screen, drawing me in at once and whisking me back in time to some of my favorite movies from days gone by, movies I'd spent hours watching. Studying.

No way.

It was Fred and Ginger. *Top Hat.*

In a rush of emotion, my thoughts shifted back to my father, to that special night when he had brought me here to see this very movie. I turned to face Jordan, unable to hold back the tears. "I-I can't believe you did this."

"Only the best for my girl." He leaned over and gave me a little kiss on the cheek. "We're creating some new memories. Some I hope you'll never forget."

I would never forget, all right. "How in the world did you do this? This is . . . crazy."

"Crazy in a good way." He chuckled. "This is when it helps to have friends in the publishing business. I'm doing an article on the theater for our magazine, so they set all of this up, hoping for a good write-up to increase their business."

"Business? But the theater hasn't been open for years."

"Not to moviegoers, necessarily, but a lot of companies rent out the space for parties."

"I had no idea."

The fact that he'd done all of this for me made my heart sing. And clearly it had all been done with me in mind. I couldn't locate another living soul in the theater.

Oh, wait. Down in front of the screen stood a couple. I could only make out their shadows, what with the theater being so dark and all. For sure, I could tell that the fella was wearing a top hat. Interesting. Probably part of Jordan's amazing plan to wow me.

"Let's make this a night to remember," he said.

"It already is," I whispered.

Jordan offered me his hand and guided me down the aisle toward the stage. Once there, I realized that the odd-looking couple wasn't a couple at all. They weren't real, anyway. My dress forms stood side by side, facing the screen. Ginger wore a beautiful crystal-covered gown I'd designed weeks ago, and Demetri—okay, Fred—looked pretty swanky in his tuxedo and tails. Almost as swanky as the fella at my side. And that top hat . . . gracious! The expensive headpiece almost made me giddy.

Still, none of this made sense.

When we reached the area in front of the stage, Jordan pulled the hat off the dress form's head and bowed low. "Thank you, Fred. Don't mind if I do."

He then eased me into his arms and began to hum the melody to "Cheek to Cheek" along with Fred. The Fred on the screen, of course. Jordan tipped his hat, gave a princely bow, and the dance began.

Seconds later, my dance partner picked up the speed, completely taking my breath away. In a good way. He spun me around our makeshift dance floor, singing in my ear.

Was there anything this fella couldn't do? And didn't he look dashing with his tails and top hat flying in the air? Well, the tails were flying, anyway. The top hat miraculously stayed perched on his head.

When that inevitable moment came in the song—you know the one, where Fred and Ginger take off like two maniacs across the stage with only the undergirding of instrumental music to guide them—Jordan held me closer and slowed the dance a bit. Still, he moved like a pro.

*Did he take dance lessons for this or something?*

Clearly some preparation had gone into making this dance number a top-of-the-line event.

As the music softened, Jordan paused and swept a loose hair from my face. He leaned down to whisper "Ginger" in my ear.

"Yes, Fred?" I whispered in response, and then a little giggle escaped.

"I love dancing with you." He nuzzled my cheek with his lips.

A delicious shiver ran down my spine. "And I love dancing with you."

We spoke the words "cheek to cheek" in unison, as if we'd planned it, and then both laughed. I felt my nerves bubble up as he swept me into a tight embrace and kissed me with a passion suitable for the big screen. Wowza. One of those tingle-all-the-way-to-the-toes kisses. I could hardly keep my feet on the ground.

"Fred is a happy man," Jordan said when the kiss ended.

Ginger was pretty happy too, but she couldn't speak right now. The lump in her throat wouldn't allow it.

The jovial expression on Jordan's face grew more serious, and I felt his hands tremble as he took mine. "Ginger, there's something Fred needs to ask you."

"O-oh?" My own hands trembled uncontrollably.

"Yes." He led me to the dress forms. Once we got close enough, I could see that Fred had a funny little piece of paper pinned to his lapel. With the paper folded in half, I couldn't see what was on the inside.

"What's that, Fred?" Jordan leaned down as if listening for an answer. "Oh? You want me to give it to her? Okay." He unpinned the note and pretended to pass it to the other dress form. Then he leaned down to listen to Fred's instructions again. "Oh? Wrong woman? Okay."

He passed the note to me and shrugged. "I think this was meant for you."

"You sure?" My hands still trembled as I opened it. Just twelve little words, but they took my breath away: *Will you be my dance partner . . . for the rest of our lives?*

The paper slipped out of my hands and floated down to the floor. Before I could reach down to snatch it—how could I, really, with the dress being so fitted and all?—Jordan bowed low and scooped it up. "What does it say?" he asked.

"I-I think Fred here is proposing." I slipped my

arm around the male dress form. "But I'm not really sure he's my type, to be honest. He's such an old stiff."

"Ah. That he is." Jordan slapped Fred on the back. "And I can't believe he was hitting on my girl. Who does he think he is?"

*Who indeed?*

Jordan drew me close, and I felt his breath soft against my cheek. "But what if that old stiff was just acting on someone else's behalf? What would you say then?"

My heart thump-thumped in rhythm with the background music on the screen above. "I'd say whoever put him up to this is a romantic at heart and perfectly suited to a girl like me."

A dazzling smile lit Jordan's face. "Well then. There's just one more thing to do." He dropped to one knee, reached inside his jacket pocket, and came out with a tiny box. "Would you like to be *my* dance partner . . . forever? I promise not to step on your toes or make you dance in front of an audience."

"I would dance with you even if you made my toes black and blue—on the big screen or in the privacy of our own . . . bedroom." A little giggle escaped as I spoke that last word. Still, it seemed appropriate, all things considered.

"Whew." He wiped his brow with his free hand. "That's good. Because I make no real and lasting promises where the dancing's concerned."

He held the ring up—a sparkling marquise. "So is that a yes?"

"Oh yes!" My heart burst into a miraculous love song, one that propelled me to the stars and back to earth again. "It's a yes."

"That's a relief. Fred's getting arthritic in his old age."

The music on the screen swelled as Jordan slipped the gorgeous ring onto my finger, and I practically swooned. He rose and swept me into his arms for an Oscar-worthy kiss, which was interrupted a few seconds later when Jordan waggled his index finger at the male dress form.

"Cover your eyes, Fred. We need some privacy. She's my girl now."

He put his hand up as if to cover Fred's eyes and then kissed me again. And again.

Another song from the movie now provided the perfect backdrop, so we continued to dance. And dance. And dance.

I could still hear the music long after it ended. In Jordan's arms, I found myself lifted to the heavens, where life truly felt as breezy as a song.

Maybe this was the way Ginger had experienced love too. Some internal rhythm had kept her toes tapping and her heart twirling long after the song ended. And maybe, just maybe, she was smiling down on us now, offering congratulations from above. I had a sneaking suspicion she and Fred were still dancing too.

# 20

## Three Little Words

I adore the man. I always have adored him. It was the most fortunate thing that ever happened to me, being teamed with Fred: he was everything a little starry-eyed girl from a small town ever dreamed of.

GINGER ROGERS

I'd no sooner said yes to Jordan than a sudden fear grabbed hold of my heart.

"Mimi!"

He looked around as if trying to find her. "Your grandmother's here?"

"No, you don't understand." I took a seat in the front row. "You and I are getting married, which means I'm moving out."

"Right. That's the idea."

"Yes, but Mama's about to flit off from country to country, which means she's basically moving out too. That leaves Mimi . . . by herself." Emotion overtook me in that moment. Would Mimi really have to spend her golden years alone? The idea made me feel sick inside.

Jordan took the seat next to mine. At about the same time, Fred and Ginger reached a complication in their romance on the screen.

"God has a plan for all of this, Gabi," Jordan said. "I know he does. So just rest easy, okay? And trust me, we'll live close by. You can still spend as much time with your grandmother as you like. Here's an idea—why not continue to office out of the house?"

My heart felt lighter at this proclamation.

"Now, I hate to cut this moment short, but we have a little party to get to."

"A party?"

"Yep. Come with me, please."

I waved goodbye to the usher as he opened the door for us and followed Jordan with my hand tightly clutched in his as we made our way to the car. I quizzed him nonstop, but he wouldn't give up any information except to say, "You'll see."

When we pulled into the driveway at Club Wed, I could see all of the cars in the parking lot and the lights on inside.

"Jordan, what in the world . . . ?"

"A real Fred and Ginger experience awaits. Be prepared to dance your heart out." He leaned over and kissed me, then got out of the car and came around to my side to open the door. Minutes later, hands tightly clasped, we entered the reception hall at Club Wed to a rousing cheer from the crowd.

The crowd?

Heavens to Betsy! The place was filled top to

bottom with friends and family. I wasn't sure how he did it, but Jordan had acquired a forties swing band, and they played a rousing tune as Jordan hollered, "She said yes!" upon our entry.

Everyone went a little crazy at this point. The bandleader shifted gears and started playing the "Wedding March," and my BFFs came running my way—all three of them. Well, four if you counted Kitty. Five if you added in Mama. And Mimi Carmen, who stood at a distance, tears tumbling down her face, made six.

I looked around, completely mesmerized, but extended my left hand to show off the ring for so long that I got a cramp in my arm.

I nudged Bella and said, "You arranged all of this?"

"With a little help from some friends." She gestured to Scarlet and Hannah. "We've been waiting on pins and needles for half an hour. I thought you'd never get here."

"But how did you know I'd say yes?"

"Are you kidding?" Bella laughed.

Scarlet jabbed me in the arm. "Because we know you, goofy. Besides, who could say no to a suave guy like that?"

"True." I gave Jordan a little wink.

"We even have presents!" Hannah took me by the hand and pulled me to a gift table fully loaded with all sorts of unwrapped Fred and Ginger items. She handed me a poster of my favorite dancing duo, one I'd never seen before. My eyes swept across the beautiful scene—the two of them flitting across the stage—and I was transported back to what had just happened at the theater. What almost escaped my notice, however, was the quote at the bottom.

"Check it out." Bella pointed to the text and I gasped as I read it:

"Ginger was brilliantly effective. She made everything work for her. Actually she made things very fine for both of us and she deserves most of the credit for our success."—Fred Astaire

"No way." I looked at my friends and grinned. "You're saying Fred actually credited Ginger with their success?"

"Obviously. He thought very highly of her." Bella leaned in to share the next part privately. "You know, there are really guys out there who think highly of women, right?"

"I do now."

"Yes, you do. And don't you love the fact that they aren't as rare as one might imagine?" She gestured to Jordan, who flashed a great smile.

I reached to slip my arm around his waist, and he drew me close, then cleared his throat. Gesturing to the older couple standing nearby, he said, "Gabi, I want to introduce you to someone."

He didn't even have to say the words. I knew

the minute I looked into his mother's tear-filled eyes. She reached over and hugged me and spoke the words, "We're so thrilled!" into my ear.

Turned out Jordan had his father's build and his mama's eyes. And as Mr. Singer—the senior—offered me a rousing "Meet the in-laws!" I realized that Jordan had also acquired his father's sense of humor.

We dove into a wonderful conversation, but it was soon interrupted by D.J. Neeley, who made an announcement. "The bride-to-be and groom-to-be are going to share a special dance."

"We—we are?" I jabbed Jordan and lowered my voice. "I thought you weren't going to make me dance in front of an audience."

"This isn't an audience. These are our friends and family." He took my hand and led me to the dance floor as the music began for "A Fine Romance," one of my all-time favorite Fred and Ginger tunes.

The crowd cheered as Jordan pulled me into his arms. Before long it didn't matter that we had sixty or seventy people looking on. I saw only one, and his eyes were glistening with tears.

When the song ended we took a little bow, received a round of applause, and then the party began. The band kicked off the dance portion of the night with some rousing swing music. Turned out the Splendora Sisters were pros at swing. Two of them—Twila and Jolene—danced with their husbands. Bonnie Sue searched the room for a partner, finally setting her sights on Bella's little boy, Tres, who seemed to have a good time.

Mama seemed to be enjoying herself too. She and Jordan's parents spent much of the evening chatting and laughing. No doubt they were already planning my big day.

My big day!

I had a wedding to plan. How—and when— would we pull this off with Mama out of the country?

Ah yes. June. She had the month of June free. Looked like we would be hosting an early summer wedding.

As I spun around the dance floor in my sweetheart's arms, my thoughts shifted to my wedding dress. A thousand images came to mind at once. How would I ever choose just one? Looked like I had my work cut out for me.

Cut out for me. Ha!

When the music ended, Bella insisted that I take another look at the gift table. I loved every single Fred and Ginger item, but the poster still took the cake. From the moment I read Fred's words about Ginger, I realized he had seen her as a person of value from the get-go.

Thinking about this reminded me of my father. I would have to tell him about the wedding, sure. I might even invite him. But someone else would be walking me down the aisle.

I turned to search out Mimi Carmen and found her wrapped in Daniel's arms on the dance floor, oblivious to the fact that the music had stopped. Oh well. I would tell her later.

Jordan and I had a blast going through the gifts, and when we were done he looked my way with a twinkle in his eyes.

"Speaking of presents, I have a little pre-wedding present for you."

"Pre-wedding?" I laughed and looked around at the guests, who all smiled ear to ear. "And again I ask, how did everyone know I'd say yes?"

He grinned. "I had faith, of course. Do you want to see your present?"

I glanced down at the gorgeous ring on my finger—truly the prettiest thing I'd ever owned—and sighed. "How could it possibly be any better than this?"

"It's not better," he said. "Just . . . different."

"Well, I'm ready."

He took my hand and hollered for everyone to follow us outside.

Outside?

We walked to the front of Club Wed, and an unfamiliar red SUV pulled into the driveway behind Jordan's car. Armando got out and walked my way with a smile on his face. He handed me the keys.

"What in the world?" I walked toward the SUV with the crowd following behind me. "Are you saying this is mine?"

Jordan nodded. "It's yours. I couldn't wait until after we were married to get you the car you need. I want my bride to be safe."

"And you need a vehicle to haul all of those amazing gowns around in," Mimi Carmen said. "This one is perfect because you can put a clothing rack right here." She gestured to the area above the backseat. "See? And there's plenty of room in the back for a portable sewing machine, and even a little area for your supplies."

"Wow." Just one word was all I could manage. I finally got control of my senses long enough to slip my arm around Jordan's waist. "You really did this for me?"

"Yep." A look of concern filled his eyes. "I know you love that old Ford Focus."

"I-I do?"

"Yeah, it's got a lot of character, I know. But to be honest, every time I saw you drive off in it, I was a nervous wreck. Now I won't have to worry." A dazzling smile lit his face. "Sorry this new one doesn't come with rust built in. And it's got that annoying little side mirror on the driver's side. I know how much you hate those." He gave a little wink.

I hardly knew what to say, so I opted to say . . . nothing. Instead, with my friends and family looking on, I climbed into the driver's seat and Jordan took the passenger side.

"Let's take 'er for a spin," Jordan said.

"Okay." I closed my eyes for a moment, blinking away the tears that threatened to emerge. As I did, I caught a teensy-tiny glimpse of Fred and Ginger waltzing across the dance floor. I giggled as I pictured Ginger carrying her Academy Award across the stage, all smiles. I now knew just how she felt.

I fumbled around with the keys, my hands shaking, and finally managed to turn on the car, which caused my guests to cheer.

Moments later, as I backed the SUV out of the drive and pulled onto Broadway, I glanced at Jordan, who looked perfectly comfortable in the passenger seat. Well, until I almost ran the first light because I was so distracted by the car's cool GPS system.

"Sorry!" I hit the brake.

He laughed. "There's a lot to learn when you make the jump from an older car to a newer one, but you'll get it."

"It's just so . . . advanced." I laughed. "Hope I can figure it out."

"You will. If you can figure out that new sewing machine, you'll get this in no time."

"New sewing machine?" Now he had me puzzled.

"Man." He put a hand on his forehead. "And I call myself a reporter. I'm lousy at keeping secrets." He gestured back to Club Wed, now disappearing from view behind us. "Your friends out there . . . they have another little gift for you. Only, it's not so little. They all went in together to get you a machine that will go the distance."

"Are you serious?" I wondered if my heart could possibly handle any more.

"Yep." He leaned in to whisper, "But please don't tell them I gave away their little secret, okay? Bella will kill me."

As if Bella could hurt a flea.

"I won't tell them." Oh, but how my mind reeled! A new machine? One of my very own?

In that moment the strangest sensation flooded over me. As much as I needed—and wanted—a state-of-the-art sewing machine, I would miss Mimi Carmen's old Singer. It had brought Jordan and me together, after all, and deserved a place of honor in my life.

"So, I had this idea," Jordan said. "You know how you told me that your grandmother's sewing machine is going to be willed to you one day?"

"Yes. But how did you know I was thinking about that?"

"Because I know you." He grinned. "I say we put it on display in our home. As soon as we find our own place, we'll set it up in a place of honor."

Wow. Great minds really did think alike. But all of this thinking ahead stuff was starting to make me dizzy. In the past few hours I'd acquired a husband-to-be, a home-to-be, a sewing machine, and a brand-new vehicle. And a lot of really cool Fred and Ginger memorabilia. Oh yes, and in-laws-to-be.

I drove around the corner, closing in around the back of the wedding facility. Minutes later, my heart in my throat, I pulled the car into the drive again, and Mimi and the others met me at the door.

We got out of the car and answered a thousand simultaneous questions and then led the way back inside. Before we headed to the reception hall to gather up our gifts, Mimi Carmen took hold of my arm. The anxious expression on her face concerned me a little. Perhaps she'd already started to worry about living alone. I would put her mind at ease with Jordan's suggestion that I office out of the house.

"Now, Gabi, I know you're busy and all, but I need to ask a little favor."

"Anything," I said.

"Maybe tomorrow or the next day, you could take my measurements?" She lowered her voice for the last few words as Daniel appeared.

"Take your measurements?" I whispered in response. "Why? The dieting thing?"

"Well, that, and . . ." Her cheeks flamed pink as she spoke louder. "Because I need you to make me a dress, and I want it to fit just right."

"A dress for my wedding?" I asked.

"No." She chuckled and slipped her arm around Daniel's waist. "A dress for *my* wedding."

"A—what?"

The most delightful smile lit her face and she giggled. "A girl can't exactly get married in her everyday clothes, now can she?" These words came out in Spanglish, so I thought for a minute I might've misunderstood.

"Mimi, are you saying . . ." I looked back and forth between the two of them, just to make sure I had the story right.

"She's saying that she's agreed to be my bride," Daniel said. "Best birthday present I ever got. But you'll need to hurry up and get that dress done quick-like. At our age, there's no waiting around to get married."

"That's right." Mimi grinned and nuzzled close to him. Joy bubbled in her laugh and shone in her eyes. "I don't mean to steal your thunder, Gabi, but we're in a hurry and some things just can't wait. We're not getting any younger, you know. We want to get married pronto."

"As in weeks, not months." Daniel gave her a kiss on the forehead. "Think you can handle that, kid?"

"Oh, my Gabi's a whiz. She can handle any-thing." Mimi and Daniel turned back toward the other guests, hand in hand.

In that moment I truly felt my world whirling around, coming loose from its axis.

Mimi Carmen was getting married.

Mama was setting sail.

And I . . .

A giggle arose. I had better get busy designing dresses for my grandmother, a host of brides . . . and myself. Looked like the closet dress designer was out—for good!

# EPILOGUE

## Shall We Dance

Oh, there's no such thing as my favorite performance. I can't sit here today and look back and say *Top Hat* was better than *Easter Parade* or any of the others. I just don't look back, period. When I finish with a project, I say, "All right, that's that. What's next?"

FRED ASTAIRE

On the third Saturday in December, I donned my dance shoes and rehearsed the steps Jordan and I had learned in our most recent class. It felt like I'd never get it right. And on a day like today, a girl really needed to have her steps down.

Jordan arrived at six o'clock, dressed to the nines, and ushered me out to the car. Mimi Carmen and Daniel followed behind, chattering all the way about their honeymoon cruise, which had—according to Mimi—been epic. I only hoped she wouldn't share the details. I'd heard more than my fair share already.

No, tonight was all about dancing, and not just for fun. Tonight I would meet one of Hollywood's biggest superstars and watch him dance across the stage at the Grand Opera Society alongside other former *Dancing with the Stars* contestants. Afterward those who wanted to join the stars on the big stage could do so for an hour of ballroom dancing.

I had butterflies.

Looked like Jordan had butterflies too.

We arrived at the event to find the Rossi family in the foyer, hyped and ready. Bella took me by the hand and gave me a little wink. "Ready to meet you know who?"

I nodded, but my feet wouldn't cooperate. I couldn't even walk, let alone dance. Jordan stayed behind to chat with D.J., and I followed behind Bella to the greenroom, a small area off the stage. The security guard gave her a nod, and she entered the room, all smiles.

"Brock? There's someone I want you to meet."

The larger-than-life hero took hold of my hand and shook it. "Gabriella. I've heard all about you."

"You—you have?" I stared up into that gorgeous face and found myself unable to speak further.

"Yes. My wife is so excited to meet you." He searched the room, finally calling out her name. "Erin! She's here."

The most beautiful young woman rushed my way, beaming with excitement. "You're Gabi?"

"I am."

"Ooo, we need to talk!" She threw her arms around my neck and gave me a big hug. "Bella showed us your designs, and I can't wait to talk to you about my gown for the Academy Awards. Do you have time to make it between now and then? I know how busy you are, since your line took off and all."

I could hardly catch my breath to answer. "Once the Christmas rush is behind me, I'll be fine. I have a lot of winter brides."

"You're going to have a lot of brides, period. Your dresses are gorgeous." She put her hand on my arm. "And speaking of which, I hear you're getting married in June. Congratulations!"

"Thank you." I could hardly believe she knew . . . or cared. But from the look of zeal in her eyes, I could tell her words were genuine, heartfelt.

"We can talk after the show tonight," Brock said. "Want to come back to Bella and D.J.'s place? We're spending the night with them."

"Bring your fiancé," Erin said. "We'll play games or something."

Um, okay. Hanging out at Bella and D.J.'s with Brock Benson and his wife. Playing games. Talking dresses.

"I'd be honored," I finally managed.

"No, I'm the one who's honored." Erin gave my neck another squeeze, then flitted off to chat with one of the other dancers. She turned back to me and hollered, "See you after the show!"

Off in the distance, the orchestra warmed up,

and the director popped his head in the room to say, "Three minutes to curtain call."

"Guess that's my cue." Brock reached to take my hand and gave it a little squeeze. "Thank you so much, Gabi. You've made Erin's night, and nothing makes me happier than seeing her smile."

"I have no doubt she'll be the best-dressed woman at the Oscars," Bella chimed in.

Brock and the others headed to the stage, and I tagged along behind Bella to the auditorium to join our families, who had already taken their seats. When I saw Jordan, I could hardly wait to tell him everything.

Settling into the seat next to him, I was scarcely able to get out a word. The orchestra stopped playing their warm-up and then dove in to the first song with a robust beginning. The curtain opened and Brock stood front and center, all of the other dancers beside him.

Jordan leaned my way. "What was it like?" he whispered. "Meeting a star, I mean?"

I turned to face the man I loved, my heart overflowing. "There's only one star in this room, you goober. And he happens to be seated right next to me."

"Good answer." Jordan flashed a smile and reached for my hand. I offered it willingly and then nuzzled up against him, overcome with joy.

Together we turned to face the stage . . . cheek to cheek.

# Gabi's Top Ten
# Fred and Ginger Quotes

I don't care what the critics say. My fabulous mom will give me a good review if nobody else does.

Ginger Rogers

Do it big, do it right, and do it with style.

Fred Astaire

When you're happy, you don't count the years. Beauty is a valuable asset, but it is not the whole cheese.

Ginger Rogers

When I was working with Ginger, it was like heaven on earth. She had all the talent anybody could have.

Fred Astaire

Even when one is of a certain age to make one's own decisions, there are many times when it is great to be able to go back and talk it over with the people one loves—one's family.

Ginger Rogers

I have no desire to prove anything by dancing. I have never used it as an outlet or a means of expressing myself. I just dance. I just put my feet in the air and move them around.

Fred Astaire

The most important thing in anyone's life is to be giving something. The quality I can give is fun, joy, and happiness. This is my gift.

Ginger Rogers

Ginger is the most effective performer I've ever worked with. Ginger's a salesman. She can sell it. She's a showman and an actress. She's quite unique. She's amazing.

Fred Astaire

I'm most grateful to have had that joyous time in motion pictures. It really was a Golden Age of Hollywood. Pictures were talking, they were singing, they were coloring. It was beginning to blossom out: bud and blossom were both present.

Ginger Rogers

Believe me, Ginger was great. She contributed her full fifty percent in making them such a great team. She could follow Fred as if one brain was thinking. She blended with his every step and mood immaculately. He was able to do dances on the screen that would have been impossible to risk if he hadn't had a partner like Ginger—as skillful as she was attractive.

Edward Everett Horton

# Acknowledgments

To my mom, Shirley Moseley, the best seamstress I've ever known. You are a whiz behind the sewing machine! If I had half of your talent, I would spend my days putting together gorgeous dresses like Gabi.

To my agent, Chip MacGregor. We're a little like Fred and Ginger, aren't we? We're quite the team. I know that you've been my "better literary half" (and have certainly offered me ample opportunities to dance). For that, I'm eternally grateful.

To my amazing team at Revell—Jennifer Leep, Michele Misiak, Jessica English, Donna Hausler, Erin Bartels, and all of the hard-working folks on the sales team. How can I ever thank you for taking me under your wing? I'm so thrilled to be a member of the Revell family.

To my precious critique partners—Janetta Messmer and Virginia Rush. You save my neck every time!

To my Weddings by Bella readers. Without you, this series would not have been possible. Thanks for asking for more! What a blast to keep Bella's story going.

Most important, to my Lord and Savior, Jesus Christ. Without you, there would be no stories to pen.

# About the Author

Award-winning author **Janice Thompson** enjoys tickling the funny bone. She got her start in the industry writing screenplays and musical comedies for the stage, and she has published nearly one hundred books for the Christian market. She has played the role of mother of the bride four times now and particularly enjoys writing lighthearted, comedic, wedding-themed tales. Why? Because making readers laugh gives her great joy!

Janice is passionate about her faith and does all she can to share the joy of the Lord with others, which is why she particularly enjoys writing. Her tagline, "Love, Laughter, and Happily Ever Afters!" sums up her take on life.

She lives in Spring, Texas, where she leads a rich life with her family, a host of writing friends, and two mischievous dachshunds. She does her best to keep the Lord at the center of it all. You can find out more about Janice at:

www.janiceathompson.com or
www.freelancewritingcourses.com.

**Center Point Large Print**
600 Brooks Road / PO Box 1
Thorndike ME 04986-0001 USA

(207) 568-3717

US & Canada:
1 800 929-9108
www.centerpointlargeprint.com